SECOND CHANCE AT US

STACY TRAVIS

SECOND CHANCE AT US

STACY TRAVIS

Cover Design: Shanoff Designs

Copyediting: Red Adept Editing

Publicity: Social Butterfly PR

PROLOGUE

ecca

I'd worked in hospitals long enough to understand one important truth—no one should ever underestimate a woman. Or her vagina.

"Do women still die in childbirth?" Sydney gasped through clenched teeth. Her bloodshot, round eyes begged me to tell her she'd survive labor pains.

I rubbed a hand lightly across her forehead and used my soothing nurse voice. "Very rarely, especially in hospitals. You're doing great, and we'll take good care of you." I wanted to reassure her but also keep her expectations realistic.

And realistically, she had no baby in sight.

Sydney's doctor had given her Pitocin several hours earlier to stimulate things, but *things*, i.e. a woman's uterus, had a way of ignoring doctors and nurses and deciding to take the scenic route through bumpy terrain for eighteen hours.

Not that Sydney wanted to hear that.

"Your contractions will get stronger, and as the head descends, you'll start to feel more pressure." It was my standard script. When I stuck to it, all went well. When I didn't, my awkward thoughts spewed forth like the faulty sprinkler that drenched everyone's pantlegs.

Sydney dabbed the perspiration from her forehead with a diaper cloth and pushed back the strawberry blond strands that had fallen from her ponytail. The rosy flush on her cheeks gave her the kind of glow that launched a thousand makeup tutorials.

"Good. The sooner, the better," she said, her voice still strained from the previous contraction. "These fucking suck. It feels like my pelvis is about to explode."

I patted her hand. "In seven years of working here, the only explosions I've seen are from pooping babies," I smiled reassuringly. When her eyes grew larger, I realized I'd overshared. "I mean . . . it happens. Not all the time. Sometimes they do come out pooping...but you don't need to think about that now. The point is you will be fine. I promise. What you're doing here is amazing—you're bringing life into the world. Let's focus on that." I needed more coffee. Or less. And an Off switch.

Sydney was right about the perils of childbirth. History confirmed that having a baby was no easy feat. In the 19th Century, five to ten out of every thousand women didn't survive to meet their babies. Modern medicine may have made the process safer, but it didn't change the fact that every woman who pushed out a baby was a certified badass superhero.

Which kind of made me Robin to their Batwomen.

"Her contractions are coming about ten minutes apart." Sydney's birthing coach pointed to her stopwatch. She wore a set of hot-pink scrubs that were much prettier than the pale blues we all grabbed from the supply closet at the hospital. Her pigtailed hair hung down her back, and she blinked at me with bright blue eyes that matched the eye shadow swept across her lids.

"We can give you something for the pain," I offered.

Sydney shook her head vigorously. "I'm not getting an epidural. No way. I'm doing this naturally. There's my birth plan." She gestured to the empty chair in the corner.

From my scan of the chart, I knew that Sydney Fulton was thirty-five and giving birth for the first time. Her water had broken the day before, and she'd come to the hospital in the middle of the night when her contractions had become more frequent.

"I already explained everything to the night nurse. Jesus, fuck. Do I have to start over with each person who comes in here?"

I inhaled a deep breath and counted backward from five, as I did every time a patient snapped at me. It was just pain that made her inner playground bully yank my ponytail—I knew this. She was probably a lovely person most of the time.

I could see the birthing coach trying to make eye contact, but I kept counting and kept my lips glued together to prevent my inside voice from slipping through. A moment later, she nudged me and told me she preferred to be called a doula, not a birthing coach. I began counting again.

Just then, the door swung open, and a tall, imposing man strode into the room with the authority of someone who owned a wing of the hospital. I briefly glimpsed the strong set of his jaw and eyes filled with concern as he made a beeline for Sydney's bedside. "Did I miss anything?" His voice rumbled like a well-oiled train car, and he reached for her hand.

"Only another mammoth fucking contraction," Sydney spat. "And according to this one, I'm not making any progress." Eyes ablaze, she flicked her hand in my direction.

He had his back to me and didn't turn away from his wife, smoothing her hair and trying to calm her. "You're doing great," he said in his velvety tenor. The soothing sound of his voice made me want to blurt that he should do radio commercials for…everything.

Purely an objective observation.

Instead, I piped in like a chirpy cheerleader. "You're making progress. You've dilated almost three centimeters." I smiled encouragingly into her glare, but her eyes stayed fixed on her husband.

"I was three centimeters when I got here," Sydney said. "I've made zero progress. And I'm an overachiever, so you know how that pisses me off."

The man laughed at her temper, handing her a wrapped bundle. "Well, maybe this will help. They only had vanilla in the gift shop, but I think it smells pretty good."

Before he could hand it off, Sydney batted it away, and it bounced to the end of the bed where I caught it before it fell. "Jesus, you went to the hospital gift shop? How lazy are you? I fucking hate vanilla," she said.

The man took a step back, running a hand through his hair and looking down at the floor.

I felt for him. Some husbands had a hard time in the delivery room. They were out of their element, and most had no idea where to stand, what to say, or how to generally avoid annoying their partners, who were doing all the work.

Not to mention that vaginas being used for anything other than hot sex made a lot of men very uncomfortable.

"If it makes it any better, you can't light a candle in here anyway. Fire codes," I said, trying to keep the peace. Refereeing birthing mothers and their partners was a surprisingly large part of my job.

"I don't need to light it. I want to smell it. But not if it's vanilla. Vanilla makes me gag," Sydney said, throwing an arm across her eyes. "You might as well pump fake cookie smell in here."

"Hmm, cookie smells sound pretty good to me. Chocolate chip?" I exchanged looks with the birthing coach, hoping for some support.

She shook her head. *Don't even go there*, her eyes seemed to say.

Too late. My rogue parade of perkiness had already left the staging area. "Or how about cheesecake? I've heard they even make candles now that smell like croissants and coffee in case you're homesick for France. Though, arguably, smelling it might make a person more homesick."

Damned. Rogue. Perkiness.

Sydney dismissed me with a wave of her hand. From the monitor and the strain in her voice, I could see another contraction coming on, but Sydney seemed determined to argue through it. "I need a calming scent—lavender or grapefruit—haven't you heard of aromatherapy?" She stopped to huff, and the birthing coach counted down her inhales and exhales.

As soon as Sydney could, she groaned through clenched teeth, "Shitty gift shop candles are *not* aromatherapy." She took another deep breath and let it out with a hiss. "This hospital smells like old people and bleach. But if you're going to bring me vanilla, I might as well have nothing." The contraction began to subside, and she glared at her husband who had a hand over his forehead.

"Syd, I'm sorry. I'll fix it." The smoothness had left his voice, leaving a croak.

Sydney rolled her eyes, shutting him out. Her birthing coach went about fussing and bringing her a water cup with a bendy straw.

I glanced at Sydney's husband sympathetically. Almost as though he knew I was looking, he turned and extended his hand. "Hi, Blake Fulton, the candle idiot. Is the hatred for vanilla a universal female thing? Am I the only one late to the party?"

As I grasped his extended hand and processed his words, I felt a jolt.

The jolt was borne of many things—the warmth of his skin, which sent an unexpected zing of heat through my body, the bedraggled look on his face, which didn't obscure the fact that he was really, really handsome, and the jarring collision of my present with the awkward days of my past.

I knew Blake Fulton.

A person did not forget the name Blake Fulton.

Or the rest of him.

And once I got over the shock of hearing his name, my brain was besieged by a whole host of memories, most of them clawing at my chest and making it hard to breathe.

Looking at his face, I held out the possibility that he wasn't the same guy I'd known—and fallen for—in high school.

The guy who'd charmed me senseless, kissed me within an inch of my virginity, made me believe in fate and love and fated love—and then dumped me.

Yeah, that Blake Fulton.

No question, it was him. And in typical Blake fashion, his charming, handsome smile told me he had no recollection of me.

CHAPTER ONE

ecca

Fifteen Years Earlier

"This is your third detention slip in a week, Rebecca. Are you proud of yourself?" Principal Franciosa asked me as I sat chomping gum in her office.

Gum wasn't allowed at Beckman Prep. "No one wants to see you chewing like a cow," she had explained at the first assembly of the school year. Given that it was now March, I knew better than to cave to my bovine instincts.

I was flaunting the rules.

Nervously.

Jutting my jaw forward, I spoke slowly. "No, actually, I'm disappointed. I was going for five." My chin wobbled as I tried to maintain the stony façade of a warrior. After an uneventful two years as peppy cheerleader, disciplined straight-A student, and outgoing bestie, acting out felt kind of amazing—if a little daunting.

"Come on, Rebecca. I don't think you mean that." She smiled, trying to coax me back to the kind of behavior she could reprimand with a slap on the wrist. She wanted me to make her job easier, but I was going for broke.

"Whatever."

I was manifesting a moody, entitled teenager, trying the attitude on like a glove, feeling my way through a meltdown that felt beyond my control.

The worst part was that no one would stand in my way or tell me to shape up.

Death had that effect on people.

My dad had passed away from an inoperable brain tumor less than two weeks earlier. It had been "expected," but is death ever really expected? I knew he was sick, I hoped against hope that the chemo and therapies would work, and then the end came too quickly.

There was no way to prepare for the loss of my favorite person, no matter how much I anticipated it.

People chalked up my actions since then to grief. My closest friends avoided me like I might cry if they said the wrong thing—and because nothing freaked out invincible teenagers like the finality of death.

Poor Rebecca with the dead dad has gone off the rails because her mom's busy dealing with her four other sisters and older brother—and who has that many kids anymore anyway? Eventually, Rebecca will figure out how to deal. She always does.

In answer to Principal Franciosa's question, nothing about my behavior made me proud. Not the fact that I'd been so unfocused in Spanish that I'd gotten a D on a test I should have aced. Not my messy hair that was somewhere between blond and pink because I was too impatient with the fuchsia dye and rinsed it out. Not my mixed-up brain that didn't know if I really wanted to make a statement with pink hair or just disappear.

For crying out loud, I was failing at rebelling. That frustrated me even more.

As a disciplined student, there wasn't a goal I couldn't crush, given a little effort. And yet...I could already see that I—along with my pinkish hair—was headed back to class, and I probably wouldn't even get dinged for being late.

I made a terrible warrior.

Principal Franciosa had seen plenty of temperamental teenagers before me and would see them long after I graduated these hallowed halls. She could tell the real delinquents from the ones who would dabble in petty rule infractions and eventually go back to the straight and narrow.

She steepled her hands on her desk and looked at me over the frames of her cat-eye glasses. I stared back, taking in her principal-appropriate, shoulder-length brown hair and pale peach lipstick. She wore a royal blue crew neck sweater under a navy blazer and had tied a paler blue scarf around her neck. No jewelry, nothing superfluous to her outfit. It was like she'd memorized a fashion manual for high school principals.

"Rebecca, I know you have a lot going on at home, so I'd like to be lenient. Please don't make it difficult."

"Okay. Sorry." My sarcasm dripped, and from the scowl on Principal Franciosa's face, I was succeeding at trying her patience. I felt emboldened. "I didn't ask you to be lenient. You're free to punish me, though, for the record, I would like to say I think the rules are stupid, and no one should be punished for breaking them."

The rules *were* stupid.

White socks were okay, but white socks with a navy stripe—blasphemy. Uniforms were about leveling the playing field and taking the focus off of fashion but giving someone detention for a stripe was putting form over function.

I'd pushed the issue further by wearing an old pair of running shoes instead of the required loafers. Then I'd opted to wear my brother's old Army-green coat instead of the navy sweater or gray blazer that was part of the uniform.

On the first day I'd come to school with my blond-pink-combo hair, I hadn't been breaking any rules, per se, but it hadn't endeared me to the faculty, who were already worried I was losing it.

I also hadn't done a stitch of homework in two weeks and had doodled on two tests instead of writing an essay. All that seemed like it would add up to more than a date with the principal where she would offer to be lenient.

I wanted a full-blown suspension so I could hang out at home and figure out how to be okay without my dad.

My mom hadn't allowed me to miss more than a day of school because she thought that feigning normalcy would help us all move on. What she didn't understand was that I didn't want to move on, not yet. And maybe I just needed to lose my shit in whatever way came naturally so the consequences would hurt me in a different way than the sadness I couldn't shake.

"I don't want to punish you. I think you're doing a pretty good job of punishing yourself," the principal said.

I rolled my eyes. "Do they give you a manual on stupid things to say to students?" It felt freeing to say awful things. I couldn't be awful to my family. They were hurting, too, so it needed to come out somewhere, and this woman—who barely knew me and was lobbing a few trite words my way—was an open target.

"Rebecca, please. I'm on your side. I don't think you're a bad person or a bad student, but I need you to meet me partway here, or I can't help you."

"How am I supposed to do that?" I was annoyed. Everything about Principal Franciosa grated on me, from her glasses, which weren't as cool as she thought they were, to her overly neat desk with a collection of apple-shaped paperweights on it. They were irritating. She was irritating.

And on that note, it annoyed me that the plaid fabric on her office couch itched my bare legs below my skirt. It was beside the point that if I'd kept my skirt at the mandatory fingertip length, more of my legs would have been covered.

Principal Franciosa inhaled deeply and studied me. "Maybe I should just assign you a week of detention. You seem to want that."

"I do. Detention sounds great."

Since I hadn't been able to push the boundaries enough to get a suspension, detention sounded like the next best option. Not that I had some *Breakfast Club* idea that detention would introduce me to new friends who would see me differently and produce epiphanies. I just felt drained. I wanted my meeting with the principal to be over.

"Okay, three days next week and three the following, detention after school. You can pick the days," she said, extending her hands like she was offering me a gift.

I nodded and waited to see if she planned to say more. Principal Franciosa stared at me.

"You can go back to class now, Rebecca. And I hope I'm not adding tea to your rebellion by saying you can do better than this. I think you know you should do better."

I squinted at her weird metaphor, but she was right. Of course she was.

It wasn't a matter of being capable of leaving the house in the correct shoes. I owned the loafers. I'd gotten up in the morning and made a choice. At that moment in my high school career, I was choosing sabotage. I was choosing to burn everything I cared about to the ground.

Even if no one noticed.

As I left the principal's office, I felt a glimmer of satisfaction.

A parting gift from my dad was that for the first time, I was enjoying the freedom of not knowing what happened next. *What did one Spanish test matter anyway when people could die, leaving a gaping soul chasm that would never be filled?*

I thought about that as I walked away from the main building and decided whether to go back to math class or pretend my principal meeting had lasted for the whole period. Then maybe I could have a moment to sit with my pinkish hair and fall apart.

The halls were empty because everyone was already in class. I'd been pulled out after the first few minutes by a student who was getting her community service credits by working in the school office. She seemed especially gratified to serve as my angel of doom. She probably had her own problems, but while I'd normally have been curious about them, today I couldn't muster empathy.

I slumped against the wall outside the door to the math class-room, deciding whether or not to go in. A wave of exhaustion seeped deep into my bones. It was hard being angry at the world. Really tiring.

Closing my eyes for a moment, I acknowledged that I hadn't really slept in two weeks. I'd tried. From sheer exhaustion, I'd drifted off for an hour here or there, but most nights, I lay awake, aware of my sisters living in the same house and unable to talk to any of them.

At first, I envisioned us working through our grief in a family kumbaya circle, but I soon realized I was alone. We each had to process the sadness in our own way, and I couldn't disturb their process by making them deal with mine. I was the middle sister, neither old nor young, and I fended for myself.

"Hey, you okay?"

I didn't recognize the voice, so I didn't open my eyes, but I sensed he was talking to me. No one else was around. Maybe if I ignored him, he'd go away.

"Hey," he said again.

I could feel his presence even with my eyes closed, and he didn't seem to take the hint from the angry girl with the ridiculous hair who was ignoring him. I figured that made him a special kind of masochist, and I was all ready to tell him so when I opened my eyes.

But I didn't speak.

Something about his face calmed me—the look of concern that wasn't a look of pity, the sweetness behind his eyes, and the curiosity about me as a human, not a hot mess who was trying everyone's patience.

I vaguely knew who Blake Fulton was, but we'd never spoken in almost two years at the same school. I'd had a class or two with him, but he was on the quiet side, and I didn't know his friends.

Yet there he was, and there I was.

I couldn't explain it at the time, and I struggled to understand it afterward, but for some reason, I wanted to talk to him. I wanted to tell him everything.

And that was how it began.

CHAPTER TWO

lake

REBECCA FINLEY DID NOT LOOK okay. I knew this because I'd spent the better part of a year watching her with fascinated preoccupation, and I'd come to know her moods. They were almost always upbeat and welcoming to anyone who entered her orbit.

Her bright personality had made me bold enough to think she might actually like me as a person. She seemed to like everyone, and I was part of everyone. I decided to extrapolate that to mean she liked me too.

Finally, a use for a math concept—extrapolation—that may not have been meant to help a nervous guy approach a girl. But it worked.

"Hey, you okay?" I asked.

She stood with her back against the stucco wall outside a classroom, her head tipped back, eyes closed. I noticed her eyelashes first. They were dark and fanned out across the tops of her cheeks. If I had to bet, I'd say her eyes were pink from crying or at least from carrying a burden no one our age should have to carry.

Her lower lip was plump, larger than the one above it. I could only describe them as kissable because that was what I wanted to do to them. Badly.

She wore a bright shade of pink lipstick, and it went well with the pinkish shade she'd dyed her hair a week ago. Her shoes would allow her to make a quick escape, and that gave me an idea.

I knew about her dad. Word had gotten around. He'd apparently had brain cancer for a year or so. I felt guilty knowing such a significant, painful piece of information about her when I barely knew her at all. But that was what high school gossip did. It made us all part of a story, whether we consented or not.

Even with treatment, glioblastoma was near impossible to beat. I'd looked it up. But no level of planning could prepare a person for her dad to die while she was still in high school, arguably the time when we needed our parents the most. No kind of preparation could make something like that feel normal.

I knew because my mom had died the year before. Most people at school didn't know because I had a bad habit of keeping things hidden. I already felt like a gawky nerd around a lot of my classmates. I didn't need people feeling sorry for me on top of it.

Nevertheless, the loss had floored me, and maybe it was part of why I'd willed myself into the woodwork at school—I didn't know how to let people in, but that didn't mean I couldn't be there when I saw someone going through pain I understood.

Rebecca had given up trying to keep up appearances. She looked broken and utterly alone. Reaching out to her felt non-negotiable.

"Hey," I said again.

She opened her eyes and seemed to have momentary difficulty focusing on me. She looked around as if to check for someone else I might be talking to, but no one else was in the hall. I had a free period and had forgotten my chemistry textbook, so I'd gone back to my locker to get it.

"Oh. Hey." She tried to pull her lips into a smile, but they resisted. "Yeah. I'm . . . I don't know what I am, but don't worry. It's all good."

That was the most she'd ever said to me, and I felt myself savoring the tone of her voice when it was directed my way. In my mind, it sounded different than when I'd heard her speaking to other people, even though I knew rationally that it probably sounded exactly the same.

"Okay, well . . . I'm glad."

Our high school wasn't that big, two hundred kids in a grade, and we'd already been there for nearly two years. But the school had cliques and groups, and we'd never been part of the same one. We knew *of* each other after being paired as lab partners once, but we didn't *know* each other. That was fine by me, all the better to observe her without being noticed.

Observing Rebecca Finley was all a guy like me could ever hope to do. She was a star. I was a fleck of space dust.

My social status never bothered me. I had friends, and I did well in school. When I went to football games or parties, it was to watch the sport and show school spirit with like-minded friends.

Then I went home, even though I knew most of my classmates were drinking beer from a keg at someone's house afterward. I was curious how high schoolers bought kegs of beer but not curious enough to see the setup for myself. Someone had a fake ID or an older sibling. It wasn't exactly rocket science.

Actual rocket science held far more sway over me. I excelled in math and STEM subjects but was a dunce at sports—to be fair, I never tried sports, but a five-foot-seven kid who went through puberty late wasn't exactly first pick.

I had so little to lose that it seemed like a low-risk proposition to try befriending Rebecca when no one else was around to beat me to it.

So I waited to see if she'd say anything else. She seemed unable to move away from the wall, or unwilling. I understood the feeling. Sometimes it felt good to have something tangible to lean against when everything else came unmoored. I wasn't about to launch into a whole Q and A on her feelings about her dad, but I sensed she didn't actively want me to leave—at least not so much that she said anything.

She stood outside one of the math classrooms—maybe it was her class, maybe it was just where she happened to pause—but she didn't want to go inside. That much I knew. What I couldn't ascertain by looking at her, was where she did want to be.

I took a stab. "So, I know we don't know each other at all, but maybe that's a good thing. I can be like a blank canvas."

When her eyes landed on me, I saw more confusion than disinterest. "You want me to paint on you?"

I squeezed my eyes shut. *No.* My metaphor was all wrong. I hadn't thought it through, and the last thing this girl probably needed was me saying stupid things. I got ready to backpedal and come up with something better, but when I opened my eyes, she was smiling.

That was all it took. I was done for.

It was one thing to see her smiling at the crowd from the top of a human pyramid with a backdrop of football players, but it was completely humbling to have her smile directed at me.

I didn't know the girl at all, but I knew I wanted her to smile at me like that for a long time. So I did what any self-respecting nerd would do when faced with a pretty cheerleader who was out of his league. I asked her out. Sort of.

In my head, that was what I was doing, but because I was a guy anticipating rejection, I tried to act cool and make her think I was being friendly and helpful.

But really, I was asking her out.

CHAPTER THREE

Becca

THE LAST THING I expected to come out of Blake Fulton's mouth was an invitation. People at school had been acting like I might spontaneously burst into flames if they looked at me wrong, and everyone had either shifted their gaze to the ground when I walked by or intentionally skirted out of my path when they saw me.

It was fine, actually, because I was tired of their pitying looks and their questions. "Are you okay?" "Should I leave you alone?" "Do you just want some space?"

The truth was, I did want most of the people at school to leave me alone. I wasn't a science experiment that had grown fungi for everyone to peek at and analyze. But my friends . . . the people I'd always trusted to have my back, they'd been disappointingly AWOL, busy in the evenings, dashing to class early instead of lingering to talk.

Death freaked people out. It was like they thought it was conta-gious or something—if they just hung out with me like we normally did, they might catch it and lose someone close to them.

It was ridiculous, but maybe I'd behaved the same way before. I couldn't even remember *before*.

The only thing I felt bearing down on me was *now*, and now sucked.

I couldn't imagine what had motivated Blake to talk to me when he'd never done so before. Apparently, I was that pathetic, such a basket case that strangers were staging interventions.

When I met Blake's eyes expecting pity, I saw steady gray that seemed more concerned than judgmental. It told me a lot, considering how I looked.

I'd given up on wearing makeup because it required too much energy. My eyes seemed to be permanently puffy after two weeks of crying, and the dye job I'd done on my hair was epically bad.

Blake stood maybe three inches taller than me, and I saw his lips moving, but I was so preoccupied by the sheer strangeness of standing in the hallway with a guy I barely knew that I didn't hear him.

"I'm sorry . . . what?" I asked.

"I said, I know we don't really know each other, but it seems like you're not having a great day. Then I apologized for being intru-sive and making assumptions." He looked sheepish but deter-mined to have a conversation.

I still couldn't fathom why he wanted to talk to me. Even my best friends had mostly hugged me and given me space. Maybe they thought ranting and getting hysterical because the cafeteria lady ran out of fruit cups was an overreaction, but I couldn't help it. I had big feelings and canned fruit pushed me over the edge.

And yet…here was Blake Fulton, acting like a friend.

"Don't apologize. You're not being intrusive. You're being…kind. I appreciate it. And you're correct, my day is pretty shitty, but that's okay."

He nodded and glanced at my hand. I was white-knuckling the doorknob to the math classroom.

"Are you going to class?"

"I was . . ." I'd never missed a class in almost two years of high school. I'd never caught so much as a cold that kept me away from school, and I'd *never* considered skipping class or even showing up late on purpose.

I was spirited, loud, and I talked a lot, but that wasn't the same thing as being a rebel.

I wondered why I'd been such a good girl for so long. *Habit?* Maybe it was because I wanted to make my dad proud. Well, he was gone now. "Do you have a better idea?"

The corner of Blake's mouth tipped up into the beginnings of a smile. "We could ditch. I mean, I'm not the guy who does it all the time, and I don't really have a plan, but . . ."

He looked so guilty. I couldn't picture him as the kind of guy to ditch classes. The look on his face slowly morphed from worried to shy, and I realized I was nodding.

"Okay," I said.

He smiled for real this time. "For the record, I'm not wanted for kidnapping, in case you were concerned," he added.

"Okay," I said, having no idea whether I was more concerned now that he'd said it. "Are we just going to...walk off campus?"

"I think...yes, we are." He cocked his head, watching me in a way that made me feel protected, not judged. Then he reached for my hand and pried my fingers from the doorknob. And I was free.

———

BLAKE LOADED me into the front seat of his black VW Jetta and drove.

We didn't talk on the way, partly because I was still a little bit in shock that I'd left school. I pictured my math teacher standing in front of the class, lecturing on Algebra II, drawing matrices, and tapping on the whiteboard with a green pen while he waited for someone to fill in the blanks. I pictured my empty seat and wondered if anyone noticed I hadn't come back to class.

I was so lost in my thoughts about whether I'd get into worse trouble than my existing three detentions that I wasn't really paying attention to where Blake was driving until we pulled up to In-N-Out Burger near the Oakland Marina. He didn't ask if I liked their burgers, or any burgers.

"This okay?" Blake pointed up at the yellow arrow sign that signified the greasy goodness within. He'd put on an Oakland A's baseball cap. I could smell the grilled-burger-and-french-fry haze before opening the car door, and it made my stomach growl. He was gripping the steering wheel the same way I'd clung to the door of the math classroom.

"It's great. I can't remember the last time I ate a meal." I was pretty sure I'd shoved down a handful of peanuts here or there, mainly for survival. My mom and sisters had practically force-fed me a granola bar a day since the funeral. *But actual hunger?* I'd lost that basic drive to all the emotional numbness that allowed me to get through each day, until now. "Wow. I'm really hungry."

Blake brightened and exhaled the breath he'd been holding. "Okay, well…good."

It was my turn to peel his hands from the security of the steering wheel he clung to, and he turned in his seat to face me.

"I know this is completely weird. You and I . . . we've barely talked to each other, and we've never hung out. Is it…? I mean, is this okay? Do you feel like you've been kidnapped? Or is it now strange that I've mentioned kidnapping twice in an hour, and are you starting to wonder if, while I may not be an actual kidnapper, maybe I'm someone who suffers from kidnapping fantasies? Because again, I assure you, I'm not."

I liked this guy. His honesty was unusual. Most people did everything they could to hide their feelings behind bravado and sarcastic comments. He seemed to have a straight line between his thoughts and his words.

"I don't feel like that. I'm glad you got me out of there. Although…I still don't really understand. Why do you even care?"

He rubbed a hand over his face and took a deep breath. His forehead drew up in ridged concentration, and I got ready for a big admission. Maybe the principal had paid him to perform an intervention. Or he'd seen my downward spiral as an opportunity to get laid. Or he had a thing for wounded birds. "I don't know. I just do," he sighed, which made me think he understood somehow.

"Okay. Then let me buy lunch."

Once our number had been called and we sat with trays loaded with burgers and Animal-Style fries, I felt surprisingly better.

"I don't know how to say this without it sounding like an insult... but the color is back in your face," he said.

"That doesn't sound like an insult. Don't worry so much. I'm not going to break apart. I'm not as unstable as I look." I flipped up the strawberry-colored ends of my hair and ran them through my fingers. "It's a little 'beauty school dropout' from *Grease*. I look insane."

"Actually, it's a pretty cool color." He grinned. Taking off his cap, he raked a hand through his brown hair. "You think it would work on me?"

"Ha. I don't think it works on anyone." I turned my burger around until I decided on the perfect bite. I moaned at how good it tasted. "You're a genius, Blake Fulton. This burger is the best thing I've ever eaten." I felt juices from the special sauce dripping down my wrist and did my best to mop up the mess with my tongue and a wad of napkins.

When I looked at Blake, he was smiling. I liked his smile.

"What?" I asked.

"I didn't think you knew my last name."

"We've had, like, three classes together. I'm not that clueless." But to him, maybe I seemed that way. "I guess you think I'm a mean girl or something."

He grabbed a french fry and popped it in his mouth, shaking his head. "Not at all. It's not about you. It's me. I keep a pretty low profile. I'm pretty antisocial."

"Why?" I took a couple of fries.

Blake shrugged. "Laziness?"

I waited to see if he would elaborate. I had a feeling it was something other than lack of effort. When he didn't say anything, I nodded. "Okay. I guess I'll have to accept laziness as the big explanation, even though I think there's more to it."

"What's your theory?"

"You don't want people to get to know you?"

"Interesting. Why would I do that?"

"Maybe you're hiding something. Are you an undercover agent?"

He raised his hand in the air. "Ding, ding, ding. She gets it on the first try. And now that you know, my cover is blown, so . . ."

I rolled my eyes. "You'll have to kill me?"

"I was going to say I'll have to recruit you as a secret agent," he said.

The food was making a dent in my ravenous hunger, and I put my burger down in its paper tray and wiped my hands. I wanted to focus on the guy sitting with me. His face held a kindness, but the lines across his forehead belied something more complicated in his thoughts.

He tended to smile without parting his lips, almost like it took an effort to smile fully or his natural smile embarrassed him. His irises were dark gray rimmed with brown, and the array of colors within was mesmerizing. A dimple in one cheek popped with his reluctant smile. Everything about his face felt comforting, and he made me want to trust that he was a good guy.

I sipped from my water cup, which was half the size of his milkshake, probably to discourage the convenience of drinking free water instead of paying for a beverage.

He watched me drain the cup. "You want to try the shake?"

"What flavor?" I hadn't paid attention when he ordered.

"Vanilla."

"Huh. I was sure you were going to say chocolate. Isn't that the default shake flavor?"

"Probably. I just happen to like vanilla. I wasn't doing it to be different." He pushed it closer to me. I slurped down a cold sip through his straw, not feeling at all weird about sharing germs with him. Nothing about the two of us hanging out was normal, so sharing a straw was the least of my concerns.

"I like vanilla too, and they make a good shake." I savored the taste.

"Want one?"

He started to get up without waiting for my answer, so I put out a hand to stop him. "I'm good. Getting full, actually." I looked at the remains of my burger. I couldn't let it go to waste, so I took another big bite. "Not too full for this, though," I said, talking with my mouth full.

He finished his burger, picked out a fry that wasn't covered with cheese, and munched on it.

It felt…normal, the two of us playing hooky and getting burgers like we did it every week. I'd been so out of sorts, so in my head. *This* was why I'd wanted Principal Franciosa to suspend me. I wondered how he knew. Maybe he didn't. Maybe he ditched school all the time. *How would I know?* I'd never paid attention to him, which made me feel a little bad, even though it wasn't out of malice. "Do you do this a lot, leave school in the middle of the day?"

"Nope. Never." He took another fry without the cheese. "At least not this year."

"Not this year. Aha, so you were a big ditcher last year?"

He shook his head. "Small ditcher."

"How small?"

He held his fingers about an inch apart.

"So why today? Why with me?" I asked. "And why aren't you eating the fries with the cheese on them? The whole point of Animal fries is the cheese and sauce, and you're eating neither."

He shrugged. "Sometimes I like them plain."

"Did you agree to split them with me even though you don't like them?"

He mock gasped. "How dare you accuse me of subjugating my fry feelings? No, I just felt like eating the plain ones."

I studied him for signs that he was telling the truth. He met my gaze, so I decided he wasn't hiding anything, and as proof, he took a cheese-laden fry and popped it in his mouth, then held up his hands. "See? All good."

"Okay, just checking."

"So in answer to why I left school with you today, the easy response, and the only one I have right now is, 'I don't know.'"

"Do you think you might come up with a more complicated answer?"

He blinked a couple of times, and I felt something soften in my heart when he fixed his eyes on me and smiled. I hadn't noticed the low-level chill that had seeped into my bones until his smile warmed them.

He looked at the sky and our surroundings, which weren't too picturesque—a freeway in one direction and a car dealership across the street. "It's a really nice day, isn't it?"

I followed his gaze and noticed for the first time in weeks that the sky was bright blue, the sun was shining, almost too enthusiastically, and a few clouds hung in the distance, too lazy to come closer. Despite the tornado in my brain, it was a nice day. "Yes, and I think you're changing the subject to avoid my question." He grinned again, and another thrill of warmth rippled through me.

"I told you I didn't have a good answer."

"It doesn't have to be good. Just come up with something. Do the best you can."

He studied me for a moment, his eyes growing serious. "Fine. I'll dig deep into my psyche and tell you why I abandoned my academic morals to ditch school with a pretty girl I barely know. But then I'll have a question for you."

"I think that's fair, given that you're the only one on the entire campus who seemed to know what I needed." I felt vulnerable admitting it, but he'd made a sacrifice for me, so I wanted him to know.

The tops of his ears got a little red, and he looked away, but he sat up a little straighter.

I was still fixating on him referring to me as a pretty girl, even though I'd been raised to know I was more than my exterior shell. I liked hearing that he saw past the puffy eyes and bad dye job.

"Let's hear your answer." I was curious what the one question would be, but I was more curious about why he'd decided to ditch.

He ran his hand over his face then rested it on the round speckled concrete table. The outdoor seating was packed, but no one seemed at all interested in why two teenagers weren't at school. As a virgin ditcher, I had no way of knowing whether the rest of the world skipped school regularly, even if it seemed scandalous to me.

"Okay. I guess I saw you outside the classroom, and I've heard… about your dad . . . I'm really sorry." When he looked at me, the pain in his eyes seemed greater than what a person would feel for a stranger. It was so…touching. After feeling stuck in sadness, my heart swelled with gratitude that he'd come to my rescue.

"Thanks. It's been…really hard."

He nodded then spoke without hesitation. "I guess I saw you standing in the hallway alone, and no one seemed to be helping you deal with what you must be feeling. And I felt like someone should. I'd seen you come out of the principal's office with your detention slip, and it killed me. You just lost your dad. So what if you lose your shit for a week or a month? Hell, my mom died last year, and I lost my shit for a lot longer. It didn't seem like you deserved detention."

He'd said so much in one breath that I had to pause and parse through all the pieces. The kindness. The understanding.

He lost his mom.

I'd cried for my dad off and on for months as he'd gotten sicker and even more over the past two weeks, but at hearing Blake say his mom had died, my eyes stung with fresh tears.

I met his gaze to say how sorry I was, and he looked stricken. "I didn't mean to upset you . . . I'm so—"

I held up a hand to stop him. "You didn't upset me. I'm so sorry about your mom. I didn't know. If I had…maybe I could have been . . . I hope I would have tried to help. I mean, I know we weren't really pals, but I'd want to be that sort of person, the sort who knows when someone needs a friend."

The way you knew. How did you know?

He took a deep breath and nodded. "Thanks. I'm okay now, but it was tough for me. That's why . . . I don't know. I thought . . ." He stopped talking and took another breath, not meeting my gaze.

I wished he would. "Thank you," I mumbled.

He looked at me then, and I saw vulnerability that mirrored my own.

"Anyway, I don't know you, obviously, but from what I've seen, you're a happy person. You're upbeat and friendly. So to see you . . ."

"...with pink hair?" I suggested, trying to lighten the mood. It seemed hard for him to spit out what he was trying to say.

"No. Seeing you unhappy...made me want to fix it."

No one had said anything like that to me before. "That's...incredibly nice."

Blake shrugged. "I'm not sure I succeeded since I made you cry, even though these burgers are pretty awesome. I might have set my sights a little too high."

He was so self-deprecating. So...real. He seemed more mature than a high school kid, but I decided that was what losing someone does to a person. I suddenly felt older than my years. "Blake, this was exactly what I needed. It's the first time in two weeks that I've felt normal. So thank you."

"You don't have to keep thanking me." He got up, threw our trash into a red bin, and put our trays on top. "So...we've ditched one class, and we could probably make it back before last period. Or…not. You want to go somewhere else?"

I nodded. "I want to go somewhere else. I don't want to go back. I want to move forward and keep moving forward until that's all I remember how to do."

He reached for my hand, and I didn't hesitate to accept it. His grip felt firm and warm and safe. We walked back to his car and drove the twenty minutes it took to get to Berkeley. He didn't take the freeway, and I relished the chance to have the window open and breathe in the fresh air. I didn't ask where we were going. It didn't matter.

I knew Blake still intended to ask me his one big question, but we'd already had enough heavy conversation. No reason to push him.

When we pulled onto the small road that led to César Chávez Park, it didn't clear up any of my confusion. Parks sprawled all over Oakland and Berkeley. Other than being on the waterfront, I couldn't tell what was special about this one.

The second I exited the car, the wind whipped my hair into my face. I tried to tame it into a ponytail with one hand because Blake had grabbed my other one. We walked to a vintage brown camper van with a dozen tiny rainbow spinners flying from an awning on its side.

"Where are we going?" I squeezed his hand, and his warm eyes met mine. I didn't know Blake well, but somehow I trusted him implicitly.

As long as he wasn't planning a threesome in the back of that camper van, I'd go with whatever he had in mind. The area was deserted. Maybe we'd look out across San Francisco Bay at the bridges and the city. Blake led me to the van, digging into his pocket with his other hand and pulling out a wallet made entirely of blue duct tape.

"What are we doing? What's the plan?" It still wasn't obvious to me.

He pointed to the rainbow spinners, which I realized were tiny airborne kites. Behind them, much bigger kites shaped like dragons and fish and jellyfish flapped in the breeze.

"We're gonna buy a couple of kites and take them onto the bluff. The wind's always perfect here. When's the last time you flew a kite?" he asked.

"I'm gonna go with 'never.'" But that day seemed like the perfect time to try.

CHAPTER FOUR

lake

IN OVER MY HEAD, no question about it. And I didn't even have the wherewithal to realize.

I *believed* in the picture unfolding before me. In that pretty tableau, Rebecca and I could fly kites together. We could laugh when our kite strings got tangled up and her kite started dancing across the sky like a big, flopping rainbow-colored dirigible.

I could grab her hand like I had the right to, even though I had no idea whether she had a boyfriend or if she was just in a vulnerable place.

We felt bound in flight like the kites, caught on a strong wind, so I didn't stop moving forward. I couldn't. If someone had asked me a month earlier if I wanted to spend time with Rebecca Finley, I probably would have shrugged at the impossibility and never given it more thought.

A bookish, quiet guy by nature, I'd never exactly been a lady magnet. After my mom died, I almost felt like I didn't deserve to be happy in a world where she didn't live, so I shut down even more and kept to myself.

"This is so awesome." Rebecca watched with delight as her rainbow jellyfish kite rose higher and higher, its tentacles waving in the breeze, following its body as it dove on the gusts when she pulled the string.

I'd showed her how to unroll the kite string and tie it to the plastic holder before re-rolling it. Once I'd made the mistake of launching a kite straight from a spindle of string. It went up, up, then it detached and flew away. No kid had to learn that lesson twice.

"You got the hang of it quickly," I said.

She grinned like a kid who'd smuggled a bagful of bubble gum into class. "I'm a kite flier, what can I say?"

She was a kite flier.

Mine was a blue shark with a long tail and rainbow fins. It was a little zippier, but it didn't have the color display of hers. She hadn't hesitated when it came time to pick the one she wanted to fly. A box kite that could do tricks had been an option, but she was set on the jellyfish, and with a small running start, it lifted straight into the sky.

We ran around like a couple of toddlers, screaming as the wind whipped our kites into the air and marveling at them when they climbed and dipped on the breeze. Rebecca charged across the field with her arm held high and the kite string trailing behind her.

I didn't know what I was doing there with her. It should have been some other guy, some football player or student body president, someone with stature on campus. She was that kind of girl, the one who would be elected homecoming queen without lobbying her friends to talk her up to the rest of the school.

She radiated light, starting with the gold and pink streaks in her hair and ending with her smile. People wanted to be around her. People didn't feel that way about me, and I was fine with that. I knew my place.

So how the hell did I end up on a grassy bluff overlooking the bay, flying kites with her?

She ran back in my direction, careening with the jumping flight of the kite. Without slowing on her approach, she ran smack into me.

"Sorry, it was the wind," she said. "I meant to run past you, but a gust sent me the other way."

"Ha. Likely story." I grasped her by the arms to steady her. "You good?"

She nodded. "I know it's crazy since I ate a giant burger two hours ago, but I'm hungry."

"It's not crazy. You're getting your appetite back. That's good. And besides, it's been more like three hours."

"Really? We've been flying kites for three hours?"

"Yup."

"Wow. I just . . . wow. I guess we're not going back before dark." She looked around, taking in the scenery in some new way. "The sun's gonna set soon. How did I not notice that when I've been staring at the sky for the past three hours?"

"You've been focused on your kite. You're a kite flier, Rebecca."

"Yeah. Totally." She smiled at me. Her lips parted like maybe she was going to say something else, but then she stopped herself.

"What?" I asked.

She shook her head. "Nothing. It doesn't matter."

"Rebecca, everything matters."

She nodded. "True. I was just thinking I like it when you say my name."

I couldn't have said why, but I loved hearing that. I tucked the morsel of information away like a lucky penny and watched our kites dance together in the sky.

Slowly, we reeled our kites back in until we could control them. Then we sat on the grass and watched the sun aim at the horizon, squinting until we couldn't bear to look at it any longer.

The timing was perfect—the afternoon light bouncing off the bay and the breeze dying down to where it felt balmy. If she were any other girl, I'd have kissed her by then. I couldn't have painted a more perfect setting, and I'd teed everything up with the kites and the romantic lighting.

But she was Rebecca. Unattainable. If we kissed now, it would be because I'd taken advantage of her in a vulnerable moment, and I couldn't bear that.

She was there because we were friends. So I took her hand again —it felt so natural that I pushed away thoughts about how I didn't hold hands with any of my other friends—and we walked back to my car, talking about the best places to eat in Berkeley.

"You really want to eat at Skates?" I asked when she suggested the seafood place just across the harbor from us.

"Yeah. It's right there. That's what gave me the idea."

It was expensive and kind of a date place, kind of an older people place. I never would have suggested it. *But if that's where she wants to go . . .* "Sure. Let's go to Skates."

CHAPTER FIVE

ecca

I'D NEVER EATEN at Skates. My best friend Lucy's sister was a college freshman at Berkeley, and I remembered being at Lucy's over winter break and hearing her sister talk about going to Skates with her date and a bunch of friends before a fraternity formal. It sounded sophisticated and cool, and since the day so far had felt like an escape from my regular life, I wanted the fantasy to continue.

We sat at a table at the very end of a long wall of windows. Our view took in the expanse of the San Francisco Bay and Angel Island, which sat between the Berkeley coastline and the northern end of San Francisco. I stared at the island, remembering the times my dad had taken all six of us kids there on the BART train with our bikes. We'd ridden the trails like banshees while our parents had screamed at us to slow down.

Everywhere I looked from then on would be tinged with bitter-sweet memories unless I moved far away. For college, I vowed, I'd give myself some distance.

"Are you a seafood fan?" Blake perused the menu.

What type of food they served at Skates hadn't even occurred to me. I just liked the idea of the place because it seemed cool and it was on the water. *Was I a seafood fan? Did it even matter?*

The sun had fallen below the horizon, and its glow still topped the blue Pacific, glowing bright and sinking fast before our eyes. I didn't care what I ate as long as I could keep moving forward, feeling something other than sadness. Blake had allowed me to accomplish that for hours on end, and I wanted as much of it as I could get.

"Enough of one to find something. How about you? Is this okay?" I asked.

What if he hates seafood? The menu had to have something he could eat. *Was it selfish of me to suggest this place without thinking about him? Probably.* Everything about me lately had been selfish—grieving, rebelling, pushing people away. "We can go someplace else," I said, not taking my eyes off the sun.

"Are you kidding? Look at this view. It's perfect," he said.

I knew he was watching me instead of the sunset, but I wasn't willing to look away from the sun until it had fully descended, and the last butter pat of yellow light had melted into the sea. When I turned back to him, his face lit up pink like the high clouds that still absorbed the sun's rays. I tapped his menu. "What are you going to eat? I'm definitely having the cheesecake."

"For dinner?"

"Well, after dinner, so I'm planning accordingly. Clam chowder and maybe a salad."

"Fish and chips. I've got English ancestors somewhere who would be very proud."

"Yeah? I have English ancestors." I felt the telltale creep of blush over my pale skin while he gazed at my face.

"From where?" he asked.

"Liverpool. You?"

"Ireland."

That made me laugh. "You know Ireland isn't England, right? It's a totally different country."

"I'm generalizing for the sake of making us seem connected."

"I'll concede, then. But I'm holding my ground on the food. Not sure they eat fish and chips in Ireland." As though it mattered.

He shrugged and snapped his menu shut. The sky was still light enough that we could see a flock of birds flying in the distance, their formation a near-perfect V. "If you were a bird, do you think you'd be the one at the point, leading all the other ones, or somewhere in the pack?" I asked. I'd always wondered how birds chose who to follow.

"I have a terrible sense of direction, so I'd probably be in the back. Otherwise, the other birds would probably revolt and kick me out of the squad when we ended up in Alaska for the winter instead of a Mexican beach."

I laughed. "Birds don't fly in squads. Aren't they flocks?"

He wagged a finger at me. "Not if they're crows. Then it's called a murder. Who's to say some birds don't hang in squads?"

"Fine. You win. Your bird gang can hang in a squad, with you bringing up the rear," I said.

Our waiter dropped off a basket of bread, and we rattled off our orders, never taking our eyes off each other. Blake dug into the bread, tearing a piece off the loaf and offering it to me. It was warm, and I happily smeared it with butter before taking a bite.

"Kite flying works up an appetite, huh?" he asked, watching me.

"I guess it does." It felt good to have an appetite. It made me believe I was creeping out of the stupor that had claimed my soul for weeks. A new normal. "Wow, this is the first day I've had an appetite since my dad went into hospice care."

Blake hadn't asked me anything about my dad or how I felt about his death, and maybe that was because he knew after going through something similar. I hadn't wanted to talk about that stuff anyway. But being with him was so easy that I found I wanted to share a little bit more of myself with him, kind of a reward for not asking.

"When was that? When did he go into hospice?" Blake watched my response as if treading carefully.

"It was home hospice, so a worker came and lived with us for about two weeks to keep him comfortable, make sure he suffered as little as possible."

"That must've been hard to watch."

"I guess it's supposed to prepare you, you know? You see it coming. The person gets sicker, you know he's going to die. But there's no real way to prepare for the complete lack of a person. The hole." I surveyed Blake to see if he really wanted to hear the answers to his questions.

Some people asked, but they really just wanted pat answers. They wanted to hear I was fine, so I told them I was. That was easier than seeing their discomfort when they struggled to know what to say or how to act. But Blake reached out and put his hand over mine, and his gaze told me he wanted to hear whatever I wanted to tell him, which made me want to keep going.

"I don't know if you know, but I have four sisters and a brother. Plus my mom and my dad's brother, who's been staying with us. So it's a full house of people, all feeling sad together," I said.

"Does that help? Or are you all circling in each other's grief?" he asked.

I hadn't thought of it like that. "Everyone's dealing with it in their own way. Honestly, I'm probably the biggest basket case because I was his favorite. And I know, no parent is supposed to have a favorite, but let's be honest, they all do, and I was his. I'm the most like him."

I took a deep breath, and when I let it out, it came out a sigh.

Blake nodded like he could tell that was all I wanted to say for the moment. "I'm sorry." He squeezed my hand.

"Thanks." I squeezed back. "What was it like for you? With your mom?" It felt only fair to see if he wanted to talk about it.

"Oh, well, she died in a car accident, so it was sudden. She wasn't sick." His words came out in a way that sounded like he was fine. His voice didn't break or waiver, but I could see in the depth of his eyes how much it still hurt.

I shook my head. "That's so...sad—and hard. If I'd known, I'd have done...something. Or at least tried to be nicer. I'm sorry if I was self-absorbed."

He gave me another small smile with his lips closed. I was starting to recognize it as his sympathetic smile. "Not at all. You didn't know me, and I didn't tell many people."

"Still . . ."

His fingers brushed the back of my hand, making circles that caused my breath to hitch. I was aware of my heart beating faster. It felt like a drum in my chest. "I'm certain that if you'd known, you'd have helped me. You're helping me now. Just being here with you feels like a gift. I'm really . . . I like hanging out with you."

"I like hanging out with you too." I blurted, not needing to think to know it was true.

It was easy to get lost in the soft kindness of his eyes, but my gaze moved to his mouth, which he must have noticed because he licked his bottom lip. I leaned in an inch, wanting to see what he would do. I looked back at his eyes, and for a moment, I thought he wanted what I did. He leaned closer, and the corner of his lips tipped up in a smile.

Then the waiter came with our entrees and fussed around our table, asking if we wanted more bread and refilling our water glasses.

When he finally left, I looked for what I'd seen in Blake's eyes before. But the moment was gone. Replaced by a plate of fish and chips.

CHAPTER SIX

ecca

WE WERE BELTING out the lyrics to U2's entire album, *All That You Can't Leave Behind*. We started with "Beautiful Day," which it had been. From the moment we'd left campus, Blake had transformed my day. I didn't question whether Blake would know the lyrics or whether he would have a CD of my favorite band. He'd said he was Irish. If he didn't have at least one U2 album, I would call him an angry expat.

I didn't know if Blake picked the specific album because he knew the lyrics about finding beauty in a hopeless place would resonate with me, and I didn't ask. I opened the car window all the way and sang louder, letting my hair blow in my face and feeling wild.

I'd lost track of where we'd driven, but at some point, we were at the top of Grizzly Peak, eating cheesecake we'd ordered to-go after dinner. Then we were sneaking over a fence to dip our toes in the freezing water of Lake Anza.

"Wowza, that's cold." He shuddered.

"It's perfect."

"Perfect for polar bears."

"C'mon, let's skinny dip. I dare you." I wasn't sure if I really had the guts to do it and felt fairly certain he wouldn't call my bluff.

"No way, not doing that."

"Fine, chicken." I smirked at him, taunting him and wondering what he would do about it.

"You really like playing with fire, don't you?" He looked me over.

I nodded. If he was fire, then yes. Yes, I did. I leaned over and bumped his shoulder, feeling a warm thrill at the contact and hoping he would take the hint and kiss me.

He put an arm around me instead and tugged me close to his side. I inhaled the scent of him, which smelled like clean laundry and pine body spray. We sat in the muddy sand, dug our toes in where the cold water kissed the shore, and looked for stars overhead. The longer we looked, the more we could see.

Later we drove up and down the streets in a seedy part of Oakland, taking photos of cool graffiti with our phones. Eventually, we had to refill his gas tank.

"Can we play the song one more time? I know you're probably tired of it," I said, already cueing "Stuck in a Moment" from the same album we'd been listening to.

"It's a good song. We can play it on repeat all night if you want." By the fourth time through, tears rolled down my cheeks. "I feel like Bono wrote this song for me. I know he didn't, but…I need to hear it again. I'm so stuck."

We parked on the side of the road and sat on the hood of the car, drinking convenience store slushies I insisted he let me buy. Mine was purple. He'd gone with classic cherry cola.

"You're not stuck," Blake said quietly, taking my hand and bringing it to his lips.

I convinced myself that all those sweet gestures were just things a normal new friend would do, even though I hoped it wasn't.

We sat quietly, listening to the lyrics, with Blake reaching over every so often to blot away a tear that ran down my cheek. The song encouraged me to get out of my own way and move toward something new.

The more time I spent with Blake, the more I knew I wanted it to include him. He felt…right.

The sun had long since gone down, and I called my mom and said I was sleeping at my best friend Lucy's house. Then I called Lucy and told her not to tell my mom I wasn't there.

Sometime over the course of our dinner, Blake and I had decided we were going to stay up all night. That was the entire plan, staying up. I had no idea if that meant we would drive around or find things that were open in the middle of the night. But I didn't care. I didn't want to go home. For the hours I'd spent with Blake, I hadn't been sad, and I wasn't ready for that to end. Going home was a sure way to bring me back to reality, and I didn't want it. Not yet.

It was the first time I'd ever lied to my mom about spending the night out, but I'd learned from Lucy, who was a pro. She'd been dating her boyfriend, Dillon, for a year, and when she wanted to spend the night at his house, she pretended to be sleeping over with me. So far, none of the adults in our lives had been the wiser, and I'd always planned to use her as my alibi when the time came to sneak out.

My mom seemed relieved she didn't have one more kid to deal with that night, and my sisters were busy doing homework and dealing with their own lives. If ever a time was tailor-made to stay out all night with a guy, it was this one. It never occurred to me to ask Blake what his excuse was to his dad. I just assumed he had a Lucy.

"Where to next?" I slid into the passenger seat of his car as though I belonged there.

Blake shrugged and laughed quietly. "I have no idea." He looped around to the driver's side and got in. When he put his hands on the steering wheel, the white knuckles reappeared, and I felt an iron weight drop to the pit of my stomach. His closed-mouth smile had returned sometime during dinner, and I'd begun to have the deflating feeling that I'd overstayed my welcome. He'd wanted to be nice, getting me out of my detention gloom, but we'd been together for over seven hours.

"I mean, we don't have to go anywhere. If you changed your mind and want to drop me at home, that's cool."

His head whipped around, and he looked at me, his face a concerned tangle of emotions. "Do you want to go home? Are you . . . is everything okay?"

"Of course. It's fine. I just didn't want you to feel obligated to keep me company. You've been amazing for hanging with me all day. I just—"

He reached out and held a finger against my lips to stop me. "I don't feel obligated at all. I told you. I like hanging out with you."

"Okay . . . well, I like…you." The air in the car felt heavy, and I wondered if the thought of kissing me had wandered through his mind at all.

What would he do if I leaned over and kissed him?

His lips were full and pink, and he had a tendency to rub his knuckle slowly across them when he was considering what to do. My brain reeled with all kinds of ideas. The mere existence of his mouth was an invitation. *Invitation to what?* I had no clue what I wanted from him, but it had something to do with that mouth and his hands on my body. Beyond that, I didn't care how it all went down.

"Actually, what about the drive-in theater in Emeryville?" he asked.

Is a drive-in movie a metaphor for car sex?

Maybe we were on the same page—only without the car sex. I wasn't about to lose my virginity in the back of a car. I hadn't thought through too many of the other specifics, but I knew that much.

"I haven't been to a drive-in movie since . . . I don't even know. Sure, we could do that. Or just a regular movie in a theater." I tried to gauge whether his interest in the drive-in was about the movie or the car sex.

"Me either. I hope you don't think it's weird, but I kind of like our little bubble in the car. I don't feel like sitting in a row with other people. Am I a freak?"

Maybe, but he was exactly the kind of freak I wanted to be with. He was right. I liked hermitting in his car, holding hands up on the cliff, holing up at our table by the window at Skates. I felt protected from the world with him, and I wanted to keep that going. "Nope, let's do the drive-in. You're right. It'll be fun."

The movie didn't start until ten. We got there an hour early and parked the car in a great spot for viewing the screen. We'd just eaten, so we didn't need snacks, which meant we had an hour to hang in the car. The intimacy of being in such close quarters might have felt weird ordinarily, but nothing about my day with Blake had been ordinary.

Mostly, we talked. It was funny that I hadn't realized I wanted to talk. In fact, I'd shut everyone down who'd tried to get me to open up about my feelings, mainly because it seemed like they were asking because it was the right thing to do or because they wanted to satisfy their curiosity. I also didn't know how I felt. It was easier to shut down.

"You still haven't asked me your one big question." I gave him jazz hands at the magnitude of the question he supposedly had for me. "Do you actually have something you want to ask me, or were you just reserving the right to ask something big in the future?"

It worked. I got the full smile from him, finally, and it was worth it. When he smiled without hesitation or worry, the dimple popped in his cheek, and his eyes danced with curiosity and playfulness.

"I have something I want to ask."

"Okay. I've been waiting. Ask away. I'm ready." I squared my shoulders and prepared for the usual questions. *How did it feel to have your dad die? Why did you freak out so much when you knew he was dying of brain cancer, and it was bound to happen? How are you feeling, really?*

I'd heard them all from my well-meaning friends and teachers. I didn't have good answers to any of the questions. My answers all seemed obvious and impossible to articulate at the same time. But Blake had been nice to me all day and hadn't asked me anything. I could do my best to answer one of those versions of the same question.

"What's the one thing you miss most about your dad?"

Oh.

That was not what I expected. I also didn't expect to burst into tears. The tears flowed uncontrollably, fat and insistent and real. I tried to stem the flood I felt coming hard and fast, which resulted in me not taking in enough air.

"Oh my God, I'm so sorry." He waved his hands like he could erase his question. "Forget I asked that. I didn't mean to upset you. Jesus, that's the last thing I wanted to do. I was hoping you'd think of something nice, and it would make you happy."

"No, it is. It does. I'm just . . . I wasn't expecting you to ask that, and it's . . . you're the first person who's asked me about *him*," I said, still sobbing. "And I appreciate it so much. Because...I miss him so much."

He gingerly reached for me and pulled me toward him, which was hard with the stick shift knob and the space between our seats, but I didn't care. I wanted to be in his arms. My head was dizzy with confounding wonder.

How does he always know the right thing to say to me?

He didn't know my dad or me, and he still cared enough to ask. I buried my face in his shoulder, and he held me tightly, his head dipped to the top of my head, his hands rubbing my back and neck.

Who is this guy? And how have I overlooked him for two years?

I felt such a rush of affection and gratitude for how he'd turned my day around—hell, maybe he'd turned my world around—that all I could think to do was kiss him.

"Blake . . ." I pulled back far enough so I could see his face. "I promise I will answer you. I'd love to tell you about my dad. But first…just let me . . ."

Gently, I leaned in and brushed my lips against his, closing my eyes to heighten the sensation of my lips against his pillowy mouth, which responded tentatively. He reached a hand around the nape of my neck, and his fingers wove through my hair while he kissed me back, delicately at first, then with more feeling and intensity.

"Can I?" I reached gently for his glasses and pulled them away when he nodded. "Can you see without them?"

"I'm nearsighted. So I can see you, but not much else." He smiled. "In other words, I can see everything."

He cupped my jaw in his hand and tilted my face to the angle he liked. His mouth covered mine without hesitation or apology. He'd been so solicitous all day, but he wasn't holding back anymore.

He licked my bottom lip, and I opened my mouth greedily. Our movements felt clunky because of the car seats and because everything was new, but our mouths melded like they were meant for each other and had finally found their way home. I reached and felt the stubble on his chin. He wasn't tall or built like an athlete, but he was more of a man than most.

After a few minutes of breathless kissing, we broke apart and looked at each other. I immediately turned away. This was so new and so strange, and I didn't usually initiate kisses with guys.

Blake shifted my face toward his, and our eyes connected. "Are you okay? Was this"—he gestured between us—"too much?"

I shook my head then nodded. "Not too much. Just…unexpected. But good. You?"

The smile invaded his face, and he ran a hand through his hair. The rumpling just made it look sexier. "Oh, I'm great. I've got the most beautiful girl in the entire school in the front seat of my car, and she just kissed me. I might as well get my GED now. High school is officially complete."

I laughed at that. "You kissed me back, you know. I might get some bragging rights too."

"Yeah? Do girls do that? I thought that was a guy thing."

"Oh, we brag, I assure you."

Though generally, I didn't. I kept my hookups to myself because my friends were anything but discreet. I'd once told my two best friends in English class that I made out with a basketball player, and by the end of the period, the entire school had known. My friends liked to have good dirt on everyone, and the basketball player and I were excellent dirt. We'd never ended up going on a date, and after that, I did my best to keep my exploits to myself unless I was really serious about a guy. And that hadn't happened over the past year.

I didn't want to think about where Blake fell on the spectrum of seriousness or what I might say to my friends about him. It was too soon. I didn't want to think about anything except kissing him again.

Fortunately, we had agreement there, a nonverbal, tongue-tangling, fused-lip agreement.

He leaned in and grazed the line of my jaw with his lips. When he reached my ear, he whispered, "I'd really like to give you more to brag about."

His breath against my skin sent comet trails of fire through every part of my body, and I dropped my lips to his neck and sucked on the soft skin.

We were barely fazed by the awkwardness of being in the front seat of a car with bucket seats and things like glove compartments and steering wheels as recreational hazards. When his knee banged into the center console as he tried to move closer and hold me tighter, we barely acknowledged the jangling of his parking meter coins and the collision of his head with the rearview mirror.

I wanted him closer, I wanted to kiss him, and I wanted him to touch me. The details of how it happened and what immovable car parts needed to be navigated felt irrelevant.

"Can you come all the way over here?" I moved to one side of my seat to determine if he would have enough space to slide in next to me.

"I can try. I'm skinny, but I think I'd need to be a hollowed-out pelt to fit there." He put his hands on either side of my shoulders, where they could rest on the back of the seat. Then he gingerly shifted his weight and threw one leg over the console, leaving the stick shift dangerously close to rendering him unable to conceive kids with one unfortunate miscalculation.

"You're not skinny," I said. "You're exactly right."

"You're kind, but I know I'm no quarterback." Then he made it the rest of the way over, tilting the seat to full recline and straddling my lap. "Okay, this could actually work." He hovered over me on his elbows and kissed me softly, edging my lips apart with his tongue and delving deeper.

"You should know," I whispered against his lips, "I don't want a quarterback."

He pulled back and looked into my eyes, and I saw that he craved me as much as I desired him. And I only wanted him. His lips crushed against mine, and I forgot to breathe as he took everything I could give him. We stayed there for a long time, kissing like it was our mission.

Even in the cramped space, I moved to the side with my back against the door handle, so he could roll to his side, facing me. He reached for my cheek and caressed it before kissing me there, then on the tip of my nose, my chin. The reverent look in his eyes shifted in a flash to something worried.

"Hey." I wrapped my hands around the back of his neck. "What are you thinking about?"

He smiled, but it wasn't his real smile. "Nothing. I'm not thinking about anything." He was lying, and it bothered me.

"Liar."

"How dare you accuse me of thinking when, I assure you, your lips have made it impossible?"

I had no retort for that, so we kissed for another ten minutes. Or an hour. But things he'd said nagged at me. I looked at him again. His face seemed more relaxed, and I liked it.

"I have a serious question," I said. "You have to promise to answer it."

"Okay, I promise, though it's kind of unfair to make me promise before I've heard the question."

"Fine, I'll ask it first, then you can decide, but I'd like you to answer . . . why do you keep saying things about how you don't measure up to football players, like you're assuming I'm only interested in superstar jocks, and this is some kind of pity date?"

"It's just my self-deprecating personality." He grinned sheepishly. He was sweet, and he had a handsome face behind his self-doubt, so why did he keep insisting he was undesirable?

I ran a finger across his lips, and he shuddered and closed his eyes for a second.

"I don't think it's that. I feel like you believe you're not good enough. Do I make you feel that way? Why do you think that?"

His eyes revealed that he realized the difference between what he was saying and what I was saying. "Oh. No, no, it's nothing you're doing. You're...amazing. It was just me being insecure about not being your type."

"Right, but you're assuming I have a type. You're thinking I have some preference for certain kinds of guys, guys who aren't you."

He nodded and looked away.

In the distance, I could hear muffled sounds, probably music playing on the drive-in channel in other people's cars. We hadn't turned ours on, and I couldn't have been less interested in hearing the pre-film soundtrack.

His voice was quiet when he spoke. "That wasn't how I meant it. It's not that you believe you're too good for me. It's me. *I* think you're too good for me."

"You shouldn't think that."

"Okay...well, some habits are hard to break. I've never really thought of myself as cool-girl dating material."

"Now you're labeling me, and that's kind of unfair. I'm not a cool girl. I'm just me. I'm cheerful and loud and confident. I don't know if people like me or if they're secretly talking about me behind my back. And honestly, I don't really care. Or at least I didn't before. Now I feel like I'm walking around with this big rain cloud over my head that everyone can see. It feels...conspicuous."

He nodded and let out a sigh. "That sucks."

"Until today. You knew what I needed. I will…always be grateful for that."

"Always? That's some pretty big gratitude right there." He smirked.

"Yeah. The kind of gratitude that might even get you to second base. Oh, wait, given that you're not an athlete, and you make a point of avoiding all that cool-kid stuff, do you know what second base is? See in baseball, when a batter—"

"Stop. I don't give a shit about baseball, but I know where second base is." He rolled me under him and showed me exactly how well he knew the game.

CHAPTER SEVEN

lake

I WAS PRETTY sure they played the movie. Didn't know. Didn't care. I spent the two hours when I might have been watching the on-screen guy woo his girl feeling like I was the star of my own romance. In my fictional universe where I got the girl, I wasn't about to glance away for a second to see if the world was imploding around us.

Kissing every inch of Rebecca's skin had been a dream but never a goal—goals implied a concrete way to achieve them.

I had no game and no plan.

I was okay with the way high school would unfold, with her shining brightly and me plodding along, waiting to grow a few inches and enter a phase of life when being smart was more important than being a good-looking jock. In other words, college or sometime later.

After a year of driving my car and wondering what I would do if I ever got a girl in there who wanted to push the limits of the car-as-bed, I quickly discovered that the passenger seat was practically made for it. Thank you, Volkswagen engineers, for making all my teenage dreams come true.

I hated that I'd made her cry. I hadn't thought my question would garner that response, but thinking back, I was an idiot. I should have stuck to something banal, but I wanted her to focus on something positive when I asked about her dad. Emotional intelligence was not my strong suit.

It seemed like a far-superior idea to keep the talking to a minimum and focus on testing the limits of my car's hookup capacity. I rolled Rebecca onto her back in the reclined passenger seat and moved to hover above her again. She was beautiful, and she looked so trusting and open lying there beneath me. I knew I should probably take things slow, but I was a teenager incapable of restraint when I watched the rise of her chest beneath me. I couldn't change course when I felt the hitch in her breath when I kissed along her jaw to the tender spot beneath her ear.

Hearing her quiet moan, I forgot about everything but doing whatever I could to hear that sound again.

It was like melted butter, and I wanted it to feed me—then drown me.

We kissed for an hour—*maybe two hours, who knew?*—and new feelings settled in. *Who was I kidding?*

I'd liked her from afar for two years, but in a matter of hours, I was falling in love with her.

It was exhilarating at that point in my life, but it was dangerous. I probably couldn't be what she wanted me to be. For the time she seemed happy to make out with me, I selfishly took everything she was willing to give. Maybe this one night was all I'd ever get.

Eventually, we redirected our attention to the on-screen drama of *Pride and Prejudice*. The movie played, but we'd turned off the volume. We'd been assigned the book in sophomore lit, so we'd both read it, but Rebecca admitted she'd already seen the movie.

"This is the part where Darcy says he loves her," Rebecca said, leaning her chin on her hand and watching Keira Knightly on the screen, mesmerized. "'I cannot fix on the hours, or the spot, or the look, or the words, which laid the foundation.'" Her voice sounded lazy and content while her fingers ran over the back of my neck.

I fantasized she was saying those words to me. I finished the line from the book, and my words definitely were meant for her. "'My real purpose was to see *you*, and to judge, if I could, whether I might ever hope to make you love me.'"

She turned to me, surprised. "You know the line from the book?"

"Of course. It's like the ultimate romantic line. Every guy should know it. Damned Darcy had Jane Austen putting words in his mouth, making him look better than the rest of us."

She smiled. "Most guys I know didn't even read the book. They used Spark Notes or read a summary on Wikipedia."

"I don't like to take the easy way out," I said, drowning in the heavy buzz of her presence. I swore, in a hundred nights like this, I would never get enough of her.

We lay next to each other and talked, our faces about four inches apart until I couldn't stand the distance anymore. Then I would run a hand over her face or lean in for another taste of her lips. It was hands down the best night of my life.

I couldn't help but worry that once we were back in the real world, with the social hierarchy of high school at play, we would both resume our normal lives. Apart. Maybe that made me a pessimist, but I didn't know if we would fit into the larger constellation of our high school experience as a couple.

"Okay, I'm ready to answer your question now." She turned sideways and adjusted her arm so it wasn't smashed.

I'd almost forgotten about my question and the fact that she hadn't answered. I had so many more enjoyable things I wanted to do with her. My arm had gone numb, pinned underneath her. I tried to wave with the other one to tell her she didn't need to answer. "Not necessary. It was a bad question."

"It was a great question. That's why it made me so emotional. I want to answer it."

"Okay. Totally up to you." I really did want to hear her answer as long as it didn't hurt her.

She traced the features on my face while she spoke, and I tried not to get distracted by her touch because I wanted to listen, but it was damn near impossible to focus.

"My dad was a heart surgeon, so he worked a lot and got called in for emergency procedures on patients. He had a crazy schedule and a demanding job, and he loved it. He used to say that fixing a heart made him feel like he was performing a miracle every time. Not so much for the patient—I mean, anyone who has a life-threatening health issue that requires a surgeon probably feels like their doctor is some kind of miracle worker. He felt like he was blessed with witnessing a miracle when he repaired a heart. The fact that he could go in and fix the part of a person's body responsible for pumping blood through their veins, he always said he felt lucky that he could do that for a living."

"He sounds selfless. And humble. Don't a lot of doctors have a sort of God complex because they hold life in their hands?"

"Maybe, but he never did. He felt like he was the one who got lucky because patients trusted him enough with their hearts to let him help them."

"Good to have a role model like that."

"Oh, he was also a total nut. He pushed the boundaries of health and safety every day of his life. Rode a motorcycle, went hang gliding every chance he got, even owned a squirrel suit, but he never got a chance to use it. He bought it when he was diagnosed with glioblastoma. He said, 'If I'm gonna go down, I'm doing it from the top of Half Dome in a squirrel suit.' He just got so sick so quickly, he was never able to go."

"Sounds like you take after him a little, the spirited part of you—from what I can see."

"Really? I hope so. I think I'm always trying to prove my spirit goes deeper than cheerleading. He showed me it's the only way to be. He said the thrill seekers had the most fun, even if they were thrill-seeking through books or horror movies. Not everyone's meant to sky dive. He didn't judge. He just wanted people to push their boundaries."

I nodded. "You were lucky to have him as a dad."

"Yeah. I know."

"Your whole life, you can honor his memory by pushing your boundaries."

She smiled. "I'm doing that right now, with you."

"Then I owe him a big one. Because I'm really glad you're here," I said.

She moved closer to me, if closer were even possible in the cramped passenger seat, and put her hands on my chest. Every graze of her fingers added fuel to a fire that I'd have a hard time extinguishing

Looking into her eyes, I felt a pang of disappointment, anticipating having to drive her home eventually. What would it be like to see her at school, no longer protected by our car bubble? My brain was always in overdrive, thinking about the future and savoring the present moment only briefly.

"Hey," she said, almost like she could see me disappearing into my head.

I was worried about a lot of things—her feelings now, my feelings later if tonight was a one-time thing.

Of course it was a one-time thing. It's not like she's your girlfriend. You helped her on a bad day, and you hooked up. Get over yourself.

She guided my face, so I was looking right into her eyes. "Are you okay? You seem like you just went someplace else. We can totally go home if you're sick of me." She laughed after she said it, but I saw the vulnerability, and it made me want to encourage her to be open. "The whole staying-up-all-night thing doesn't need to happen. I'm good. You really helped me today."

"I could never be sick of you," I said before I had a chance to stop the truth from tumbling out. I worried my honesty would freak her out.

"That's the nicest thing anyone's ever said to me." She giggled like a kid.

Her lips grazed mine, and I immediately snapped to the present. It was stupid to waste my time worrying about tomorrow. I kissed her back harder with all the intensity I felt for her. I wanted her. Physically, I wanted everything from her, even if it was too soon.

My body didn't want an explanation for why it was wrong.

She pressed harder against me, the heat building between us until our clothes were too hot, too constraining, too much. She pulled at my shirt, tugging it from the waistband of my jeans, and I did the same, pulling her white uniform shirt from the sweatpants she'd grabbed from her locker when we left campus.

We went from zero to a million in about four seconds. It was fumbling and awkward, but we felt right together, at least to me. I was too much in my own head and my own world of wonder to tune in to what she might have been thinking, so I just listened to her words and the noises she made and decided to believe them.

I marveled at her luscious breasts with their pert pink nipples. I kissed them. I fondled them. My eyes fluttered shut when she ran her hands over my chest and licked her way down to my belt buckle.

I didn't know what she wanted or how to give it to her, and I didn't ask. I wrapped every emotion I'd been carrying for her into my touch as I worshipped her body. I hoped it was enough. I knew she needed something I was probably powerless to give her, but damn if I didn't want to try. I wanted to be everything she sought in that moment.

When she went for my belt buckle, I panicked.

"We can't," I said, breathless and stupid, but trying to take the high road that was rising further from my reach with every moment I was with her.

"We can, and we should. Please, Blake . . ."

She was going to melt my resistance with those words, but I couldn't take advantage of her, and that was what it would be. She probably wouldn't regret ditching or spending the night with me, but she might regret sex.

"Are you sure you're thinking clearly? You don't just want this because you're upset?"

"I'm not upset."

"But you were. It's been a rough couple of weeks for you."

"Blake, stop overthinking it. Just go with it."

How badly did I want to do exactly what she was asking? If a ten-minute period went by that I wasn't thinking about having sex with a girl, it was only because I'd only made it for five.

Everything felt great. Maybe that was why I hesitated. Because I had the delusional nerve to think that if I took it a little bit slower —if I didn't give her what she was asking for—maybe we would become a couple, and I would get to have sex with her all the time as her boyfriend.

It was possible that was what I was thinking. Or I was just trying to be a good guy in the moment. The details were blurry.

"Are you a virgin?" she asked, studying my face. "Is that why?"

Her question held no judgment, but she wasn't going to let go of the discussion until I explained myself. *Fine.* Maybe talking would cool the moment. Talking was probably good.

"No. Negative. For sure not." I watched her face to gauge her reaction. And her reaction was…surprise.

"Oh. Well, I am, actually."

"Okay. Cool." *Was there any way that was an appropriate response?*

I did my level best not to act as shocked as I felt. It wasn't that I thought Rebecca was a slut, not by any stretch of the imagination. But she was every guy's dream. I knew she'd dated a bunch of different jocks at school, or at least they'd made it sound like she'd dated them.

Come to think of it, almost nothing I thought I knew squared with the person I'd spent the past twelve hours getting to know. Maybe she hadn't dated many guys. Maybe she was waiting for someone special to do the deed. *Well. Okay.* In no way did I imagine that person to be me.

"Guess it's good one of us has experience, then." She smiled at me like no part of our conversation had dissuaded her from her mission.

Except that I'd lied. I was a virgin with a capital *V*, but I'd been trained early by my horny pack of dude friends to never admit to my lack of experience, especially in the presence of a girl when there was a sliver of a chance of getting lucky.

"Actually, if I'm being honest...I haven't...done that before. I'm sorry I lied. I just didn't want you to think . . . I don't know."

She nodded. "I get it. It's okay. But please don't lie to me again."

"No, never. Of course not."

My brain was exploding with the possibilities that lay before me. *Sex? Tonight? With Rebecca?* I was lucky my whole head didn't blow off my body. That was how severely my brain was working to figure out if there was any way it was a good idea. *Sex! Tonight! With Rebecca!* began playing on a loop.

It wasn't that I'd put her on a pedestal. Okay, I had. That made me want to be her first even more. Even though I didn't know what I could do to make it necessarily memorable, I would at least take care to make sure she felt good. A part of me wanted to be that guy for her. But not now, not like this. Not in my goddamned Jetta in a parking lot.

"We can't. We shouldn't," I said.

"We should, and we can."

"Well, maybe I can't," I said because I was an idiot.

"Like literally can't? Because from what I can tell, you seem like you can."

"I don't mean physically. I mean it's too impulsive, we barely know each other. I don't want you to do something you'll regret."

"I feel like I know you," she whispered, and it made my heart ache.

I wanted to believe her, but caution took over. *How could I know what sex meant to her?* I stalled some more, my hand clinging to the zipper of my pants to prevent her from getting to it. "I'm just not sure . . ."

What am I even saying?

I was sure. I wanted to be with her so badly my dick was throbbing in my pants, and the energy it took to tell her no was making it harder and harder to think clearly.

"Will you regret it?" She looked incredulous.

"Not in a million years, no. But I don't want your first time to be on a night you're upset."

"I don't feel upset. Although the more we talk about it, the more I'm starting to get upset."

"Argh. This is terrible."

"Yes. At least we agree. Now what are we going to do about it?"

Fuck it. I tried to be a stand-up guy, but a horny teenager could only take so much when he's been given the gift of the girl he'd jerked off to for a year, and she was begging him for sex.

"How about this?" I hated the sound of the words as I said them. "We put a pin in this tonight. Not because I don't want to do this with you, because I do. So much. But let's get to know each other better. If it's good now, it will be even better when we're more connected, right?"

"Okay, Mr. Debate King. Is this where I offer a counter argument with evidence?"

"No. This is where you'll thank me later for not taking your virginity at a drive-in theater."

"Fine. I was just trying to live according to my dad's ideals, but if you can't handle that . . ."

"Oh no, you're not gonna guilt me with the dead dad. No, no, no. Remember, I have the dead mom. I know all."

"So, what do you suggest? When will we do it, if not tonight?"

"I don't know. Sometime soon. Let's make a pact, okay? Whenever it is, we'll be each other's first. What do you think your dad would think of a virginity pact?"

She laughed and kissed me. "I think he'd think it was crazy. Which makes it perfect."

I could live with perfect.

We stayed there until the sun came up, and reluctantly, I drove her home. We were both exhausted, but I could tell she was happy. We stopped for breakfast before I dropped her off, and she programmed her cell phone number into my phone.

I promised to call her. I kissed her goodbye. Then I fell apart.

CHAPTER EIGHT

ecca

I DIDN'T KNOW what I expected to happen on Monday when we got to school. I knew what I didn't expect to happen—I didn't expect Blake to be a no-show for two days and then reappear and pretend he didn't know me at all. But that was what he did.

We didn't have any classes together, which was why I didn't know him well before the day we spent together, but our paths crossed in plenty of places—the lockers, the lunchroom, the field after school. He knew where to find me if he wanted to.

We'd connected. We'd talked about U2 and recited the lyrics of the entire album, *All That You Can't Leave Behind*. People didn't share a love for U2 and know every lyric to every song and end up not having anything to say to each other afterward. Singing those songs together was a bond. Knowing we were at the same concert across the stadium from each other was a bond. Making out all night in the passenger seat of a cramped car was a bond.

So where the hell was he?

I'd left him a few messages on his cell phone and sent him an email, nothing earth-shattering. Just a note to say hi. He hadn't gotten back to me.

It had worried me at first when he wasn't at school. Maybe he'd come down with a bad cold after staying out all night with me. In my head, I knew I was exhausted, but after our night together, I felt alive for the first time in forever. Sure, I could have stayed home and slept, but I managed to haul myself into the shower and get myself to school before first period.

I was excited to see Blake. I didn't know what would happen with us, and the newness and hope felt exhilarating.

I hadn't spent time with his friends, but I knew who they were, so by Thursday afternoon, I staked out the area outside his Honors Chem class and tried to casually jump into a conversation with two of them. One's name was Max.

"Um, hey," I said to them as they exited the classroom and tried to navigate around me. I stood directly in their path, so it was pretty obvious I wanted something.

"Hey," said Max.

"You're friends with Blake, right?"

"Um, yeah." He looked confused as to why I would be bothering him about Blake.

"Do you know where he is? Is he sick?"

The other guy piped in, shaking his head. "I saw him yesterday. He seemed fine."

"Here? Was he at school?" I asked. Maybe I'd just missed him. The campus was a decent size.

He shook his head again. "Nah, we prepped for the Mock Trial together last night at his house. I haven't seen him yet today."

"Oh, okay. Cool." I didn't know what else I could ask them. *Did he say anything about me? Did he seem happy? Does he want a girlfriend?*

My dignity prevented me from asking them anything. Stupid dignity.

But I could take other routes. Since I was still in the doghouse with the principal, it wouldn't hurt to swing by her office and show her that I was one hundred percent in uniform and feeling better about my future at her academic institution. And while I was in the office, I could find out if Blake was at school. Maybe he was just holed up in the library, preparing for the Mock Trial.

That errand went nowhere fast. The principal was out of her office, and the attendance ladies didn't seem inclined to discuss another student's attendance record.

Fine. I could check the library myself. And the study center. And the debate classrooms.

I didn't find Blake in any of those places, and the fact was I didn't know him well enough to guess where he'd hang on campus. So I resorted to the only other thing I could think of—I checked the student parking lot for his car. I found a lot of students and a lot of cars. But no Jetta. He wasn't at school.

His disappearing act bothered me throughout the rest of the day and through the night until I arrived on campus the next morning and decided to check the parking lot first. *Bingo.* His car was there.

Okay. Maybe he'd been under the weather or had an emergency with his family. Maybe he just stayed home to prep for the Mock Trial. I had no reason to get my panties in a twist.

I walked down the hallway toward my locker, knowing full well I was taking the long route, which allowed me to pass by his locker, and there he was, behind the open door, loading books into his backpack.

By the time I got close enough to see his face, he'd hoisted the backpack by its twin straps and turned to go the other way.

"Blake," I said, not wanting to shout. I was close enough for him to hear me and turn.

The look in his eyes was not what I expected. The depth and warmth that had swallowed me up three days earlier had been replaced by a hollow deadness. He seemed uneasy and gave me a tight-lipped half smile, tilting his head. "How are you?" he asked, his voice strained and stiff.

"I'm…um, fine. Are you okay?" He did not look okay. He looked awful.

"Yup, all good." If a person's face could be expressionless, that was what I saw when I looked at him. He would have needed to make an effort to look that blank. "Anyway, I should get to class. Take care, okay?"

"Sure," I said, watching him go. Those were the last words we spoke to each other for the rest of high school.

CHAPTER NINE

ecca

Present Day

THE MAN STANDING in Sydney's hospital room was . . . wow. He was almost aggressively good looking, if that was possible. Like he could send his face into battle and return having vanquished lesser humans with mere regular gorgeous faces.

The Blake Fulton I'd known in high school was shorter than this man, judging by the way he now towered over me by nearly a foot, and far less sure of himself.

It was almost like that Blake wanted to fade into the peasant outliers of the high school caste system.

For one day, his presence was bigger and more significant than anything I'd ever felt before, and he swept my heart to a place it wanted to stay forever. And just as suddenly, he'd left my heart in the garbage, tossed away without an explanation.

The episode had left a deep impression on me, making me wary of trusting people who seemed to be well-intentioned. Coupled with the loss of my dad, Blake's vanishing act served as a one-two punch that left me gutted back then.

It took me a long time to recover.

I no longer actively despised Blake—I was a grownup, after all— so seeing him standing in front of me only unearthed feelings of…nausea and intense dislike.

He probably didn't mean to be a jerk. He's probably spent years plagued with guilt that's nearly destroyed him. That's why he looks so...

Freakin' hot.

Blake hadn't suffered life's outrageous misfortunes. Even henpecked by Sydney and suffering from what seemed like lack of sleep, he still managed to pull off the rakish look of a guy who'd intentionally not shaved in order to look just so.

He was *so* so.

He was also the first jerk among an escalating parade of jerks in my dating life—the founding cautionary tale followed by a downward spiral of bad dating luck. There was tattooed amusement park ride operator with the wheat allergy who wouldn't kiss me if I ate pizza, the shy orthodontist with a swearing disorder that was set off by guilt each time we kissed, the emotionally unavailable kite surfer who liked dirty talk involving his mom, and so, so many more—if there was a dating misfit, I found him.

Then I'd settled into my current state, in which I worked too hard, took time for myself, looked out for me, and dated no one except dudes who liked coffee, so I could schedule morning dates when my shifts ended and get home in time to sleep.

Oh, did I mention? I work the night shift almost exclusively. Today was the once in a baby blue moon I'd switched shifts with a friend who needed the day off. And what did I get for my good deed? Blake Freakin' Fulton.

I couldn't exactly blame Blake for my ruining my expectations of men, but he seemed…involved.

Thus, I kind of still hated him.

I knew it was irrational to feel the wellspring of anger for someone who's ghosted me fifteen years ago, but that didn't stop my feelings from multiplying like gremlins eating poundcake after midnight.

Here he was married to Sydney, who, by the look of things, was about to give birth to Satan's spawn.

Why couldn't he have aged poorly, gained a middle-aged paunch and pockmarked skin, and come to resemble a balding ogre, and not a cute one like Shrek?

Meanwhile, Blake stood with his hand shooting sparks through mine and a look on his face like maybe I could rescue him from the verbal beating from his awful wife, who I now believed was his perfect match.

"Are you okay?" the doula asked me quietly. It wasn't fatigue that had me in a sudden daze.

"I'm Becca," I snapped, reclaiming my hand. I turned away from him and busied myself with whatever nurse activities I could find. I moved an IV cart from one side of the room to the other. I washed my hands, put on a fresh pair of gloves, and fussed with Sydney's monitors and the height of her bed.

Then I answered his question. "And yes, heightened hormone levels can lead to all sorts of sensitivities—smell, taste. So vanilla could be particularly nauseating to Sydney." Did he not bother to get to know his wife at all?

Sydney smiled at me for the first time since I'd entered the room. "Thank you, Becca. I'm sure that's what it is."

The poor woman was suffering from labor pains. She needed empathy. I could give her that, and suddenly—inexplicably—I wanted to protect her from Blake.

If I could get her to agree to some pain meds, she'd love me even more. Maybe I could help her relax so she could yell at him some more about his smelly candles. It was easier to play the good cop, now that I knew Blake was all bad.

"I'm pretty sure I told you to look for a holiday scent, Blake." Sydney's eyes bored into him with such intensity I thought she might set him aflame.

"You did say that. The problem, Syd, is it's the middle of April. The holiday-scented candles are long gone. I asked. Vanilla seemed innocuous enough." He shrugged and shook his head, befuddled and clueless.

"It's not. It's the most overused candle scent. To me, it smells like a bathroom after someone took a shit. Please take it out of here before I vomit."

As Sydney continued to let loose on Blake for his candle selection, another contraction kicked in. So I stayed focused on the monitor in front of me and let the doula coach her through the breathing while Blake stood uselessly, giving me a blank look.

He doesn't remember me.

So many feelings warred for me to acknowledge them—shock, anger, embarrassment, and dammit, attraction—and I was doing my level best to ignore them all. Heat crept over my cheeks, courtesy of my Irish family genes, which made my skin extra pale and the resulting blush extra noticeable.

Why does it bother me that Blake doesn't remember me?

It wasn't like he should. It was a really long time ago. I'd probably changed a little bit since then, for the better. My hand went to my knot of hair, and I looked down at my baggy scrub pants.

Okay, maybe not for the better.

If I reminded him of our shared high school experience, it would likely all come crashing back to him, and I would have to lie to his pregnant wife and tell her what a good person he'd been back then.

I didn't want to lie.

Or worse, he could still draw a blank. He could remind me that all those years later, I still wasn't worth recalling.

When the contraction subsided, I wiped Sydney's forehead with a damp washcloth and made sure she had everything she needed. I still had to finish my rounds on the other patients.

I turned and found Blake's gaze fixed on me.

His eyes still had the power to make me feel…things. The man was absolutely stunning, with his strong jaw and luscious lips. But that wasn't what got me. It was the memory of how kind he'd been when no one else knew how to handle me.

You need to stop.

Shaking myself out of the Blake haze, I told Sydney I'd be back to check on her in a bit.

"I know you have your birthing plan, but if you start to feel like you'd like something for the pain, call me anytime. And your doctor will be in later this morning to check on you."

"Okay, thanks, Becca." Sydney smiled sweetly at me. "I'm still determined to do this the natural way."

"Why hasn't the doctor been here yet?" Blake barked, checking his watch. "We got here at eleven last night, and we've only seen nurses."

Ugh, he was one of those—willing to accept help from nurses all day and night but held doctors up on a pedestal for the real medical knowledge. Little did he know, the labor nurses were the ones he needed to befriend. We had access to the good snacks and the secret cable channels. Blake would be getting neither.

"Dr. Kelley usually rounds after nine, but she knows Sydney's here, and I'll keep her in the loop on her progress," I said.

As I walked toward the door, Blake stepped in my path as if to block my exit. I was forced to meet his eyes, and I felt simmering rage at the hard stare that said he didn't like me despite not recalling who I was.

"Nurse...Becca." He made a point to read my nametag. I didn't make enough of an impression on him five minutes earlier for him to keep my name in his head.

"Yes?" I put a hand on the doorknob to imply that I was done and needed to leave.

"In your opinion, am I in danger of missing Sydney giving birth if I jog out for an hour to find another candle?"

Ever the doting husband. And from the looks of him, he does more than jog.

I shook my head and tried to smile, but I could feel how stiff my face felt. "You should be fine. She's got a while to go."

He glanced from my eyes to my nametag again and back to my face. Then he nodded. "Okay. Thank you."

Mercifully, he backed away so I could push the door open and walk away from him before I blurted out all the things I really wanted to say. It shocked me a little that after all these years, I still didn't have closure. Until now, I hadn't needed it. I was over him. I didn't think about him anymore.

But with him staring me in the face, getting ready to be a first-time dad, I had to admit that I was still a little hung up on the past. And he was still a jerk.

CHAPTER TEN

lake

 EITHER SHE'D FORGOTTEN ME, or she was doing a great job of pretending.

I was just an ugly stain on her past. And she was…still the brightest damned light I'd ever seen.

I recognized her the moment my eyes met hers in my sister's delivery room.

How could I not remember Rebecca Finley when I'd probably spent a decent part of the past fifteen years thinking about her?

So much regret, so much self-loathing. And a big, giant what-if that had gone unanswered for over a decade.

We'd spent one day together. Well, most of the day and the entire night. And for a besotted sixteen-year-old, we might as well have been Romeo and Juliet, star-crossed and torn apart by my own doing.

What if? What if I'd done things differently? What if I'd been a better guy?

Instead, I'd fucked it all up, and I only had the memory of the one night. We were bumbling and hormonal and teenaged. It could have been the beginning of something—*should* have—if I hadn't gotten scared out of my wits and screwed up so royally that we never spoke again.

I didn't discover sports or anything requiring athleticism until college, and by then, I'd grown five inches, gained muscle, and learned to use the same academic discipline to push myself at the gym. When I went out for the crew team, I earned myself a spot in the boat. But that all happened later. My college years were awesome, and I finally understood what it must have been like for some of the guys I'd envied.

Rebecca's gorgeous exterior blinded people to the fact that she was ridiculously smart—I knew that from the few classes we had together—and she never bothered to correct the mistaken impression. There was a lot more to her than she got credit for, and she was too modest to outshine her peers. She just cheered for the football team, aced her studies, and acted confident when most of us felt awkward, which made her all the more spectacular in my eyes.

Sometimes I wished she'd blown me off, so we could have stayed in our high school castes like we were supposed to, and I wouldn't have hurt her.

The name she said when she shook my hand threw me initially. In high school, she'd been Rebecca, never Becky, and certainly not Becca. She wasn't the type to let her name dictate the kind of fun she planned to have in the world.

Rebecca sounded responsible and straitlaced, yet she'd colored gleefully outside those lines. It was what I'd liked—and if I were honest with myself back then, what I'd loved—about her. She didn't need to be called Becca in order to be fun and carefree. She just was.

I wondered if that had changed.

I wondered about it as I drove away from Alta Bates Hospital and made my way to College Avenue, where I was pretty sure one of the shops would sell candles in scents other than vanilla. I parked near the BART station and walked through the Rockridge Market Hall, ignoring the cheese shop, even though I would have liked nothing better than to sample a few types of cheese.

If my sister had trouble with a vanilla candle, there was no telling how bent out of shape she would get if I showed up with smelly washed-rind cheese breath.

Better to keep my head down, find the candles quickly, and try to avoid making Sydney any angrier than I already had.

The market was too tempting though, and before I gave it more thought, I found myself at a bakery counter, staring through the glass at fruit tarts, frosted cakes, and meringues. Then my gaze landed on the row of cheesecake slices.

Was it kismet that Rebecca had mentioned a cheesecake candle?

I hadn't eaten cheesecake in years, and I avoided analyzing why. But if forced to come up with one, I would say it had something to do with her, with the one night we'd spent together and the slice of cheesecake we'd shared. And the gorgeous way she'd smiled through the first bite like it was perfect. She was perfect.

"What'll it be?" The bakery owner snapped me out of my reverie. Her gray hair was pulled into a topknot, and her blue eyes were winged by laugh lines. Baking and laughing seemed like a great way to live.

I pointed to two strawberry tartlets, two individual pots de creme, and two butterscotch puddings. Without realizing my mouth was moving, I heard myself order two slices of cheesecake.

Maybe one of those things would make Sydney happy.

I was bringing them to Sydney.

Nurse Becca's feelings about cheesecake—if she even still ate cheesecake—were irrelevant.

"It's like Noah's Ark, all your pastries in pairs." I knew she owned the place because a framed magazine article sat next to the register, and the identical pleasant face featured on the page was smiling at me.

"I know. It's a thing. I can't buy just one of anything, and three seems like an awkward number."

"I won't complain about doubling up. It's the only way to eat sweets, with someone sweet," she said.

It felt like she was telling me to eat them with Rebecca.

My eyes burned, and I rubbed them, knowing it was the wrong thing to do, but it felt good for a moment. Sydney's labor had kept us both up all night. I felt like I'd experienced each contraction with her—not the pain, but the agony of her squeezing her eyes shut, moaning profanities, and taking out her discomfort on me.

It was fine. I loved her, and she was the one going through labor. The least I could do was support her, even if it meant getting yelled at. A little sugar rush couldn't hurt either one of us. After a momentary reprieve, my eyes burned more. It served me right for not leaving them the fuck alone.

"Would you like anything else?" The bakery owner interrupted my thoughts as she packed the sweets into a white box and tied a blue string around it.

"No, that's all. Thanks. Everything here looks amazing."

She looked into the box where she'd arranged the items amid crumpled tissue paper to separate them. "You picked the best ones." She winked.

"I'll report back next time I'm here. I'll need to try the rest of these." I was always looking for food ideas, especially desserts, and if I saw something that looked good, I filed that information away for later.

She wiped her hands on her apron and bent to reach into the bakery case, where she delicately slid one of the small berry tarts onto a sheet of tissue paper before handing it to me. "You seem like someone who won't want to wait to open that box until you get wherever you're taking it. Have this on the house."

She grinned with her lips pressed together, the crinkles around her eyes proof of her extensive experience taking delight in people eating her baked goods. And I was hardly the kind of man to turn down a fruit tart with ripe raspberries and strawberries bleeding red under a sugary glaze.

I accepted the gift and immediately took a bite. The juice from the berries trickled down my chin, and I slurped the fruit and custard before it ended up all over my shirt. If I went back to the delivery room looking like I'd just won a pie-eating contest, Sydney would have my head—again.

Then I thought about Rebecca some more, reliving the first moments after I walked into the labor room at the hospital. Had her expression shifted at all when she saw me? Did she really have no idea who I was even when I introduced myself by name?

Maybe she did, but she still hates you.

Suddenly, my heart felt like I'd been gutted by a fishing knife. It ached so much that I unconsciously put my hand over it and rubbed the spot. I should have said something to her.

You could have pulled her aside and . . . what? Apologized for being a dick fifteen years ago and dredged up the awful past?

I'd be lying if I said I hadn't imagined running into her, hadn't hoped for a chance to explain myself now that I had the benefit of time and distance. But there she was, and I'd been tongue-tied, unable to remind her that she once knew me.

The fact that she didn't even remember me should have been a sign that I should fucking let her go. But I didn't want to.

The stupidly optimistic side of me wanted our chance encounter, the serendipitous fact that she was Sydney's nurse, to be a sign. *A sign of what?* I had no idea. Maybe it only meant something because I wanted it to mean something. Story of my life.

That was a problem—getting distracted by hopes and dreams when reality was supposed to be the priority. I needed to get back to the hospital. Sydney was about to have a baby, and I was dithering around with pastries and thoughts of a girl I'd lost years ago.

I left the market in search of a candle that didn't smell like my favorite flavor of ice cream. It was the least I could do for Sydney. She'd weathered her whole pregnancy with hardly a complaint. The fact that she was uncomfortable and cranky now was all the more reason to stay focused on her needs.

And yet...Rebecca was my first real love. *What was I supposed to do with that?*

CHAPTER ELEVEN

ecca

WHEN I WENT to check on Sydney a couple hours later, I was surprised to find that Blake hadn't returned from his candle errand. Surprised, and a little relieved.

And also disappointed.

After getting over my shock at seeing him, I had an insatiable urge to remind him of who I was and pin him into a corner until he admitted he never forgot me, explained everything that had gone unsaid back then, and apologized. Or at least admitted he sort of remembered me.

For a while after high school, I'd anticipated running into him at a reunion or even a local coffee place, assuming he stayed in the area. We'd have a frank conversation, and I'd get some closure. To this day, it still didn't make sense.

But he'd never turned up at a reunion, and my casual inquiries among people I'd remembered as his friends gave me no clues as to where he'd gone. We had zero coffeehouse run ins. I didn't bother to look for him on social media because by the time college ended, I'd moved on. I never forgot him, but at least I didn't think about him constantly and wonder.

Yet here he was. I should have felt confident on my own turf, comfortable in my workplace, but instead, one look at him sent long-buried emotions bubbling to the surface.

What if I reminded him who I was, and he was just as blasé about me now as he'd seemed back then?

Do I really want a reminder of how he walked away and forgot I existed at all?

Gah—I could do this. Even if it meant admitting that I cared more than I wanted to, I needed to know if some part of our high school experience resonated with him the way it had with me.

Or maybe it was the goofy part of me that loved bad horror movies. I wanted to see a real-life version of a man screaming and leaving a Blake-shaped hole in a hospital door. That would be fun.

Damn you, Blake, for stirring up the past and making me feel...feelings.

I didn't have time to dwell on it because I had a job to do. Sydney was writhing and huffing through another contraction, and I needed to reassure her that she could do this. Her doula stood near her head and began counting while Sydney worked on breathing through the pain. She inhaled for a long breath, then let out a series of puffs while the pain in her uterus gripped her.

"Ahhhgggh!" she screamed, looking at me.

I nodded and handed her a squeeze toy to grip while she endured the contraction without pain medication.

I'd learned the hard way not to let a patient hold my hand. One had pulverized my bones so badly I couldn't pick up a pen for a week afterward.

A minute later, the pain subsided, and Sydney's breathing slowed. I checked the monitor. "You're doing great. They're getting stronger and closer together. Just keep doing what you're doing."

"Am I there yet?" she panted desperately. "I want this kid out!"

I did a quick exam while the doula changed the playlist on her phone to a symphony of horns with a backdrop of ocean waves.

"Fuck that music. Can you play Lizzo? I'm way more *that bitch* than ocean mermaid at this point."

"You're dilating, making good progress. But you've got a ways to go."

She grabbed my arm. "Level with me, sister. Am I gonna make it, or am I dying in childbirth?"

"You'll make it. No question. Just not...yet." I hated to give her false hope. She was only about halfway dilated. Her brow was slick with sweat, and her hair stuck out in all directions after pressing her head against the pillow.

"Okay, done. Fuck it. I wave the white flag. No more." She waved her hand in the air, beckoning me closer. "Give me the drugs. I don't want to feel these anymore. Just...make it stop."

I nodded, exhaling relief on her behalf. "Sure thing. Let me call the anesthesiologist. We'll get you an epidural, and I promise you'll feel so much better."

"Better is good. Better is what I want," she said as the door swung open and Blake returned holding a white bakery box that I recognized from Rockridge Market.

Sydney glared at him. "Seriously? Two hours, Blake? What the hell took you so long? One candle for a mood, that's all I asked. I've had like fifty mammoth contractions since you left. I think my uterus blew up while you were gone. Did you enjoy yourself? Do some shopping? Have wine with lunch?"

Some relationships thrived on people bickering with each other. I wasn't about to judge theirs, but I did wonder about it.

From what I remembered about Blake, he was a calm guy, but he didn't seem passive. He was on the debate team, which probably meant he could make a good case for his argument, but I'd yet to see that here. He let her walk all over him.

"I found you three different candles. Maple, Christmas Tree, and Forest Fir. Want to smell them?" His voice stayed level. He didn't seem perturbed by her mood.

Smart man. This was not the time to argue or antagonize.

Sydney smiled at him for the first time. "I trust you. Pick whichever one you think smells best. Oh, and I'm getting the drugs. Fuck my birth plan. I don't need to be a hero. It's enough that I've been pregnant for nine months and I'm having the baby. My body doesn't need to prove anything else."

"I support your decision." Blake turned to me. "Will the pain meds slow down her labor? I've done some reading and saw that it can take a little longer once the patient gets an epidural."

He's done some reading.

It bugged the crap out of me when patients or their families came in with all kinds of medical gems they'd gleaned from the internet because most were half-baked and only made patients second-guess actual medical knowledge. But he wasn't entirely wrong. Damn him.

"It can slow the process a bit, mainly because Sydney might not be as aware of feeling when she's ready to push out the baby, but I promise it won't hurt her or the baby, and it will make everyone a lot more comfortable."

Read my lips, Blake. She'll probably stop snapping at you once she gets the drugs.

"Great," he said. "I can see she's in good hands with you."

It was a nice thing to say, even if he had no real reason to think my hands were better than anyone else's. But it still didn't make me abandon my dislike for him.

A couple of minutes later, the anesthesiologist placed Sydney's epidural, Blake had decided on the Christmas Tree candle, and Sydney was starting to calm down.

"Okay, well, everything looks peaceful here—and it smells pretty good too—so I'll leave you alone and update your doctor with her progress."

When I was in the hallway, I checked my watch, certain it must be getting close to quitting time. It felt like I'd been at work for a week.

Nope. Four hours to go.

Four long hours until I could put the sight of Blake Fulton and all the memories he dredged up to rest. For good.

CHAPTER TWELVE

lake

"BLAKE, can you ask one of the nurses for a cup of crushed ice?" The epidural had kicked in, and Sydney was feeling better. Thank fuck.

"Sure. Let me see if I can find someone." I grabbed the pink pitcher that contained the dregs of what had been ice a couple hours earlier.

I thought my sister was nuts for trying to push a baby out of her body without the benefit of modern medicine, and I'd shared my opinions, but she was determined to do it her way.

Even if I didn't understand it, I had to respect it. What I didn't know about women and childbirth could fill an encyclopedia.

Sydney had reminded me of that fact plenty of times, and yet she still chose me to be by her side while she gave birth. There was no future dad in the picture—she'd used a sperm donor and confidently laid out her plans for single parenthood for me one night over beer and potstickers as though she was explaining her choice of wallpaper for the den.

I was her person, and she deserved my best self. There was no way I'd risk hurting her by implying the birth plan was a pointlessly painful idea. So much better that she came to that conclusion on her own.

"I'm a little obsessed with the ice they have here," she said. "I'm going to have to invest in an ice maker after this because I don't think I can live without these little ice pellets."

"They'd be even better with a little Diet Coke mixed in. You want me to find some for you?" I asked.

"You're sweet. Nah, I'm good just munching on ice." She smiled at me for the first time since we'd arrived at the hospital, and I exhaled a sigh of relief.

"Okay, be back in a bit." I took the empty pink container out of the room, wondering if hospitals were like hotels, with a communal ice machine I could find for a refill.

Doubtful, I decided. And probably unsanitary.

In the hallway, I didn't see anyone who might be able to help with the ice issue. No nurses. In particular, no Nurse Becca. I hated to admit that I was as almost excited about the possibility of having a conversation with her as I was about witnessing the birth of a new baby.

She'd defined what a love story should be.

Every woman I'd met in the past fifteen years had had the misfortune of being measured against Rebecca. It wasn't their fault I'd been ruined at sixteen because I'd had a shot at love, witnessed perfect happiness, then destroyed it all.

I'd decided I didn't deserve to be happy after what I'd done.

Right. Ice. Sydney. Focus, asshole.

The hospital had to have a cafeteria or something where I could get a cup of ice. That idea cheered me. I wondered what kind of food they served and whether it would feel more like a restaurant for families of patients or a quick stop for hospital employees. I was a geek about food-service places.

Five years earlier, I'd opened a restaurant I'd been dreaming about since college. Back then, like most wayward freshmen, I'd been undeclared and had no idea what I wanted to do with my life.

By graduation, all signs pointed to law school, at least according to my father. He was a lawyer and couldn't imagine me finishing college and making any plans other than law school. "It's a good degree to have, no matter what you decide to do with your life," he told me, over and over again.

"What if I want to open a restaurant?" I asked. At the time, I had no interest in opening a restaurant. It was just the first non-law idea that came to mind, and I needed a retort.

We sat at a high-top table at a bar and grill in Ann Arbor, where he was visiting me at college. I'd learned the useless art of flipping cardboard drink coasters off the edge of the table with one hand and catching them. My dad was watching me with an expression that said he regretted wasting four years' worth of tuition on my new talent.

He'd taken a sip of his beer—some sort of lager that looked like apple juice—and rubbed the stubble on his chin. It was one of his signature lawyer moves, not that I knew what his actual lawyer moves were. I'd never seen him in court or with a client. But I imagined him rubbing his chin in that way, which implied whoever he was listening to was a fucking idiot and only had thirty seconds to figure that out before my dad eviscerated the room with his incisive logic and facts.

That was how it always happened in my head.

The problem was I could never see myself as a stubble-massaging master of persuasion, in court or anywhere else. And because I was stubborn as shit and lacked creativity, when my dad asked me what I planned to do after college if I wasn't headed to law school, I scrambled through the recesses of my brain for anything that would stick.

Then I lied and told him I was applying to culinary school, all the better to open that restaurant I'd conjured up in my fit of collegiate insubordination.

Then I had to make good on it.

My dad nodded and actually seemed pleased that I was so focused. He applauded my drive after I applied to the Culinary Institute of America, along with a few lesser schools. I hadn't honestly expected to get in. Especially since I'd written my applications late one night after returning from a bar crawl with my roommate.

In a moment of drunken stupidity, I'd decided to write my essay in the form of an epic poem, "Ode to a Blueberry Muffin."

And because I was just that young and stupid, I also fired off an application to the Cordon Bleu cooking school in France. Might as well aim for the Eiffel Tower.

All of it was a giant joke at my father's expense. I was prepared to parade my rejection letters in front of him so we could both lay to rest the charade that I was actually going to do something as concrete as graduate school when really my plans were to bum around Europe, drink beer, and fuck Scandinavian women like a

Viking. The way I saw it, I had years of high school acne, shyness, and self-flagellation to make up for.

Then I got in.

Not only did I get into the schools in the US, I got into Cordon Fucking Bleu. So I went. I figured a couple of years living in Paris, dating French women, and learning to cook would serve me well in life.

Once I got to the Left Bank, I went full Julia Child. I attended all my classes with utmost seriousness and learned to crack eggs with one hand while whisking a bordelaise sauce on one burner and a hollandaise sauce right beside it. I spatchcocked chickens and learned how to cook their entrails. I was indoctrinated into the cult of butter and swore never to try passing off margarine as a real food again.

I learned to cook like a chef, only to come home and take the lowliest line cook job at the San Francisco mainstay, Zuni Cafe. And despite the whole thing being born of a spiteful conversation between the college twerp I was and my dad, who probably knew a lot more about me than I knew about myself, I fell in love with cooking. Real cooking. Restaurant cooking with multiple saucepans going at once and a flat-top grill and knives imported from Japan and secrets I learned from other, better chefs.

The point was, I could cook. And I loved restaurants, all restaurants, even the ones with troughs of gravy-covered food.

Which brought me happily to the hospital cafeteria, where I started poking around at the food options in a big refrigerator case, noticing that there were several types of hummus and only unsalted butter.

My cell phone pinged with a text.

SYDNEY: Where are you?

ME: Cafeteria. Getting u ice.

SYDNEY: Nurse came by with ice.

ME: Sorry. Be right there.

I hightailed it back to her room, feeling like a useless lug with my empty pink container and thoughts of chickpea products. I fought the question in the back of my mind about whether Nurse Becca had been the one to bring Sydney ice and whether she was still in the room. Because it didn't matter.

And she wasn't.

"Sorry. I thought I could get ice in the cafeteria." I hoped Sydney wouldn't flip out at my incompetence.

"I told you to ask a nurse."

"I know. I didn't see anyone."

"It's fine. I'm good. But can you take these pastries out of here? The smell of the sugar is making me nauseous."

Normally, I would have wondered aloud if a person could smell sugar. But since I'd botched the ice errand, I picked up the full box of pastries so I could stash them in my car.

"Sure thing. Back soon."

"Don't worry. I'm gonna nap a little." Sydney shooed me toward the door as her eyes drooped, and I silently thanked the inventor of the epidural.

Outside the room, I took a wrong turn and ended up back near the cafeteria instead of the parking garage. When I spun around, I caught sight of Rebecca's light brown hair at the end of the hallway. It was a darker shade than it had been in high school, less blond and more sandy brown, and her sun-streaked bun lit my way like a beacon on a moonless night.

Suddenly, I was sixteen again.

I followed her.

I could pretend I had no choice, that her pull was like a tow rope that made all my logical decisions moot. But I wasn't that guy anymore, the one who ghosted women and claimed to have no control over his actions. I had complete control and I wanted to talk to her.

We could go another fifteen years without seeing each other, and I'd waited long enough for this conversation. I didn't want to wait anymore. So I pursued her down the corridor like a fanboy.

Hospitals had always freaked me out a little bit, something about the white sterile hallways and all the life-saving machines, almost like they were protesting too much. People came to hospitals to get better, but for a lot of people, a hospital was their last stop before they died. Even being there for the complete opposite —*what could be more life-affirming than the miracle of birth?*—I couldn't help feeling a little bit depressed because I knew how many people were there for their last days on earth. My mom had died in a hospital like this one.

"Rebecca," I said to her back as she moved quickly and grabbed the file from the door pocket outside a patient's room. Even if everyone called her Becca now, she would certainly answer to her full name if someone used it. *Right?*

She stopped walking, and I could see her adjust her shoulders, squaring them as though she were getting ready for a confrontation.

I remembered her doing that back in high school as well. It was one of the things I'd noticed before I really knew her. Whenever someone asked her a question, she would pause and think about her answer before speaking. She'd blink a few times and look upward, then square her shoulders and calmly answer, her face aglow with confidence.

Now her face was a professional mask of indifference. "Yes?" She looked at me warily and pushed the loose tendrils of hair back with both hands. I liked them loose, like a halo framing her face.

Not the right time, Romeo.

"Um. Yeah. I knew you in high school. You went to Beckman, didn't you? I was in your class. Not sure if you remember . . ."

She folded her arms across her chest and stared at me, but it wasn't a long-lost friend kind of stare. Her eyes hardened, and she looked the exact same way I remembered all those years ago when I would accidentally miscalculate and end up crossing paths with her. "I remember."

"Great!" I said. It was the exact opposite of what I saw on her face.

My mission of hope suddenly felt painful.

I should abort mission. Leave the past in the past.

And yet...

"Um . . ." I sputtered.

Say something charming.

"You look exactly like I remember you in high school."

A pink blush crept over her cheeks, and her hand again went to tuck the loose tendrils of her hair even though there were none. "Thank you . . . I think? Or should I be insulted that you're implying I look like a miserable cheerleader?"

"It was a compliment. You don't look miserable . . . At least, you didn't until I showed up." I saw the tiniest glimmer of a smile play at the corner of her lips. Maybe I could still scale the mountain ahead of me.

"Do you have that effect on a lot of people?" Her voice was quiet, but I detected a hint of the playfulness I remembered.

"I . . . I think mainly you."

That made her smile ever so slightly, and that was the tiny opening I needed. Every time over the past fifteen years when I imagined seeing her again, the first things I planned to say were the apologetic words that were so long overdue. I had those words memorized. I'd thought about them, dreamed about them, rehearsed them.

The couple of times I hunted for her on social media, I found limited information—she hid everything but a profile picture so obscure I couldn't be sure it was her. So I hoped for a chance encounter, our eyes meeting across the citrus fruit aisle in the grocery store, followed by dinner, or maybe . . . I was still a dreamer.

But never in my planning did I expect Rebecca to be Sydney's nurse, and the reality of Rebecca in front of me looking so goddamned beautiful made the thoughts and excuses leave my brain like the air I exhaled. I had nothing.

Just...don't let her leave.

The time was now, so I teed up whatever apology I could scrape together. "Anyway, I know it's been years, and you probably remember some not nice things I did, so I'd really like to apologize. I'm sorry, Rebecca. Really, really sorry. I was an idiot when we were in high school, and I should have done better. It wasn't fair to you, and I had...reasons...for what I did, which I won't trouble you with now. I just really hope you can accept that I know I was an asshole, and I regret it more than you can possibly know."

Then I had to take a breath because I'd spewed out everything so fast, I was in danger of hyperventilating.

I had more to say, much more. She deserved to hear all of it. So I caught my breath and began again. "They say time heals all wounds, which is a cliché and it's stupid but hopefully true, and it's been fifteen years, so that's potentially a good amount of healing. So maybe—"

She stopped me. Literally stopped me by putting her hand up and touching two fingers to my lips, which halted their movement and shot an unexpected jolt straight through my veins and threatened to derail my whole speech with an embarrassing hard-on.

I shifted a little to try to calm the horny teenager who'd resurfaced at the sight of her.

She shook her head, causing a few of the recently tamed strands to come loose again. She stared at me, looking positively dumbfounded. "I don't normally work days, and I'm still not sure if you're just an out-of-body hallucination or if maybe I fell asleep in the break room and screwed up my own revenge fantasy. Did you just apologize?"

I watched her try to make sense of me and couldn't help smiling. "I did, but that was the abbreviated version. How about a cup of coffee? Then I'll apologize some more, and if you still need revenge, well, I'm here for that too."

Slowly, she nodded. "Yeah. Okay."

CHAPTER THIRTEEN

ecca

So he did remember me.

"Can we start over? Hello." He extended his hand after we'd ordered coffee and found a table in the cafeteria. "It's good to see you again."

I reached out to shake it and tried not to react to the blaze of heat that raced up my arm at the contact with his skin. He grasped my hand, and an unrecognizable part of me didn't want him to let go. Then I remembered feeling something similar a long time ago, along with the gut punch that came afterward, and the hurt started to creep back in.

"You . . . you look a little different now."

I wasn't about to say that his face had shed a little bit of softness, replaced by angles, gorgeous angles that offset high cheekbones against flawless skin and a sharp jawline that could cut facets on diamonds.

He's married.

Yup, a married man whose baby face was now all man with rough stubble and crinkles around his steel-gray eyes that were so, so sexy. He didn't need to hear that the only thing stealing focus from his face were the hard biceps I could see straining against his shirt sleeves as he crossed his arms over his broad chest.

He's MARRIED.

"Yeah, I grew in college." I wasn't just talking about his height, which had to be well over six feet. His face was downright beautiful, and I stared unabashedly, despite his married state, because this would be the last time I'd see him.

He ran a hand over his face and leaned chin on his fist.

The gesture was something I remembered him doing in high school, and back then, it was kind of charming. Now, the little bit of anguish he scrubbed from his face bore the complications of age. And dammit, he wore his years well.

Everything about him screamed dangerously hot sex appeal, and I was doing my best to find places on him where I could look that didn't make me want to touch him.

"Nice job. The growing, I mean. You succeeded. Tall." As if to emphasize, I demonstrated what height looked like by raising my hand above my head like a love-dumb cavewoman. He smirked.

"Apparently, the gods of puberty decided it would build character if I suffered as a shrimpy stick figure throughout high school. All the better for being completely ignored by girls."

"You weren't ignored. Well . . ." I had ignored him before I knew him, and then again when I couldn't bear to look at him without deeply felt pain.

He held up a hand. "I didn't mean . . ."

My eyes closed for a long blink. It was going to be a tough conversation if neither of us could complete a thought without hurt and guilt taking over. "I know. Let's just . . . it's fine."

The benefit of years gone by had blunted most of the pain. It no longer required practiced intention to keep Blake Fulton from drifting into my subconscious. But that had taken years to perfect.

I didn't want to backslide after one interaction. I couldn't.

I wouldn't.

It had been fifteen years, and I wasn't that girl anymore—vulnerable, innocent, hopeful. I knew better than to get emotional about men, and I didn't let life throw me for a loop. I had nice sturdy boundaries and rules that kept my heart safe. Blake had helped put them there, so I supposed I owed him some gratitude for warning me about heartbreak.

I'd gotten to experience it a couple more times in my twenties with other men who at least explained themselves before they bailed, albeit poorly, "I'm not ready for a relationship," "It's not you, it's me." But I didn't even care. They weren't Blake.

Maybe—probably—I'd romanticized him into someone he wasn't, but it didn't matter. In my mind, I'd found perfect love once, and nothing else compared.

The one-two punch of losing my dad and a guy I really connected with had pushed me to self-sufficiency. Maybe I could have withstood one of them, grieved in whatever way a teenager did, and eventually gone on with my life.

But both?

I also hated how much he'd flourished. Even in his sweatshirt and old Levi's, he looked casually stylish, confident, and hot. He'd gone to the gym a few thousand times and learned how to rock a pair of jeans and a hoodie like no one's business. And found a life partner.

"Anyway...It's really great to see you," he affirmed. He still had the same damn bakery box he'd been holding earlier, and now he shifted it to a corner of our table.

My mind drifted to curiosity about what treats lay inside the box because it allowed me to avoid the feelings I feared might pour out if I gave them half a chance. That could not happen. There could be no feelings. Only explanations and attempts at understanding.

Even though I had questions—so many questions about why he'd ghosted me like I was toxic—I also really wanted to know what was in the box.

And because present-day Blake still possessed the same telepathy he had when we were young, he opened the bakery box to reveal not one, but two slices of cheesecake. Among other things.

I tried not to ogle another woman's cheesecake in the hands of another woman's husband, but it was difficult. Especially when he took one of the pieces out and put it on a hospital cafeteria napkin and sliced it in half.

"I remember you used to like cheesecake."

"I can't eat Sydney's cheesecake."

"It's not Sydney's cheesecake."

"Fine. I should not be eating your cheesecake. Jesus, that sounds even worse."

The cheesecake beckoned me like a siren to the dark side.

If I eat this man's cheesecake while his wife labors alone, who knows what I'm capable of?

He handed me a fork, and I wasted approximately zero seconds before taking a bite.

Yeah, I was going straight to hell. But it was so worth it. Maybe they served flaming cheesecake there. In my version of hell, they did.

Blake took a big forkful of his half. "Oh my god," he said with his mouth full. "This is amazing. I had a feeling when I saw it in the display case. Have you been to the pastry place in Rockridge Market?"

"It's new, right? I have."

Blake emptied a creamer into his coffee and stirred it longer than he needed to mix it. "So, you're a nurse. That's awesome."

I sipped my own coffee before answering. "I like it."

"Do you always wear scrubs? Or do they sometimes have you wear those little nurse's outfits with the short skirts?"

I almost spit out my coffee. "You're kidding, right?"

He looked unsure. "Right...?"

"Blake, do you watch daytime soap operas or something? Because that's the only time you'll see a nurse wear what I'm certain is a slutty Halloween costume."

He closed his eyes, but it didn't stop the red flush from coloring his neck. Ah, so grown-up, hotty-hotpants Blake was human and prone to embarrassment. I was infinitely relieved.

Blake held up a finger. "First, yes, I've been known to indulge in daytime TV. And two, I hope you don't mind me saying you'd rock the slutty nurse costume." His smile took over his face—literally, the beautiful white teeth and cheek dimple overwhelmed even the chiseled cheekbones until all I could see was radiant joy—and I knew my cheeks matched his neck.

"I do mind you saying it."

"Sorry."

Say it again.

He smiled as though he could hear my thoughts.

Damn him. And damn my traitorous hormones.

He was so hot. And so cocky. This wasn't the guy I knew in high school. That guy was shy, thoughtful, earnest…and also a fucking ghoster, but my hormones were begging me to let that go.

This guy, with the Hollywood face, the firefighter biceps, and the confident attitude could only be that much worse. He still made my stomach do backflips and caused red-hot havoc everywhere below that.

I shook my head. "Just…stop." There was no denying that the old blaze of attraction hadn't even needed a breath of oxygen to rear up and reignite. It didn't hurt that his unsure gaze had evolved into a smug certainty, and he'd gotten control over the pout of his lips and now wielded them like a weapon.

His wife is your patient.

That knowledge should have been enough to set me straight. On a normal day, with a normal good-looking guy, yes, I might appreciate objective beauty in the same way a person would admire a fine work of art hanging on a gallery wall. But I would never dream of stealing it off the museum wall.

Today…I was shamelessly donning a cat burglar suit.

"So, have you stayed in touch with many people from our class?" He seemed as unaffected by me as I was gobsmacked by him.

"What?"

"Beckman Prep. Are you still friends with any of the cheerleaders? Do you still talk to your senior prom date?"

I felt a sickening shot of unease pierce my chest. "I didn't go to prom."

He looked surprised. Then contrite. "Oh. Okay. Well, neither did I. It was probably lame," he said with a stiff laugh.

It probably wasn't, but I didn't have anyone I wanted to go with, so I dragged my younger sister Cherry to a movie that night instead. My sister was my pity date.

"Anyhow," he continued, rubbing a hand over his forehead and pushing it into his hair.

"I feel like I should apologize for my earlier apology. I know it wasn't sufficient."

"An apology for an apology? Seems like a slippery slope. What if I'm not satisfied with the second one? You'd find yourself in a meta loop. Look, joking aside, all I want is an explanation."

"An explanation?"

"Yes. Of what happened back then. Why did you disappear on me?"

He looked briefly uncomfortable, but then he recovered enough to say, "Oh. Okay. Does this mean you might accept my apology?"

"I don't know, Blake. Maybe."

The gray of his eyes darkened, and his features settled into seriousness. "Well, I'd like to explain. I think I owe you that much."

"Okay."

He reached out and put his hand on top of mine. I really wished he hadn't because it made me want his hands everywhere. My breath hitched, and I looked at him, immediately remembering how it felt to get lost in the depth of his eyes, which were currently locked on mine.

Doctors, nurses, and patients' families bustled around us, and I didn't notice any of them. If my brother had been sitting at the table next to ours, I wouldn't have recognized him. Blake still had that effect.

Parts of our time together would always haunt me, but I thought I'd compartmentalized them enough that I could keep them locked away. They were the past. I wasn't prepared for how I would feel when the past reappeared and stirred everything up.

I hated being unprepared.

Finally, amid the liquid lust coursing through my veins, I found the sense to say what I should have said when he suggested getting coffee. "Blake, I'm sorry. This is wrong . . . we can't do this. It's not okay."

I pointed to his hand on mine as evidence.

He should have understood what I meant. It was wrong for him, too—more wrong, actually. He was the married one.

Aren't the married people supposed to mind the shop? Are they supposed to abdicate responsibility for turning down coffee dates to single people who hadn't gotten laid in months?

That really didn't seem fair.

"What's not okay?" he asked.

"This. Us. We shouldn't be here, together." I gestured all around, making hand signals like I was guiding a small aircraft into the cafeteria, and he was looking blankly at me.

"Having coffee?" he asked.

He was the most blasé husband I'd ever met. But again, maybe the kind of guy who spent an amazing night with a person and ghosted her afterward was the same kind of guy who didn't feel the need to hang with his wife while she was in labor.

Regardless, it was weird. Maybe something was wrong with him. His emotional thermostat seemed glitchy.

"Blake, this baby's only going to be born once. Don't you want to be in the room for the whole experience? Even if Sydney says she doesn't want you there all the time, it's just the hormones talking. You should be with her."

He shrugged and forked a bite of cheesecake. "I know. You're right. I'll go. It's just…I'm sure you noticed Sydney can be a bit exhausting. I figured, if she wanted to nap, I'd take a little break."

My brain fired messages at me at rapid speed. *That's so…not nice. Who says that about his wife? This guy is still the king of all clueless, soon-to-be-father dicks.*

"Contractions are painful, Blake, and the whole process of giving birth is scary as shit. Just think for a minute about what her body is getting ready to do. All first-time moms get freaked out. I'm sure she's lovely most of the time."

"I wouldn't necessarily say lovely."

"Jerk."

"I'm sorry?"

"You heard me."

"I did, and I don't understand where that came from. Is this about high school? Because I am truly, truly sorry I hurt you, and I do want to do that repair work."

"Fucking hell, Blake."

"What?"

What?

"You're married to Sydney. You're going to be parents together. If you're not into your wife, I'm sad for you, but you could at least be nice while she's in there trying to have your baby."

Now it was his turn to have his eyes bug out of his head. He stared at me like I'd just suggested we eat his newborn baby with another slice of cheesecake. "Rebecca—"

"It's Becca. No one calls me Rebecca anymore."

"Becca," he said pointedly, "I'm not married to Sydney. She's not my wife. I don't have a wife. And I know I'm an asshole. We've established that. But I've been at her beck and call for half her pregnancy, and I just needed a break. I also really, really wanted to talk to you."

I was dumbfounded. And also dumb. "Sydney Fulton, Blake Fulton, you're not married? So why does she have your last name?"

He laughed because I wasn't going to grasp it unless he verbalized something. "Because she's my sister."

Oh.

Oh.

CHAPTER FOURTEEN

lake

OH.

Oh.

Things were starting to make a little more sense. I didn't know why I assumed that even if Rebecca remembered me, she would know I had a sister. At four years older than me, Sydney hadn't been in school with us.

And now, with a possible second chance at—I don't know—reconciling something with Rebecca, I wasn't about to screw it up by allowing her to think I was the kind of married guy who flirts with his wife's delivery nurse.

For a relatively intelligent person, I couldn't have been a bigger idiot.

"This is actually sort of funny," I said, unsure if she could possibly see it that way.

From the look on her face, she hadn't come around to my point of view yet. "I'm just . . . I don't know what to say. I thought . . ." She shook her head, and I replayed the conversations from the day in my head until I could see very clearly why she'd mistaken me for Sydney's husband. "I feel stupid."

"*I* feel stupid. It didn't even occur to me that you'd think we were married, which is the obvious conclusion someone would come to when two people have the same last name and appear to be having a baby together."

"Well, we're both stupid, then." She looked at me warily. "Is there another piece of cheesecake in that box? I think I need it."

I thanked my neurotic genetics that forced me to buy things in even numbers. "There is." I took it out and put it on the napkin, replacing the one we'd devoured, and Rebecca took a forkful.

"Okay. So...sister. Tell me more. Is there a dad?"

"Sperm donor. She got tired of waiting for a guy and was ready to have a baby." He shrugged and tipped his head to the side.

"Do you not approve?"

"Oh no, I think it's great. Our father, unfortunately, is not such a fan. I'm sure he'll come around once the baby's born and he meets her, but he's been kind of an ass, and she doesn't need that right now. So I'm her person."

"And once the baby's born?" she asked. "Will you be the cool uncle? Surrogate dad?"

"Much more the uncle, hopefully cool—thank you for the vote of confidence."

She took another forkful of cheesecake. We were going to polish off two giant pieces between us, and it wouldn't put a dent in my appetite.

Because I was hungry for *her*.

Being with her for the past half hour only dredged up the pain of regret I'd carried for so long. It resurrected the abject longing I felt after spending only a day with her. Eventually, I told myself I was over her. But if I was honest with myself, I never could be.

And maybe I imagined the hint of relief that crossed her face when she realized I wasn't married to Sydney—or to anyone. I'd cling to maybe. It caused a feeling I hadn't experienced in a long time—hope.

"It's insane that you brought these. I'm probably the only person on the planet who'd eat cheesecake at any hour of the day, but I swam last night, and that somehow ramps up my metabolism the following day."

"You swim?" I tucked away the piece of information like it was a gold nugget I would stare at later. I felt ravenous to know Becca —the woman she was now—and I felt my heart surge at the possibility of learning more.

I wondered if she'd let me.

Becca exhaled a peaceful breath and grinned. "I love the water. I'm not so fond of exercise for its own sake, but if I'm in a pool or an ocean—doesn't matter where—I can go for hours. I've done some long beach swims, and except for the cold, I'm pretty happy out there."

"Do you wear a wetsuit? Or are you like the Octopus Teacher guy, communing with wildlife at forty degrees?" I couldn't imagine swimming for hours in the ocean, even in a hermetically sealed suit. As a dry land exerciser, I had only admiration for people who liked to swim.

"Um, no. Wetsuit definitely. I like water, but I'm not crazy."

I closed the bakery box before I was tempted to dig into any of the other treats. Rebecca pushed the cheesecake toward me so I could have the last bite. "I insist."

"You have a heart of gold, Rebecca Finley."

She looked at me strangely for a minute, her eyes tracing my face with a puzzled expression. Then she shook her head. "I don't think I can take you calling me Rebecca. It's...not who I am anymore."

Talk about a loaded statement.

"Care to elaborate on that?" I fought my desire to pepper her with questions.

"No."

"Okay, so you'd rather I call you Becca?" I felt acutely aware of how awkward the name felt rolling off my tongue. I didn't like it as much as her full name, but people changed, and their names sometimes changed with them. The least I could do was give her what she asked for, especially since I was preparing to ask her for something so much bigger—her forgiveness.

Why haven't I been able to articulate what I need to say to her?

Every time I'd come close to starting my preamble—yes, my explanation had a preamble and a coda, plus it could be sung in three-part harmony—one of us would get distracted by an observation or a joke. Or cheesecake.

I looked at the woman sitting across the table from me, noticing the way the light brown strands of her hair curled under her chin on either side of her face, falling loose from the bun, where the rest of the waves were pulled back into a twirled knot. The strands touched her face in the way I wanted my fingers to graze her pale skin, and I had to shake myself out of staring at her unabashedly.

Suddenly, I was sixteen again and gazing at the girl I never thought I'd be lucky enough to have to myself.

I was pulled out of my reverie by her phone ringing. She pulled it from her pocket and answered, "Hi, I'm on break . . . okay, I'm heading back." She clicked the phone off and gestured for me to come with her. "Sydney's fully dilated." It took me a moment to process the meaning of her words. Becca was already on the phone with Sydney's doctor and moving through the cafeteria.

I trailed after her, suddenly nervous. "Wow, okay."

I'd watched Sydney's belly grow for nine months, but I'd had a hard time wrapping my brain around the correlation between her baby bump and a living, breathing human who was about to be born.

I had to man up. Maybe if I could be the man Sydney needed me to be in the delivery room, I could be the one Rebecca might want me to be someplace else.

I could do this. I had to do this. Even if I felt like I was in over my head on all counts.

ecca

"JESUS, Blake, where the hell have you been?" Now I recognized her glare as something I'd surely directed at my own brother. "Hi, Becca."

It amused me that she was still annoyed with him and happy to see me.

He scowled at her. "You should be nicer to me, Syd. You're gonna need me to babysit that little nugget, and if you're mean now, I might not do it."

"True. I do only want you for your babysitting and hospital chauffeuring." She rubbed a hand over her belly, which protruded like a mountain in front of her as she lay reclined on the hospital bed.

"Pain levels still okay? On a scale of one to ten, ten being the most, how would you rate your pain?"

"I'd say I'm at a two. I feel some pressure but not really pain," she said.

"That's good. Pressure is good." I looked at the monitor, where I could see little peaks and valleys of her heartbeat and the baby's. On another graph, her contractions were larger peaks and valleys, and they'd gotten much closer together. "Let's see if the baby's descended into the birth canal."

"Meaning I can heave this kid out of my belly, finally?" She looked refreshed after getting some sleep.

"Yes, you can," I said.

Standing quietly next to the doula, Blake watched the two of us and didn't move from his spot near the wall. I glanced at him as I washed up and put on gloves. He looked nervous.

"Blake, why're you so quiet?" Sydney asked.

"I'm not. What do you want me to talk about?" He stood about as far away from the bed as he could get and still be in the room.

"You're being weird. Come over near my head and talk to me. No hanging out down by my swollen vag."

"Jesus, Syd. Way to paint a picture." He inched closer to her.

"Here, you can grab that chair over there. It has wheels. Just roll it wherever you want." I pointed to a metal chair with a beige leather seat. He grabbed it and rolled it over to the head of Sydney's bed, wrenching his neck to the side to make sure he didn't catch any vag.

"How's it looking?" Sydney asked when I finished the exam.

"Ten centimeters, zero station. I already called your doctor. You're complete and fully effaced. Time to have a baby."

Sydney's eyes bugged out and she bit her lip, terrified. "Okay, you just freaked me out. Blake, tell me I can handle this. Say I'm going to be a good mom, even if it's not true."

"You're gonna be an amazing mom. Are you kidding? The best."

He grabbed her hand, and the two of them teared up when they looked at each other. He *was* her person. He was there for her the way he'd been there for me all those years ago.

I wondered about the rest of their family. He hadn't mentioned any aunts or uncles in the waiting room or anyone who was waiting for a phone call, but then, we'd had other things to talk about. And there had been cheesecake.

I watched Blake holding his sister's hand and fought back my own surge of emotion. I'd seen hundreds of families experience the emotions of childbirth, but watching them made me choke up. I didn't understand why, and I knew they didn't need me bursting into tears when I had a job to do.

I slipped out of the room to compose myself and wait for Dr. Kelley. A few minutes later, she and I entered Sydney's room together, and I wore a mask of professionalism.

***

"PUSH, PUSH, PUSH." I held Sydney's knees to the sides while she squeezed the ball I'd given her earlier in one hand and bruised Blake's knuckles in the other. "Okay, relax."

She'd been at it for forty-five minutes, and we were just starting to see the top of the baby's head.

"She's crowning. It's just going to be a few more pushes," Dr. Kelley said.

"Okay, relax, relax and breathe," I told Sydney, who was panting and blowing out breaths so hard I thought she might hyperventilate. "Slowly, slower . . ." I waited until her breathing ebbed a little bit and nodded at her. "You're doing great. You okay?"

"Yeah, trying to be," she said. "I'm tired though . . ."

Blake smoothed the hair off her forehead tenderly, and the loving gesture tugged at my heart. I was lucky to have five siblings. I took the chaos and the occasionally excessive outpouring of love for granted sometimes, but I couldn't imagine having only one brother and none of my sisters. Blake and Sydney only had each other.

"You can do this, mama. You've got it," Blake said quietly, putting his other hand over the one Sydney grasped. "Almost there, and then you're gonna have a baby."

The way he was looking at her, with those warm gray eyes that took on her pain and absorbed some of it, cracked my remaining resolve to hate him. He was one of the good guys, even if he hadn't always been one toward me.

"Have you got one more push in you?" I knew she was tired, but she was so close.

"The head is right there. Do you want to come see?" Dr. Kelley asked Blake.

He looked uneasy at the thought. "I think I'm good over here." He glanced at Sydney to gauge whether she wanted him to watch the baby come out.

"We're close, but we're not see-my-vagina close." Sydney groaned as she watched the monitor and saw the next contraction hit. She knew it was time to push.

"One more time, push, push, push," I told her, watching the doctor and checking the monitor to make sure the baby's heartbeat looked normal with every contraction. If the heart rate dropped, we'd have to stop and wait until it normalized. But everything looked good. "A little more, just a little more," I told her. "One good push . . ."

Sydney gave it everything she had, and instead of watching the doctor bring the baby out like I always did, I found myself watching Blake—the way he looked at his sister, eyes filled with wonder and admiration for what she was going through.

This wasn't the appropriate time or place, and later I would chastise myself for getting distracted, but in that moment, all I could think was that I hoped someone would look at me that way someday.

"Okay, ten fingers and ten toes. She's perfect." The doctor held up a cranky pink bundle with her face scrunched up and eyes closed.

I counted the fingers and toes myself to be sure, force of habit. The baby wailed as its tiny lungs got used to breathing on their own, and her small body reacted to the cold outside world. I always wondered if that first moment of life was stored somewhere in all our collective memories. *Did it register as a trauma or a gift?*

"You did it," Blake whispered to Sydney before kissing her on the cheek and smoothing her hair again. "You have your baby, and she's beautiful."

Sydney's eyes erupted with joyful tears, and Blake wept along with her, both of them holding each other by the hands and grinning in wonderment at the baby Dr. Kelley held up for them to see.

"Would you like to cut the umbilical cord?" the doctor asked Blake.

"Um, I'm not sure." His face went ashen, and his eyes darted to me.

"You should do it," I said quietly. He held my gaze, and I felt the warmth spread to my toes. I nodded toward the baby. "We don't get a lot of moments like these. This is one you'll want to be a part of."

Sydney nodded at him, and I helped her sit up a little higher in the bed so she could watch. Blake took the scissors and cut through the cord where it had been clamped off. So many times, I'd seen a partner's face morph from slightly freaked out to slightly victorious in the delivery room. Blake was no different, and when he finished and turned around, his eyes shone with wonder and adoration.

In the deep recesses of my memory, I remembered him gazing at me with reverence and a version of that adoration after we'd kissed for the first time—a reminder of why I'd fallen so hard for him.

Now, his eyes didn't leave Sydney's face, and I reminded myself that I had no claim on his affections anymore.

I cleaned up the delivery aftermath and helped Sydney rearrange her hospital gown. Then I pulled up a sheet so she wouldn't feel exposed. Measuring and weighing her baby took a few minutes, and I dictated the vital stats for Doctor Kelley to put in her notes. Soon I had the baby bundled in a swaddling blanket and a tiny pink hat, so I could hand her off to Sydney. Her tears sprang forth anew, and Blake huddled by her side. His jaw was slack with wonder as he ran a finger across the baby's cheek.

They were a family, and I excused myself because this was their moment. I'd done my job, and they didn't need me to linger.

I felt emotionally drained, and I knew it wasn't from helping Sydney deliver her baby. I checked my watch, hoping my shift was almost over, but I still had three more hours. The night shifts never felt so long. Maybe that was because Blake Fulton never showed up during the night shift.

I straightened up the room and told the doula to call me if anyone needed anything. Then I went for the door. "Rebecca." Blake's deep voice stirred something in my gut. In three strides, he stood in front of me.

"Congratulations!" I blurted. "I'm not sure I said that earlier. But you're an uncle. So awesome."

He scrubbed a hand over his face. "Thanks. For everything. Pretty unbelievable."

"Not the first time I've heard that." I forced a smile and put my hand on the doorknob. They'd be moved into a postpartum room, and unless I made a point of visiting, I probably wouldn't see him again.

We'd reached a détente. He'd apologized, and now I had some kind of closure. It made me feel choked up, which was stupid.

I NEEDED to get out of the room before I got emotional, so I steeled myself and met his eyes. "It was nice seeing you. So...I guess this is goodbye."

It surprised me when he said, "I'd really still like to talk some more if you have time. We never really got to my explanation. I feel like I owe you that much, and I'm sorry it's taken me running into you here to get around to giving it to you. Would you be willing to…maybe grab some dinner with me?"

"Oh, I don't think I can." The words rolled out before I had a chance to edit them. I always said no when someone asked me to dinner. I was a coffee-only girl. *But why? Because I don't risk getting my heart broken by guys like Blake?* All the more reason to conquer that issue. Maybe I'd start trusting people again.

"Actually, I have some time off in a couple of days. We could have coffee Friday if that works."

He smiled—his real smile where his dimple popped, and he exhaled as though he was worried I'd say no. "Friday. Coffee. Done."

So I gave Blake Fulton my number.

For the second time.

CHAPTER SIXTEEN

Blake

THE MORNING SUN beamed through the hospital window, straight into my eyes, so I got up and adjusted the blinds. But not before taking in the view. It was a beautiful day.

"Oh, that's your unquieted love, Rebecca? You have good taste, Romeo. I'm impressed," Sydney said once I filled her in on how I knew Becca.

Her sleeping baby was curled up in a blanket against her side. I'd gone home to sleep after Katie was born—Sydney was exhausted and insisted I sleep in a real bed, thank God—but I was back with her in her postpartum room the next morning, this time with a bag of croissants. What can I say? Decadent food is my go-to for most life situations.

"It was a long time ago, but thanks." Feeling like I hadn't slept, I scrubbed a hand over my face. I hadn't slept much. The conversation with Becca, the thrill of seeing her, the recollection of how well she'd handled Sydney's birthing process ran through my mind on a loop. I was desperate to see her again. But I didn't want to steal focus from my new niece, so I vowed to keep those thoughts to myself.

Sydney searched through the bag, as though one croissant was better than the next, and chose the one she wanted. She bit off the end and didn't seem to notice the flakes falling on Katie's blanket, so I reached over and brushed them off.

"In that case, I forgive you for leaving me in my moment of need," Sydney said.

"What moment of need? You were sleeping." She would find any excuse to guilt me, and I wasn't having it. Not after I'd sent my dog to stay with a friend for three days so I could be at her beck and call. I'd missed him and he'd given me the stink eye when I returned home last night. There was only so much guilt I could take. Howard would get over it if I took him on a hike later, and Sydney needed to let it go as well.

She swatted the air with her hand. "I'm just teasing you. I'm glad you had a coffee date while my uterus was exploding."

I grimaced at the image. "Again, you were fast asleep. And it wasn't a date. It was just two old friends catching up."

"Whatever you need to tell yourself, honey, but don't forget, I knew you when you were sixteen, and I remember how wrecked you were over her." She held the baby on her forearm and tried to support her head in her hand, but she couldn't quite balance it. "I'm supposed to be able to do this football hold, but it's not working. You want to try?" She huffed out a frustrated breath.

"Sure." I reached for the sleeping bundle in her arms. "Come here, Katie. Can Uncle Blake hold you like a football?"

Sydney had decided to name her after our mom, whom everyone called Catherine or Cath. I was glad she'd chosen Katie instead of our mom's exact name. I knew it was superstitious, but I didn't want a new baby to have a legacy of an early death.

I held her on my forearm the way Sydney had been trying to do and gazed down at her perfect face, her tiny slits of eyes squeezed shut and her perfect pink lips quivering like she was in the middle of a dream. "Like this?"

"Yes. And now I'm even more frustrated that I can't do it." Sydney looked tearful. She'd been emotional since the birth, and I didn't want to set her off with a skill I didn't think I really possessed. My arms were just bigger.

"It's probably just that I have a big, fat forearm, so there's more room for her. Here, let's try again." I handed her back.

Sydney got her settled on her forearm by bringing her arm against her stomach and holding her there.

"See? She's the most beautiful, perfect football I've ever seen."

I wasn't a baby guy. I'd never looked twice at someone holding a baby or asked to peek inside a stroller at whoever was inside. Maybe it would be different someday when I had kids, but generally, I could be counted on to be emotionless around small humans.

Until Katie. Maybe it was because she was my niece, or maybe it was because Sydney and I only had each other for family, but I felt protective of her tiny life and even a little bit fascinated by her.

"Back to what we were talking about," I laughed at Sydney. "You were a college sophomore out of state. I'm sure I was the least interesting thing in your life, and I'm pretty sure I didn't talk to you about girls. Ever."

"Oh sure, I was busy being fabulous at NYU, but you were a mess over her, and it was obvious even to me. Over the phone. Even though we didn't talk about girls."

I still wasn't buying it. "Dad told you."

"Yeah."

"Strange, because I don't recall talking to him about girls either."

"Well, he knew. Maybe you're just that transparent. Or maybe she rocked your world so much that it was obvious even to a middle-aged man with negligible emotional radar."

"I was a mess." At the time, I'd thought my stoic, brooding routine was a brilliant cover.

Who'd suspect a moody teenaged boy of anything other than hormonal irritability?

Apparently, everyone.

Sydney's chocolate eyes flashed with excitement. "Are you actu-ally coming to me for advice?" She looked a little too excited, and I grew wary.

"Um, I'm not sure. You're scaring me a little." I figured I could always hear what she had to say and decide whether to abide by it later.

She waved a hand dismissively. "Oh, please. Nothing scary. Though . . ."

"What?"

"You have to tell her the real reason you bailed."

"I'm not sure that's a good idea. It was...complicated, and I don't want to open up things that are better left in the past."

"If you don't tell her and she finds out…it won't end well for you, dear brother."

"I just don't feel like it's my place to tell her. If her sister has gone this long without explaining, I don't want to start a family drama."

She reached a hand for mine, a rare gesture of affection and support that we siblings didn't usually extend to each other, each of us being stoic and stupidly independent.

"Just be open and honest. If you're still interested in her—and the way your eyes get all sparkly when you mention her name tells me you are—you need to take her out to dinner, show her what a great guy you are now, and move forward from there. The whole point is to be in the present so you can have all the good monkey sex and report back to those of us who will be busy making food for a small person in our breasts and won't have a chance for monkey sex for a very long time."

"There are so many things wrong with what you just said. I'm . . . I can't even unwind all of it, and I'm really busy blocking so many images from my brain."

"Monkey sex, monkey sex, monkey sex!"

"That does not sound appealing. Have you seen monkeys do this? It's . . . never mind."

She laughed. "I'm sorry, it's just been so long…and I've been as big as a house, and no one was gonna date me when I was knocked up with some sperm donor's kid, and I haven't slept, and I'm trying to be supportive, but you're my brother. I don't know what kind of sex you like to have," she explained like that was the only thing wrong with the conversation.

"Please stop talking about sex. I…can't have this conversation… about that…with you. And also, I'm just trying to get her not to hate me. There was no mention of sex. Ever."

She shook her head and took a sip from the bendy straw sticking out of a can of Diet Coke. "If you think after all these years that you're just going to make up a lame explanation to save her sister's hide and be charming, you're fooling yourself."

"Why? That sounds great." It didn't sound great, but I wanted it to be enough because I didn't dare think about *more*.

"Because you could love her. You may not want to admit it, and I'm sure you've got PTSD from all the ways you screwed it up before, but all the more reason to do it right now. You loved her then, and I'm pretty sure she's the same person, ergo . . ."

"I can't believe you said 'ergo,'" I said. "Giving birth has made you a smarty-pants."

"I've always been wise."

"Great. So, what, in your great wisdom, should I say to her now so we can put the past behind us?"

"Make her understand you're really sorry, for starters. Don't just say the words. Explain."

Katie cooed, and Sydney kissed her cheek. I loved seeing her so happy as a mom. It scared the hell out of me to think about her being a single parent, but Sydney had been all-in from the moment she decided she was going to have a baby and never looked back.

I hated that I'd never apologized when Rebecca and I were still in school together. I had no excuse since I'd had two whole years, but I'd rationalized that I'd already waited too long by the beginning of our junior year. And by senior year, I'd decided she'd probably forgotten all about me.

Katie's eyes snapped open. They were a milky dark-blue color, but Sydney said they would probably change to brown like hers.

"Ooh, she's awake." Sydney rocked her from side to side. "Are you hungry?" she cooed, starting to unbutton her pajama top.

"Whoa, whoa, 'danger, Will Robinson.' You gotta warn a guy before you do that."

She looked at me like I was a Neanderthal and rolled her eyes. "Seriously, Blake. Are you scared of breasts? Because if you are, I'd say you've got bigger problems than getting her to accept your apology." She continued unbuttoning, and I continued to look away.

"I'm not scared of them. Please. I'm one of their biggest fans. But I'm not interested in a face-to-face with *your* breasts. You're my sister. It's...not sisterly."

She laughed and whipped a yellow-printed cloth over her shoulder, which hid her upper body and Katie from view. She adjusted herself under the cloth and looked back up at me.

I was shocked. "That's it? She's...eating?"

"Um, yeah. That's how it works. Basic biology."

"I don't mean that. I mean, how are you so good at it already? You just had her yesterday."

She smiled. "I guess it's instinct. She's hungry, and I'm her food source. And thank God she latched on right away because I get so engorged while she's sleeping. I feel like my breasts are gonna burst."

I waved my hands. "Too. Much. Information. I don't need to know about 'engorged.'"

"You are such a guy."

"I am. I wear that label proudly."

Someone knocked on the door, and two of Sydney's friends peeked past the curtain with tentative grins.

"Is this a good time for some guests?" asked the one who I recognized as her friend Terry. She shoved a giant teddy bear at me and gave me a peck on the cheek on her way to Sydney. She peeked under the cloth with no concern for the engorged breast attached to Katie's face. "Oh my God, she's the most beautiful baby in the whole world."

"Oh, she's really sweet, isn't she?" Sydney said. "Do you want to hold her after she's done eating? Hand sanitizer is on the wall."

Sydney pointed, and Terry went straight there.

"Hey, Blake," Sydney's other friend said.

When I turned to see who it was, I felt the pain of a knife twisting in my gut. Her friend Isabel had been my blind date a couple of months ago. It hadn't gone well, and I hadn't called her afterward. I'd assumed we both saw the writing on the wall and knew we weren't meant to be after an awkward dinner of strained small talk and an uncomfortable peck goodnight at the end of the evening.

Later, I learned that she'd been "really interested," according to Sydney, and was offended that I hadn't called her. I told Sydney I wasn't going to put myself through another night of hell, no matter how interested she was. I had no idea how Syd translated that message to her friend, and I'd forgotten all about it. Until I saw Isabel glaring at me like I'd murdered six bunnies in the hallway for fun.

"Isabel, how's it going?" I asked, trying for friendly but feeling like I sounded glib.

She nodded. I shrugged. We were still incapable of making conversation, and I knew that if I stayed in the room one more minute, I was likely to make her even more upset.

I had enough trouble on my hands with Rebecca, so I took my cue to leave and told Sydney I was heading home to pick up Howard. "I've got a meeting later with my investors, but I'll come by with dinner." I gave her a quick kiss on the cheek. "Do you need anything?"

"Nah, thanks. I've got my girls. I'm good."

I couldn't get out of there fast enough.

ecca

"Hey, you're early. You must want to talk," my youngest sister, Tatum, practically shouted as she ushered me through the door of our brother's house in the Berkeley hills.

"Being early doesn't mean anything except that traffic was light," I denied, hoping to abort the conversation before it began. Of all my sisters, Tatum was best at reading me. She was one of those hyper emotionally intelligent people who heard a tiny sigh and could tell people half of what they didn't even know they were thinking.

Maybe I did want to talk about Blake, even if I didn't know it.

"I brought lemon cake." I held up the box, trying to distract her with sweets.

"Delightful. I made cookies, but you'll hate them." Tatum was a good cook, but she'd recently gone vegan, and not all of her recipes tasted great. "I think I ruined them. I started with a whole grain recipe and ended up substituting raw sunflower seeds for the chocolate chips and banana for the coconut oil."

"Yeah. Pass. That sounds awful." I shivered at the thought.

"I'll just pretend I brought this. No one has to know about my cookies." She grabbed the cake box from my hands and carried it into the kitchen, where our brother and his fiancée bustled from the countertop to the stove in matching yellow aprons.

They carried handfuls of colorful chopped vegetables to waiting sauté pans and set them sizzling as though coordinated by an invisible symphony conductor. The way they moved wordlessly in synch provided one more bit of proof they were made for each other.

I was surprised to see none of my other sisters hovering nearby. I rarely arrived early, as Tatum had pointed out, but the rest of them did.

"Hey, guys." I leaned in to kiss Annie on the cheek and hug Finn. "The anal sisters aren't here yet? Isn't being on time the same as being late to them?"

"They're driving together, and they hit traffic," Finn said, wiping his hands on his apron before hugging me back.

I wandered closer to the stove, where the three pots and two pans sat on flaming burners. "Can I peek?" I couldn't see through the metal lids on the pots. I'd need a potholder to satisfy my curiosity.

"Nope. You know the rules." Finn pointed me to a chair around their large kitchen table and waited until I'd sat before taking one of the pot lids off. "Tater Tot, tie her hands behind her back if she misbehaves," he said. I loved that our childhood nickname for Tatum had stuck for so long.

"Not gonna do your dirty work, Finn," she said. I high-fived her —sisters needed to stick together, even if we outnumbered Finn five to one.

Finn had never done much cooking when he lived in Los Angeles, but once he and Annie moved to Berkeley, they started taking a weekly cooking class together. That meant we tromped over for dinners once a week to eat whatever they'd learned to make. As a bachelorette with silver-spoon tastes, I was never one to complain.

I hadn't thought Finn would ever leave LA, but Annie loved the Bay Area, and he loved her. She worked at a law firm in Oakland, he taught Economics at Berkeley, and the house they bought was amazing.

Nestled high in the Berkeley Hills, it was two stories with sun porches overlooking the bay and a rooftop deck with stellar views of the Bay Bridge, the San Francisco skyline, and the Golden Gate Bridge. There were enough bedrooms for all of us to stay, even though none of us lived more than a half hour away. It was just a thing with Finn—ever since our dad died, leaving him as the only male, he felt the need to take care of us.

My favorite part of the house was the kitchen. The space was decked out with every top-of-the-line stainless steel appliance, a giant ceramic farm sink, and exposed brick walls that made it look like a French provincial kitchen in a farmhouse somewhere charming that I'd yet to visit. I loved that it was huge, and we could all congregate there for hours.

Annie had hung pots from a rack attached to the ceiling and loaded its upper shelves with baskets and cute bunches of wheat and lavender. I had no idea where she found half the stuff she used for decoration, but it all seemed tailor-made for the room.

The highlight was the oversized round kitchen table made from reclaimed barn wood.

Finn had bought a giant lazy Susan, which sat in the middle of the table, and when we had our family dinners, that thing never stopped spinning. My family was not shy about food.

Right now, the table beckoned me with two bottles of red wine, which were open and "breathing." Ever since Annie and Finn had started their Italian cooking class, there were rules about wine.

"Can I drink this wine, or do I have to behave and wait so it can do its aerobics or jazzercise or whatever?" I took a bottle in my hand, ready to pour.

"Aeration." Annie smiled at me. "I opened these an hour ago just for you. All ready to go. Will you grab me a glass too?"

I poured one for Tatum too. Finn didn't like to drink wine while he cooked. He claimed the smells and the heat of the food ruined the taste for him.

"Finn, I'm not even gonna offer," I said. "But if you don't finish cooking soon, I will drink it all." I wasn't a big drinker, but if I started sorting through my thoughts about Blake, I could envision some wine as wisdom.

"See? You came early. You're threatening to drink all the wine. Something's up," Tatum said, pointing at me as though her finger were a laser that could see through to my soul.

Before I could decide what to say, I was saved by the arrival of Isla, Sarah, and Cherry. Immediately, the decibel level in the house went stratospheric.

We siblings were tight, but the friendly bickering that came with us often turned loud and ruthless. It drove our mom crazy, which was why she usually passed on our weekly dinners. Her excuse was that she wanted us to have bonding time "without the influence of a mother hen," but we all knew that we sometimes gave her a headache.

"Hey, sorry we're late. You didn't start without us, did you?" Isla rushed in, tossing a large loaf of bread to Finn. She was the second oldest after him, and she hated being late almost as much as I hated being early.

"Ahh, that's the stuff. You know I don't care when you show up as long as you come bearing bread." He buried his nose in the paper and sniffed the loaf.

"Yeah, you only love me for my bread. I know. I've come to terms with it."

"Good, because that's the reason the rest of us love you," teased Sarah, who had dark brown hair like Isla and was sometimes mistaken for her twin. She fell between Isla and me in the birth order, making me the middle girl. Sarah was a science nerd, a little goofy, and very trustworthy, but she and I fought the most as kids. It had taken until after I graduated college for us to start liking each other.

"Careful, or I will withhold the goods, and then you'll have to buy that Centinela Bread Company crap that gets shipped here frozen." Isla wagged a finger. She was serious about her bread.

Baking sourdough had started as a hobby for her when she was in high school. She'd created a science fair project about bacteria and fermentation, which had led to some pretty disgusting odors around our house. We had foul-smelling dishes of yeast growing in our kitchen for weeks. But the project had won her first prize and had turned into a career. She owned the hottest bread bakery in San Francisco, which provided loaves to five-star restaurants. She worked long hours, but her bread was heaven.

Isla plopped into a chair next to mine and signaled for me to fill a glass for her. I stopped at the halfway point, but she gestured for me to keep going.

"Oh, I see I have competition tonight for lushy lush," I said.

"You have no idea. The bakery has been nuts. It's always nuts."

"A glass of wine a day is good for you." Cherry was the second youngest, just a year older than Tatum and nothing like her. Cherry was the dreamer in the family. She worked for a tech company in Silicon Valley, but her job was on the creative side, coming up with the graphics for fantasy games and building worlds that amazed me when she gave me a demo and helped me create an avatar. Sometimes when I had nothing to do on a weekend, I would do a deep dive into one of her games, and I was always impressed with what she'd created.

I didn't have a wild creative side. I was a people person, always had been. Creative projects made me nervous. I was too competitive to let art be art, or whatever. I wanted it to be good, and no amount of rationalizing from Cherry that all art was beautiful made me agree.

"Wait, I have to get a look at this." I held her arms out before letting her sit at the table.

She was wearing a two-layered burgundy-and-black silk top that changed colors as she walked, making the two layers move over each other. She wore dark skinny jeans and cool peep-toe boots with spiked heels.

"I love it. I could never pull it off myself, but I love it," I said.

"Oh, you could too pull this off, but it would require you actually going into a store to purchase clothing, which I know you don't do."

"Haha. I shop sometimes."

But really, what's the point of shopping when my social life consists of coffee dates and scrubs at work?

"Really? Because if I see those stonewashed jeans one more time, I'll stone wash you."

I looked down at my pants, which were old enough to have authentic rips and a very faded hue, and I didn't see anything wrong with them. Cherry had fashion sense, while I had common sense.

"Why spend a fortune on a pair of jeans? Just, why?"

Cherry twirled a tendril of her auburn hair and shook her head at me like I was hopeless.

Isla laughed, then prodded me with a long breadstick before breaking it in half and taking a bite. "So, talk to me. Why are you competing with me for the lush prize tonight? Something bad happen at the hospital? Oh, please tell me there wasn't a bad baby."

"I hate when you call it that." Tatum rolled her eyes. "There's no such thing as a bad baby."

"We know, we know. It's a figure of speech," Isla said. "Do you always have to be the political correctness police?" She was already halfway through her glass of wine, which was unusual for her.

"No bad baby. All the babies I helped with today came out healthy and happy. Well, maybe not happy. Imagine leaving the warm, cozy womb for the harsh real world," I said.

Isla leaned back in her chair, seeming to relax after the horrors of walking in late to a family dinner. Where no one cared. "That's why they cry. They probably know more than the rest of us.

Babies are smart," she said. "So, what's going on with you? You're not the last one here, and you're drinking wine. Spill."

"Traffic was light—" Four sets of eyes rolled, and even Finn and Annie's faces called bullshit from the stove.

"Fine." I gave them the broad strokes of how Blake had reappeared and tried to downplay our upcoming coffee date as anything but an overdue catchup.

"Yeah, no. It's a date. You're dating him. Or you will be soon." Tatum studied me, waiting for the reaction she knew was coming.

She remembered how I'd been in high school when everything went down. I'd gone from loving him to hating him in the span of days. Even though she'd only been ten when our dad had died, she'd watched me career around like a broken windup toy until I'd worked my shit out and "come back from outer space," as she'd referred to it.

"Hardly. One coffee, just so he can explain what happened back then and I can have closure."

"The lies we tell ourselves . . ." Finn piped in from the stove.

"Seriously, out of sight, out of mind. I'm happy to be here and not think about him." I drank more wine and thought about how gorgeous he looked now. And how tenderly he'd looked at Sydney after she gave birth. My face suddenly felt hot, and my heart rate kicked up a notch.

"Which means all you've done since you left work is think about him. So...what's he like now? Do you still have a thing for shy debate guys?" Tatum asked.

I really wished she would stop reading minds the way she did. "He's fine. The same, only better looking. He's *so* not a shy debate guy. I don't know. What difference does it make? I'm just looking for closure."

"Do you remember how she wore black for weeks and just stormed around everywhere?" Tatum asked everyone as though I weren't even there. "You were in double mourning. You loved him."

"It was so high school. We were so angsty back then," said Cherry, which was short for Cherimoya.

By the time the fourth girl was born, my parents had apparently resorted to naming us after fruit. "Our friends took all the good names. We didn't want to be derivative," our mom had told us once. Then, for the youngest Finley girl, they'd come up with the name Tatum, a very unfruitlike name, and their whole rationalization ceased to make sense.

"You're still angsty," I told Cherry. "I've seen you lay in bed for an entire weekend, mourning a Friday night date gone bad."

She shrugged and twirled a tendril of ginger-blond hair around her finger. "I have big emotions. There's nothing wrong with that."

Just when I thought we could annoy Cherry and stop focusing on me, Finn brought the subject back around. "Well, if you want a rational person's opinion, I say you need to hear him out and decide if you want to start things up again. You're not sixteen anymore. That's a lot of water under that bridge, or it should be."

I jumped up and grabbed the loaf of rosemary bread Isla had brought, along with a cutting board and a knife. Maybe bread would distract them from dissecting my love life.

Tatum nodded at me. "Yes, good idea. We need an appetizer for this conversation."

"Leave it, I beg you," Sarah said. "Just…leave the past in the past."

She'd been the one who'd had to deal with my moods the most when she was a senior in high school and I was crying over Blake. I might have ruined her prom night. I might have gotten drunk on leftover champagne and made a scene. Not admitting to anything.

"Thank you, Sarah," I said.

"No way. You need to hear it all," Isla said. "He's the one who started you on your run of bad dating luck. At least find out why."

It took a long swig of wine, willing my family to disappear.

"You can't chickenshit out of getting the full scoop, not when fate brought you back together," Cherry said.

"Great. Gang up, why don't you?" I hated when my family was right, and I had an inkling they were, despite Sarah's protests.

"I promise, whatever happens, I won't drag your ass back into it," I told Sarah.

"Eh, I don't care. I don't have another prom for you to ruin." She waggled an eyebrow at me.

"Very funny. How was I supposed to know you were going to have people over to our house to pre-party? Isn't that the kind of thing a person tells another person?" Her prom had the misfortune of falling a week after Blake disappeared on me, and Sarah suffered as a result.

After I'd barged in on her making out with her boyfriend and puked on her dress that night, she spent an hour making sure I was okay before her friends could get in their limos and go to the prom. I'd apologized. Several times.

Sarah didn't hold it against me anymore, and I knew her desire to have me avoid all traces of Blake came from a place of love. She didn't want me to open my heart again and have it crushed by an explanation that would dredge up old hurt.

"I know you thought he was your unrequited love, but is it worth it to spend time with him at all? If he bailed once, who's to say he won't do it again?" She was getting worked up, as she frequently did.

"I agree," Tatum said. "I think you should make up the best possible reason in your head why he bailed back then and leave it at that. Make it romantic. He fell in love with you so hard back then that it scared him, and he ran. Something like that. Make yourself as gorgeous and desirable as you want. It's your fantasy."

Annie and Finn had finished cooking, and all seven of us sat around the table drinking wine. Cherry had brought two bottles of red herself, so there was no danger of us running out. She grabbed a wine opener and uncorked them so they could breathe.

"Good idea." Isla gave her a high five and topped off her glass. "Someone's thinking."

I cast a sideways glance at her. She wasn't normally a big drinker, and this was her third glass before dinner. Something was off, and I wondered about her relationship with Tom, a venture capital millionaire who she'd been dating for over a year. I hadn't seen him in months, and her excuse was always that he had to work. But maybe something else was going on.

Right then, Annie jumped up. "Hey, we need to serve this stuff before it gets cold. I just put mozzarella balls into the sauce, and if they sit too long, they'll melt into one big blob."

"No blobs allowed in Italian cooking class," Finn said. "Let's eat."

"What did you guys make?" I sneaked toward the pots. I just wanted one peek, but Finn shooed me away.

"Sit yourselves down and drink your wine. We made osso buco, linguini with tomato and mozzarella, wilted garlic greens, and polenta. And it all looks amazing." He smiled at Annie and pulled her in. "Because my lovely fiancée did most of the work."

Annie grabbed his apron straps, pulled him toward her, and kissed him. "Gotta love an honest man."

I loved watching them together. They were so perfect for each other. Relationship goals. And maybe it was the wine, but my mind immediately wandered to Blake, wondering if he and I could be that way.

Then I banished the thought from my head. We weren't dating. We were meeting for coffee. But for the first time, I admitted to myself that I was looking forward to it.

CHAPTER EIGHTEEN

Becca

"Talk to me, Island." Our childhood nicknames died hard. She used to hate it, but now she accepted that it was a term of endearment. We were exiting an Uber we'd taken back to my house, where I insisted she spend the night after she polished off almost an entire bottle of wine herself.

She didn't say anything, so I herded her to my living room sofas and grabbed us each a tall glass of water.

"What's going on? You're trying to bury something in a vat of grapes, and I'm not letting you." She turned to me, and I could see the pain in her face. It was unusual for her. She *always* had her life together. "Is it Tom?" When I saw the pain turn to sadness, I knew. "I'm gonna kill him. What did he do?"

"I think we're done." She stared blankly out the front window. They'd been together for over a year, and this was the first I'd heard of any trouble. But Isla didn't exaggerate, so I took her at her word.

"What happened? Did you have a fight? Did he say something?" I asked.

"Well, considering he's been phoning it in for the past two months, I don't think I'm wrong for calling time of death. Also, I want more from a relationship than a cardboard cutout of a good-looking rich guy, and that's what he's become." Isla leaned her head back on the leather headrest and took a deep breath, then exhaled. "Wow, it felt good to say that out loud. I haven't told anyone because I haven't been ready to do anything about it. You have to promise not to mention this to Mom."

"I won't say anything." I was shocked. Guys didn't phone it in with Isla. She was the one men wanted, the famous bread maker and café owner with a fiery personality and a wicked sense of humor. Most guys couldn't keep up. "Are you okay?"

She shrugged. "I think I'm still coming to terms with the idea of being single again, honestly." She was holding her navy blue leather purse in her lap, playing with the tassel. Her eyes looked blank. "I'm also exhausted. Maybe after eleven-teen glasses of wine, I'll finally get a decent night's sleep."

I knew I wasn't asking the right questions or saying the right things. The problem with avoiding relationships was that I was ill-equipped to talk about them.

I reached for her shoulder. "Tell me. I thought you were crazy about him. Where'd the love go? Is there a chance you can get it back?"

She let out a bitter laugh. "Um, no. I don't want to get it back. He needs a woman on his arm, and I fit the mold, but he's distracted half the time, and I don't want to be arm candy. I want passion. Am I crazy?"

"No. Absolutely not." If I knew anything, it was that Isla knew what she wanted. "You should not only have it, you should demand it. Not to make this about me, but…I'm making it about me for a second . . . If Blake and I ever did date, there'd be passion. It's built into the way we relate to each other."

She nodded. "Which proves my point. I'm the pretty thing he can bring to business dinners and seduce with a closed-mouth kiss, but he's not my Blake. It just took me a while to see it."

"You deserve better." I was getting angry because I hated to see Isla hurting. She didn't deserve it. I moved to an overstuffed chair so she could stretch out on the couch.

"Thank you. It's gonna be okay. I just need to get some sleep so I can think clearly. Every time tonight when someone said you should get answers from Blake, I heard them speaking to me. I should confront him. I should. But I also kind of want to live in the world of not knowing it's over for a little longer."

"Maybe it's not over. He could still surprise you and really bring it. Maybe you're not done with him yet."

She shook her head and pulled her hair into a topknot. She always did that when she'd made a decision. Hair out of her face, ready for action. "No. I don't want to be the kind of person who a guy takes for granted and lets him get away with it."

"So I guess you have your answer."

"Yeah."

"I welcome you to the dark side, where perfect relationships don't exist, and dating is just a comedy of errors. We have fun over here."

I waited for Isla to agree and tell me I was right. Instead, she gave me the side-eye and shook her head. My worldview on relationships *was* the superior one, wasn't it?

"What?" I asked, the wind slowly deflating from my sails.

"You're hardly one to play the superiority card."

"What's that supposed to mean?"

"Your coffee date bullshit? You don't let men in, ever. That's not healthy."

"I beg to differ. I think it's extremely healthy to be self-sufficient and enjoy my relationships for what they are, fun until they're not fun. Then, goodbye."

"And that's going to satisfy you for your whole life? Get real, Becs. A part of you has been fearful of people deserting you for most of your adult life. And I know you and Dad had a special bond, and I know you felt something real for Blake, but you need to let that shit go. Start taking risks with your heart because your coffee dates are a cop out."

It was too late, and I'd had too much wine—or not enough—to have that conversation. My eyelids were drooping, and I needed to be able to glare at her while arguing my point. "My coffee dates are . . . ugh, I don't know." Suddenly, I wasn't sure what my point was, and Isla pounced.

"Exactly. I call bullshit on your whole self-sufficient non-relationship thing. Blake is back and maybe you have a chance to get it right this time. Don't blow it because you want proof of your dumb relationship worldview. It's better to be in love than to be right."

Wow. A few glasses of wine and the knives came out. I wanted to argue back, but I took a moment to allow for the fact that she could…possibly…be right.

"I really liked him," I said quietly. "I can't explain why I felt so connected, but I did. He *knew* me…and when he bailed, it brought out my biggest fears. I . . . what if I can't trust him not to do it again?"

"You can. I promise you can." Isla looked tired, but I could tell she was determined to have her say. "But first, you need to get over your old shit. So go to coffee, talk to him, and get some closure. Whatever it takes. Because you deserve more than coffee dates with weird surfer dudes who cry." She was fully laid out on the couch, eyes closed.

I knew she'd be asleep in a matter of seconds. I grabbed a couple pillows and put them under her head, then pulled a big down comforter out of my armoire and laid it over her.

"You're saved, for the moment, from telling me everything about what he's like now, but I'm not done." Isla barely got her last words out before she was asleep.

CHAPTER NINETEEN

ecca

I woke up the next morning to the life-affirming sound of cats getting frisky against the neighbor's fence. Or "making kitten love" if you were the animal whisperer sort.

My neighbor and tenant, Carla, was not.

"If this isn't a bad omen for the day, I didn't know what is," she yelled, from where she stood holding a broom handle in our shared backyard. The sight of her—untamed silvering hair ablaze in the morning sun, threadbare pink robe gaping to show a tie-dyed Grateful Dead shirt underneath—wasn't even the most concerning thing.

I worried more about what had happened to the bristles of the broom. I feared they'd been shoved up the backside of a fertile yet unsuspecting cat.

My bedroom window faced the backyard and I'd cracked it open to let in a little breeze at night. Carla sounded like she was practically in my room.

Twisting my hair into a knot, I pulled the curtains wider and leaned out. "It's spring. That's what they're supposed to be doing, making babies," I said, jockeying for a peek at feline fluff before Carla batted their furry bodies away.

"Phooey. Those are just loud kitty harlots with no shame."

It would've been pointless to notify her that she was much louder than the cats. "Morning, Carla. Want some coffee?"

"Oh honey, yes, please. That's the kind of morning song I can get behind."

She favored her left hip as she strode toward the back door of our duplex, which gave her direct access to my kitchen. I left my inner door unlocked since she was the only one with a key to the back, and after years of living side-by-side, I trusted her implicitly.

At age sixty-two, Carla wore her years outwardly, her light Black skin freckled and creased from gardening in bright sunlight, her tight curls cut in a pragmatic bob, the hip injury she attributed to too many years on the tennis court and a surgery that left her worse off than she was beforehand. But inside, she was but twenty-five, feisty, well-read, and way savvier about pop culture than me.

I listened to New Kids on the Block and read romance novels in paperback, and she thought I was ridiculous for not embracing the poetry of rap music, making Tiktok videos, and listening to audiobooks on wireless earbuds.

On so many things, we agreed to disagree. But good coffee was our love language.

After brushing my teeth and pulling on a pair of sweats, I went to my kitchen to find Carla measuring grounds into my French press and wagging a finger at me because she wasn't done making her point. "It's not just mating season, those cats are a sign. They chose this house for a reason."

"Yes, the reason being that you leave food out for them."

Carla shot me a look—guilty because it was true, annoyed because I knew about it.

"I'm not about to let an animal go hungry, but they *chose* us first. I'm telling you."

Carla, despite her complaints about the cats, was an animal lover, feeding countless neighborhood strays, hosting hummingbirds at two feeders outside her window, and leaving out ripe fruit for the squirrels. I loved Carla, so I was there for it, even if it meant extra bird poop on my car. Spoiler alert: it did.

Skeptically raising an eyebrow, I watched in a daze as Carla bustled in my kitchen. Cats or no cats, I was not the world's best morning person.

Nor did I believe in omens, fate, destiny, or any other version of life that wasn't firmly in my own control. We made decisions and then we lived with them. Period.

If I had to come up with a metaphor for my life philosophy, it would be a game of racquetball, where each time a ball hit the wall at a certain angle, it determined where it went next, and so on, and so on.

Everything we did in life shunted us off in another direction, chasing after a new version of the same dream. Nothing happening by omen.

For that reason, I knew that running into Blake Fulton at work meant nothing. So I hadn't given it much more thought. Only some.

While we waited for the water to boil, Carla looked me over and pointed a dainty finger at my face, drawing a circle in the air. "What's happening here? You look like you just woke up."

"That's because I did."

"But you work nights."

This was true. I was a dedicated night owl, happy working the shifts other people dreaded. I didn't mind being awake while most of the world slept.

"Yes, but I'm filling in for a friend who's out of town. I'm working days this week."

Carla looked horrified. "So you were sleeping while I was yelling in your window? Did I wake you? Or was it the damn cats? Please say the cats."

"I was already up, don't worry," I said, still half-asleep and glancing down to make sure I'd put on pants.

My tea kettle whistled, and Carla whisked it from the stove and poured the water onto the coffee grounds. "You're a terrible liar. Let's get some caffeine into you if you're heading to work."

"Right. Work." I really wasn't a morning person. I'd already forgotten what I was supposed to be doing.

Carla rooted around in my fridge for some almond milk for my coffee and half and half for her own. Then she heated a bit of both in the microwave so they wouldn't cool down the freshly steeped brew.

By the time the coffee was ready, Carla was herding me toward my shower. "Loads to do today for both of us. Much as I love your company, I'm gonna let you get ready," Carla said, shooing me along with a wave of her hand. "Besides, I've got a fresh canvas calling me."

She was semi-retired, living off disability insurance after her hip injury prevented her from sitting for long periods of time. After giving up her job as a city bus driver, she spent her time reading, painting, and birdwatching. Rent control allowed her to live in my nextdoor unit without fear of rent hikes, which was fortunate because she'd become one of my closest friends.

I exhaled a sigh. "I'm not kicking you out, but you're right, I oughtta get ready and join the *day* people," I said, resigned to being a responsible adult.

"You make it sound like we're another species."

"Your point?"

"Adorkable girl, when are you gonna get yourself a man who will make you *want* to work the day shift so you can do the good stuff at night?"

"That man doesn't exist, Carla. Trust me, I've looked."

And he isn't a heartbreaker who woos people with cheesecake.

She smacked my shoulder with the back of her hand. "One day, you'll find someone who will teach you to hope."

I rolled my eyes. "Now you're quoting *Pride and Prejudice* to me? And badly, I might add."

"Fine. Be that way. Go work your day shift, and if you see a handsome man, by all means ignore him." Turning to leave, she shook her head like I was a lost cause. Maybe I was.

Carla leaned in and kissed me on the cheek before she left with an oversized mug of coffee. "I'm making a stew if you want some later. But for the love of God, if you show up at my door in those baggy work pants of yours, I'll send you home hungry."

"I need to wear finery to come for stew?"

"Not finery. Just not clothes that say you've given up."

That was going to be a tough one. Because when it came to hope, I'd given up a long time ago. A coffee date with Blake wouldn't change that.

CHAPTER TWENTY

ecca

Somehow Blake convinced me to switch our coffee plan to a dinner plan. That was the first problem.

The second was that I had nothing to wear, and he knew I didn't have work that day, so I couldn't show up in scrubs and pretend I had no time to change clothes.

I looked at the pile on the yellow-striped high-backed chair in my bedroom and realized I could no longer see the stripes or any evidence of a chair under my wardrobe. That should have been a sign to me that I was in over my head. I never spent a half hour—okay, an hour—getting ready to go out with a guy. And this wasn't even a date.

This was an apology meeting. That was it. Once Blake finished explaining why he'd felt the need to blow me off entirely during the most vulnerable time in my life, my curiosity would be satisfied, and I'd be free to forget about him.

I'd have closure. I'd be free.

That was the plan.

It was a stupid plan, I acknowledged, because as Isla said, I was not over Blake. All the emotions I'd felt eons ago, when we were flying kites in the park, felt as fresh as if I'd experienced them two days earlier.

So as much as I told myself we were having dinner as part of an effort to close a dusty old chapter of my life, I was going through outfit changes like I was having dinner with the Royal Family.

I stood in my bedroom in front of a full-length, wood frame mirror propped in a corner. It was probably too big for the space, but I loved it. What I didn't love was the image of myself in a bra and panties because I'd rejected all my clothing options so far.

So I flopped on my bed, dramatically threw an arm over my forehead, and glanced at the now-empty drawers in the closet where everything I owned was too frumpy, unflattering, or just boring.

The walk-in closet was part of why I'd bought the craftsman duplex when it first came on the market. Rental income from Carla's unit next door was also a perk.

Inside the closet area, a full dressing table sat under a window. I pictured women sitting there, brushing their long hair for one hundred strokes each night and slathering on cold cream before bed.

I'd turned the table into a sewing area, where I kept a top-rate machine and used the tiny makeup and toiletry drawers to hold thread and fabric patches. The window let in a gorgeous stream of light in the afternoons, and since I usually worked nights, I used the afternoons before my shifts for sewing projects.

I mostly sewed decorative objects, starting with throw pillows and working my way up to quilts, placemats, napkins, chair cushions—whenever I found a fabric I loved, I bought it first, then figured out what to make from it later.

Unfortunately, I didn't have time to sew myself a perfect outfit for tonight, if I was even capable of doing it. So I decided on a pair of dark jeans that weren't too baggy with a pair of black wedge-heeled boots I couldn't recall buying. I checked the mirror and decided my bottom half looked pretty good.

Looking at the piles of clothes everywhere, I felt overwhelmed. I grabbed a plain white T-shirt before I passed out from the stress of choosing an outfit.

It used to be fun to care about what I wore and how I looked. Cherry was right—I needed to do better than the same ripped pair of pants and my hair in a bun. Maybe my scrubs should be relegated to work. I could hear Carla's approval in my head, along with her anthem, "Accessorize, always accessorize."

I searched my bedroom for inspiration, hoping the perfect necklace would appear or, better yet, a fairy godmother with a wand. Instead, thanks to my fabric habit, I'd accumulated a trove of extra swatches, which I'd hemmed into scarves that I'd tied onto drawer handles and wrapped around plain pillows to make them look more interesting.

It wasn't lost on me that I was much better at accessorizing my house than myself. I grabbed one I'd sewn from Indian silk, and I wound the orange-patterned fabric around my neck and grabbed my dark-brown suede jacket.

Surveying my look in the mirror, I felt like it said semi-put-together but at the same time careless enough that I hadn't spent an hour on the outfit.

How have I spent an hour on this?

I glanced at the discarded pile of bulky sweaters, peasant blouses, button-down shirts, and jeans that should have hit the giveaway pile years ago and vowed that sometime over the weekend, I would meet up with Cherry and do some shopping. She was always bugging me to let her make over my sagging wardrobe options. She'd be thrilled.

I dabbed on some eye makeup and thanked whichever ancestor had gifted me with long lashes that barely needed a coat of mascara to look like I'd spent a fortune on extensions. With a swipe of red on my lips and my hair freed from its usual bun torture, I decided I'd done the best I could for my first dinner with a man in eons.

My doorbell couldn't have rung soon enough, just as I was talking myself back out of my dark jeans and second-guessing the height of my shoes. Fortunately, Blake was tall. He would tower over me no matter which shoes I chose.

And this wasn't a date. None of it mattered.

"Hey," I said, swinging the door open. I started to yammer before I'd even looked Blake in the eye. "How's it going? I thought we could grab a drink here, on my back patio, if you want, then maybe walk somewhere since it's not too cold. But that's just a suggestion. We can do whatever. I'm fine with anything." I realized then that I hadn't eaten lunch, and I was ravenous. I also realized Blake hadn't said anything, which was when I stopped talking and looked at him—really looked.

I noticed that his hair was still wet, slicked back from his face, which made his jarringly handsome features that much more striking. His dark-gray eyes were serious and...gorgeous. It would be a challenge to avoid staring at them all night long.

Then it occurred to me. "You don't wear glasses now." I ran a finger over the edge of his cheekbone before realizing what I'd done. The ignition of heat when I touched his skin brought me immediately back to reality. "Sorry. Boundaries. Didn't mean to do that."

"It's fine." Blake laughed. "Are you okay? You seem . . ."

"I'm fine. I'm good." I didn't want him to finish his sentence. I didn't want to explain why I seemed nervous. I had no logical explanation.

He was a guy from my past—from when we were babies. A lifetime ago. Now we'd catch up. He was going to tell me a story over dinner about a stupid thing he'd done when he was younger.

I was going to listen and maybe even laugh. It would all be water under the bridge, as Finn had said, and we'd go our separate ways afterward. Forever.

"I got Lasik surgery a few years back. Tried contacts for a few years, but I was starting to become a guy with a lengthy bathroom routine, and that felt . . . I don't know. Indulgent? The surgery helped."

"Sorry?"

He pointed to his eyes. "You asked about the glasses."

"Yes. Right. That." I needed to calm down. I needed a glass of wine.

I needed ten.

He grinned at me, and I had no idea why. Then he calmly took one of my hands, which was whirling about, and brought it to his lips. I almost fainted as he lit my body on fire with a feather-soft kiss.

"A drink on your patio sounds good," he said.

"What?" I'd already forgotten about offering him a drink. All I could think of was how much I wanted him to kiss me in other places. How I wanted his tongue to lick my throat and, what the hell, my entire body. I was a hot mess.

"Oh, yes, right. Come on in." I backed up in my entryway and caught my heel on the area rug, almost toppling backward before he caught me.

"Are you sure you're okay?" He smiled in a way that made my stomach do its own set of toppling moves.

"Of course." I turned and led us through the living room to the French doors that opened to the patio. "Totally okay," I muttered.

I was not okay. I was flitting around like a hummingbird, moving furniture as I passed it and rearranging some sunflowers in a vase because they weren't all facing the right direction.

When we got to the patio, I gestured for Blake to sit wherever he wanted and darted back into the house to find the bottle of wine I'd bought earlier and the opener I'd spent ten minutes unearthing from the mess in my utensil drawers.

"Okay, here we go." I held up the bottle, the opener, and two glasses, managing not to drop any of them.

"Perfect. Want me to open it?" he asked.

Blake took the bottle and the opener from me while I put the glasses on my coffee table. I'd found the reclaimed wooden gem at a yard sale a few years earlier for ten dollars. Its legs were mismatched, but it looked great with the red-and-orange pillows on the old Balinese daybed I used as a couch.

Because it was the only couch out there, we sat on it side by side, which immediately felt way too close. With only a couple of feet between us, I was highly aware of Blake—of the pull I felt between us. I wondered if it was a scientific phenomenon.

"You're a science guy, did you take a lot of physics?" I asked.

He raised an eyebrow while working the corkscrew into the bottle. "Some. Not a lot. Why?"

"I was trying to remember how reactions work. Like with a collision, does the force transfer if only one of the objects is moving?"

"Well, if you drove a car into a brick wall, the force would transfer from the moving object to the wall. Is that what you mean?"

I didn't know what I meant. "I guess. So the wall doesn't have its own force. It doesn't pull on the car, right?"

"It doesn't pull the car into the collision, if that's what you're asking. But it has its own mass, and that factors into the distribution of the force from the crash. Did you crash into something?"

"No, not at all. Just…wondering." I wondered if it was possible to feel the crazy pull of him if he didn't feel anything at all. Physics or some law of the universe had to be involved—empirical science and hard evidence.

The electric shock wave from grazing his skin couldn't be one-sided.

Right?

My physicist sister would be able to tell me. Damn her for not being here right now. "Where's Sarah when I need her?" I muttered under my breath.

"What?" Blake's eyes darted to mine.

"Nothing. The science stuff. I was thinking of Sarah. Do you remember her?"

"Vaguely," he said, looking away. "Two years older than us, right?"

I nodded, and he handed me a glass of wine before leaning back against the pillows. I did the same, acutely aware of the empty space between us, the thumping of my heart, and my desperate desire to move closer.

"Cheers." He held his glass up toward mine.

I raised mine to toast, but I didn't want to pollute the moment with some platitude about new beginnings or old friends. So I said nothing, then gulped down half the wine in my glass.

Blake's relaxed attitude and bright smile had all the hallmarks of a new beginning, but I still felt guarded and wary. He'd broken my heart once, and I was afraid of the power he still seemed to hold over me.

Neither of us spoke for a moment. I found it easier to sip the red wine in my glass than to think of things to say, and before I realized it, I'd finished the entire glass. Blake silently refilled it and topped off his own, even though I noticed he hadn't drunk very much. Great. I was the only one drinking nervously.

"So...is it me, or is this really awkward?" I might as well call a spade a spade and see what he would do to counter.

He exhaled and gave me the tight-lipped smile I'd grown to dislike. "I wish it weren't. I guess . . . man, I really fucked this up, didn't I?"

"What part? Ditching me when we were sixteen or asking me to dinner now?"

He huffed a laugh and raked a hand through his hair, messing it up a little bit, which made me feel better about him. Taking in the beauty of his face and body felt like an assault. "I guess maybe both?"

I drank a little more wine, then I put my glass down and turned to take in the man sitting next to me. I tried to see him for what he was now.

First, there was the confidence. The guy in front of me sat back, with his knees splayed open, certain of his place in the world. At least from his appearance, he was a man I didn't really know.

But is he? Are any of us really different from the origin stories that define us?

He wore dark-green cotton twill pants and brown work boots. His white oxford shirt was partially unbuttoned, revealing a gray T-shirt that matched his eyes, and the brown blazer he wore over it gave him a casual professor vibe. I liked it, and a part of me wanted to forget he'd ever hurt me and start fresh.

"How long have you lived here?" he asked.

I looked around my patio and tried to see it through the eyes of someone who didn't live here. With the pillows and carefully chosen minimalist decor, it looked planned but comfortable. "About four years. When I first moved back after college, I had a tiny, rent-controlled apartment in Berkeley with two roommates. It was a disaster, but it was dirt cheap. Now I'm a landlord with a tenant in the other unit here."

He nodded. "I scoured the city for a place like that when I got back from Europe. I even went door-to-door trying to meet apartment managers and hoping they'd like me enough to keep me in mind if something opened up, but . . ."

"You went to Europe?"

"Yeah, for cooking school. I'm a chef."

"Seriously? I wouldn't have pegged you as a chef."

He looked amused and swirled his wine, eyes never leaving my face. "What would you have pegged me to be?"

"I guess…something having to do with science? Or computers? I'd guess you did something in Silicon Valley. Coder or tech guy."

"Yeah, that all went out the door when I took my first computer science class in college and discovered I don't like coding and I'm not that good at it." He poured the last of the wine into our glasses.

We'd gone through the entire bottle in what felt like fifteen minutes. I had a sneaking suspicion I'd been the main one drinking, based on the fact that I felt relaxed around him for the first time since I'd seen him at the hospital.

"You're talking to a strict humanities major, so I'm not judging," I said. "What made you decide on cheffing?"

"Cheffing? New term. I like it."

He smiled, his cheek dimpling, and I swooned a little bit. I felt my chest stir and unconsciously put my hand there to tame it. As his gray eyes moved over my form, I felt an eruption of heat in my belly that made me blush. If he noticed, he gave no indication.

"How'd you pick cooking school?" My voice came out in a hoarse croak.

"Started as college-aged rebellion, but turns out I found my way into the perfect career for myself." He told me about his dad's law school aspirations. The guy I knew in high school didn't seem as cocky and rebellious as the version of himself he described.

But it fit the man I saw next to me. He was handsome and smart enough to be very cocky, and my pulse ticked up at the idea of an unpredictable, rebellious streak in him. He kept talking, which allowed me to stare at his full lips unhindered and imagine how they'd feel grazing my skin.

"I was looking for a dream to chip away at for years. I'd been thinking of cooking as an escape from work, but suddenly I saw that it could *be* my work, and it could be really consuming and satisfying work."

He'd finished talking. I forced my eyes away from his lips and stammered to answer. "I—I get that. It's how I feel about my job most of the time."

Right then, a small black ball of fur darted across my tiny yard full of weeds, heading for the hole in the fence where Carla had stashed her broom handle. Soon after, a second gray-striped blur of fluff streaked by, chasing it. Then their chorus began.

"Welcome to my world," I said. "Those are the neighborhood feral cats, and this is their mating ground. My tenant feeds them."

"Well, they'll never leave in that case."

"She'd never admit as much, but I think she's counting on it." I wondered where Carla was. If she heard me on my patio, she'd probably want to join us. But her side of the duplex stayed silent.

"Do you have pets?" he asked.

I shook my head. "Not unless you count plants as pets, which I kind of do. I talk to them and take care of them, and some are the longest and best relationships I have." I huffed a self-deprecating laugh and saw Blake's eyes searching my face. I looked away. "How about you? Gerbils, goldfish?"

"I've got a dog, Howard. He's a corgi."

"The cute ones with the big ears and the short legs, right? The queen's dogs?"

"Howard would be offended at that description, but yeah, pretty much." He pulled out his phone and scrolled through pictures. "This one's good—no, wait—this one's better." He reminded me of the parents at the hospital, glowing over pictures of their kids. I leaned closer to look at the photos and took note of the woodsy aftershave scent that was very male and sexy. I sighed a little and hoped he'd think I was just breathless over his dog.

"Oh, he's super cute." Blake showed me a video of Howard trying to herd two cows and eventually moving the big bovines with his tiny, insistent nudges. "Where was that? Do you also have pet cows?"

"Nah, that's at my buddy's place in Sonoma. He opened a winery up there a couple of years ago, and we've been working together on the wine list for my new place, so I'm up there a lot. I always bring Howard. He loves it."

"New place, as in restaurant?" I asked.

"Yeah. If everything stays on schedule, it'll be live next month. You should come to the opening."

I tilted my head to the side and nodded to imply it was possible I'd come—if I was free. But I wouldn't be.

"Really, you should come," he said again.

I could imagine a restaurant opening being some sort of who's who of models and fabulous people all hobnobbing and fawning over Blake. "I work a lot of night shifts, but yeah, maybe."

He nodded slowly. He knew I wouldn't come. I wouldn't need to because I'd have closure by then. "Okay, sure," he said stiffly. "No pressure."

Better to change the subject. I told him about my sister Isla's bread bakery since they shared common foodservice careers, and then I shifted back to the dog. "I can't believe he herded those cows!" I reached for his phone so he could show me more pictures.

Blake seemed to relax again. "It's the breed. He tries to herd me, too, but I'm more strong-willed than the cows, I guess."

I caught another heady whiff of his cologne and found myself leaning even closer to inhale more of him. My heart beat wildly, and I forced myself to back away before I reached out and licked him.

He sipped his wine and looked out at the view from my back porch. Three months ago, there wouldn't have been much to see. My tiny yard had been a patch of half-dead grass and a composting bin left by the previous tenant. But one weekend, Carla and I gone Home Depot crazy and spent two days installing a lighted pathway and small areas of planter boxes. I'd even put in a fountain with a relaxing trickle of water that I could hear whenever our conversation died down, which rarely ever happened.

"You said you mainly work nights. Is that a seniority thing? Will you eventually get moved to days, or is it by choice?"

"It started out as a low-person-on-the-ladder kind of thing, but I discovered I like it. I'm a night girl. No friend of the light. Vampire." I held up my hands to shield my face from imaginary sun.

"I don't see you that way." He tilted his head to look at me. "You've always radiated light." Because I'd moved so close to him, his breath brushed my skin like a feather.

It was sweet, and sweet was hard for me to resist. I forced myself to laugh at his comment and scooted a little farther away. "Thanks. That's nice of you to say."

He grew quiet again, staring at the lights in my yard. I focused on the burbling sound of the fountain and tried to relax. The air between us felt heavier, and if I sat next to him any longer with him saying sweet things to me, I was going to reach over and kiss him.

"We should . . . should we go to dinner?" I sounded unconvincing. I wanted him to disagree and say he wanted to stay on my couch and make out all night like we did in high school.

"Sure," he said quietly. He stood and picked up our wine glasses, which were still half full. "Maybe we should save these for later? We can finish them when we get back." He swept into the house and put the glasses on my kitchen counter. I followed, still slightly off-balance from the feel of his breath against my skin.

"Do you have a place in mind?" I asked, trying to snap myself back to full consciousness. My world was pretty small. My house in Rockridge was close to my job at Alta Bates, and most of my family lived within a ten- or fifteen-minute drive—except for Isla, who lived in San Francisco near the bakery, and Tatum, who lived down south in Palo Alto. I could recite the restaurants within walking distance of my house without thinking about it, even after two drinks —the Italian place, the Japanese place, the Irish pub, the American grill. I'd figured we would go to one of those places because it was easy, and I was a creature of habit.

Blake was busy on his phone, and when he looked up, his gray eyes melted me into a puddle of acquiescence. I would go wherever he wanted, and I hated that my rational side wasn't in control of my emotional side. "Do you like Italian? This place in Northside has a gnocchi dish I'm addicted to. It's kind of a problem. I figure if I get you hooked, I'll feel better about my own habit."

"So you're a gnocchi pusher. Is that legal?"

He laughed. "Probably not in some circles."

"There's Italian near here. We could just walk somewhere, make it easy."

"Don't you go to the places in your neighborhood all the time? Let me take you someplace new. I called a Lyft."

While we stood waiting outside my house, I looked up at the clear night sky. It had been foggy for the past few nights, but as I fixed my eyes overhead, I could see a few stars, then more, then even more the longer I looked.

Blake followed my gaze upward. "What a perfect night. The place I have in mind doesn't have outdoor seating, but maybe we can take a walk afterward."

I gave him a sideways glance. Dinner, a walk, coming back to finish our wine—we were mapping out a long evening together. It didn't feel like a utilitarian mission for information.

Here we were again all these years later, looking up at the stars. It had a grounding effect on me, as well as blurring the line between our past and present.

And yet…

"I'm game," I said without looking away from the sky. It felt safer than looking at his face.

But then I felt his fingers graze my jaw, and he tilted my face to look at him. I was only aware of the burn of his fingers on my skin and the way my eyes sought his like they were the vital life source I needed. I couldn't look away.

"I'm sorry. I'm so sorry, Rebecca—I mean Becca. I'll get used to that. But I hate the way you look at me, like you don't trust me. I know I did that. I wish I could undo it."

We'd been having a relatively nice time so far. Nothing deep, but it felt easy. And now it felt heavy. I'd spent so many years wishing for this moment, wanting and needing to understand what had happened back then. Suddenly, it felt exhausting, and I didn't want exhausting. "Maybe we should leave it in the past, whatever happened back then. Maybe we can just reset."

"Do you really think you can do that?" His thumb caressed my chin like a lit match, igniting everything in its wake. I needed to tell him to stop. He hadn't earned that intimacy.

But…I *wanted* it. Breathlessly, desperately.

"I don't know." My breath was choppy and rough, so I cleared my throat. "It seems easier."

His laugh was hollow. "I don't want easier. I want to make things right with you."

With every second his fingertips seared my flesh, my resolve was weakening. I was losing my carefully honed grip on the walls I'd built to keep my heart safe. If the past had taught me anything, it was that he had the power to break it again.

Where's the damned Lyft? They were never more than five minutes away, and this one seemed to be taking an hour.

Blake cupped my cheek in his hand, and I fought against melting into his touch. It muddied everything—an inescapable heat that threatened to burn me to the ground if I didn't learn to control it.

"Why?" I asked him.

"Why what?"

"Why are you doing this? Now. Why do you need to want to make things right?"

"You said I owed you an explanation, and you're right. Things need to be said."

"I don't know. Maybe it doesn't matter."

"Everything matters."

His words pierced another part of the wall around my heart. He was right. Everything mattered, as much as I tried to believe nothing did.

He'd said the same words years ago, and it was part of why I'd felt so drawn to him then. Not everyone thought that way, but I did. So many words were spewed with no thought about where they would land or who they would hurt, but Blake had been economical with his words when we were younger, and a big part of me wanted to know more about the person standing in front of me now.

"You said that before." I wondered if he held onto the moments we'd spent together in any modicum of the way I had.

He looked confused. "I did?"

"I mean when we were in high school. I remember you saying that before." I didn't feel embarrassed about remembering something from so long ago. If he was going to explain himself, he might as well understand the effect he had on me. It would give him more to apologize for, but he should know everything.

Almost as if he could see my resolve caving in on itself, he removed his hand and tucked me under his arm, pulling me close. "How about this?" he said softly, breathing into my hair and sending a roar of tingles down my spine. "Let's go eat Italian food and talk about whatever we want—we'll keep it in the present. No drama over gnocchi. But then we'll come back here, and we'll hash everything out. Deal?"

I looked up at him, his clear eyes, his open, expressive face. This was the guy I wanted when I was too young to understand how hard it was to find someone like him.

Blake Fulton had the power to make me feel things that left me powerless to walk away from him. If he crushed my heart a second time, I might not recover.

"Deal," I said. Light conversation over bruschetta would be okay. I would try not to think about what came next. I'd live in the present—until I couldn't anymore.

CHAPTER TWENTY-ONE

lake

"HERE WE GO, MOMENT OF TRUTH," Becca threatened, looking at the plate of green pesto gnocchi in front of me and holding her fork over it like a weapon. She'd ordered a pizza with prosciutto and artichoke hearts but had promised to try my favorite dish. "Wait, no. You should have the first bite."

"Oh, I insist. You first. You're like a guest participant in my food obsession, so you get first pick at the fluffiest potato dumpling."

"Well, now there's pressure. Which one to choose...?" She looked over the plate then up at me, a gleam in her eye. "You're not in a hurry to dig into this, are you? I should just take my time . . ."

I picked up my fork. "Okay, maybe I'll take the first bite."

"Oh, no you won't." Becca batted my hand away, speared one of the perfect green pillows, and popped it in her mouth. She let it melt on her tongue before chewing it slowly. "Oh my God. You weren't kidding. That's amazing."

I put one in my mouth and briefly closed my eyes as the familiar sensory bliss washed over my tastebuds. It had been a couple of weeks since I'd eaten at the restaurant, but each time was equally delicious. "So good, right?"

She rolled her lips against her teeth and looked again at my plate.

I tipped my head to encourage her to have another bite, which she did zealously.

"I've had gnocchi before. I've had pesto a bunch of times. Is it just the combination? What makes this so damn good?" She put the bite in her mouth and savored it, and I couldn't stop staring at the ecstasy on her face and wish it were the result of my hands on her body. But I'd be patient. For now.

"I've been trying to figure it out. It's not just the pesto. I think it's the way they cook the gnocchi. I'm working on replicating it myself, but I'm still missing something they do to get that slight crisp on the outside. Maybe animal fat. And they're probably growing their own basil, and it's a strain I haven't seen."

She looked surprised. "You've put a lot of thought into this."

"Yeah, it's chef ego. I'm not looking to cook this exact recipe, but I want to crack how they do it."

She glanced toward the kitchen, which was partially hidden in the back, where a wood-fired pizza oven was visible. "I bet if you asked, they'd tell you how to make it," she whispered conspiratorially.

"Nah, where's the fun in that? I'd rather lurk here like a spy and experiment on my own until I nail it."

Our waiter swung past our table and refilled our water glasses. *"Tutto bene?"*

"Tutto delizioso, come sempre," I told him. Our waiter nodded and made the rounds at his other tables.

"You speak Italian?" Becca cast me a side-eye and I noticed breath hitch. She liked it.

"Un po. I worked in a few Italian restaurants and picked it up." I met her eyes and didn't look away.

Becca nodded, her jaw slack. She picked up a piece of her pizza and took a bite, chewing slowly. Her skin looked a little flushed. She was mesmerizing.

And I was a goner.

"Good?" I could only muster a caveman response.

She nodded. "Really good. What's their secret?" she whispered.

"The pizza oven." I leaned in, starting to believe the conversation was foreplay. She had to know how sexy she looked and sounded with each bite. Another two inches forward and I could kiss her. I wanted to kiss her.

Then…she leaned back in her chair and wiped her lips with her napkin, breaking the spell.

"No wonder I can't make a decent pizza in a normal oven, not to mention I'm impatient, so I usually put it in before the oven's hot enough, and the crust ends up soggy in some places and burned in others."

I swallowed hard and blinked a couple times, processing what she'd just said. "You put pizza in before the oven's hot?"

"I know, blasphemy. I just eat the parts that end up cooked properly and toss the rest. Benefits of being single."

"Ah, I'm familiar. That's why it's good to work in a restaurant. I can cook for many and eat little bits of whatever I want."

"You always were a smart one, Blake Fulton," she said around another bite. Fuck trying to eat. I could barely coordinate eating a meal when all my mental energy went toward fighting the deep desire to kiss her.

I wanted to taste her lips again and feel her soft skin. But I couldn't. Not yet. I hadn't won her over, so I took a forkful of gnocchi instead, trying to convince my tongue to be happy with that. It wasn't, and this gnocchi was my favorite damned dinner.

Becca watched me spear another little green pillow and frowned, glancing at her pizza. She squared her shoulders in that way I loved, readying herself for the path she'd chosen, and took another bite.

"We can share both dishes if you want. I'm a big prosciutto pizza guy, so if you don't mind having a little more of the gnocchi . . ."

I *would* win her over any way I could. And I wasn't too proud to use a plate of pasta to do it.

"Great idea," she said as her fork dove into my dish.

I rearranged our plates into the middle of our table so we could share them more easily. I grabbed a slice of pizza, delighting in the tang of the artichokes with the thin crunch of the prosciutto.

Our hands occasionally brushed each other's as we both reached for the food, and I was hyperaware of Becca's reaction to me, mentally recording each instance of contact and assessing it. *Did she linger for a moment after we accidentally touched? Did it seem to affect her the way it did me?*

She was an iron vault of mystery.

But our dinner was lovely. Light and fun and devoid of heavy conversation. Soon, we were sharing a panna cotta and drinking cappuccino.

I mentally congratulated myself for making the decision to enjoy dinner and leave the heavy talk for later. Looking at Becca—I forced myself to call her that, even if I didn't want to—I felt the glimmer of hope build in my chest. Maybe she was right. Maybe we could start fresh in the present, and I didn't need to spend the evening wrapped in teen angst that didn't matter anymore.

But we couldn't build anything on a foundation tainted by my bullshit actions. I had to tell her everything, even if things didn't go my way after that.

So when she left to go to the restroom, I paid the check and fired off a quick text, hoping to get an answer that would set my mind partially at ease.

Me: Hi. Wanted to see if you talked to your sister.

Sarah: Not yet. But I will.

Me: When?

Sarah: Soon, okay? I promise.

Me: Thanks.

Becca and I were getting along so well, and the last thing I needed was to explain her sister's role in what happened back then. I felt like it should come from Sarah herself, which was why I'd reached out to her.

And family was family, so I had to tread lightly. It wouldn't be right to throw her sister under the bus to save myself. Even if I wanted to.

Becca returned and stood next to my chair. "Ready?" Her smile was wide, her face open, and I saw the earliest buds of trust.

I wanted to take her by the hand, pull her hard against my body, and wrap her in my arms until no distance separated us. I wanted to bite those full lips and savor their perfect taste of strawberries and honey. I wanted her, even if she wasn't mine to have.

I'd promised a casual evening out, two old friends catching up and me explaining. Ergo, no kissing. I had to respect propriety.

Fucking propriety.

AN HOUR LATER, with a box of biscotti in hand, Becca guided us through her house again, stopping to put the cookies on a plate. I took in her kitchen setup, as was my habit whenever I visited someone's house for the first time.

I liked to see what I could discern about a person from the pots and pans they kept. Everything in Becca's kitchen was put away, and none of the cabinets had glass doors, so I could see nothing but built-in appliances that had probably been there for twenty years and cabinetry that could use a fresh coat of paint.

"You're checking out my kitchen," Becca said, her back to me as she pulled a couple bottles of water from her fridge.

Before I could think, the words were out of my mouth, "If by *kitchen* you mean I'm admiring your gorgeous ass while you lean into the fridge, I guess I'm caught."

"Stop." She held up an admonishing finger, but I could see the blush creeping over her face. "No flirting when you still have plans to make me cry tonight."

"What makes you think I want to make you cry?" I really hoped I didn't make her cry.

"You may not want to do it, but I'm a sensitive soul, and I just might do it anyway. Green tea? Chamomile? Mint?" She filled a yellow tea kettle and set it on the stove.

"Any kind is fine." I didn't give a shit about tea flavors. I was worried about the idea of her crying. My guilty soul couldn't take it if I hurt her again.

She looked at me and squinted. "Why do you look like you're in pain?" She reached a hand for my shoulder and gave it a squeeze.

"The last thing in the world I want is to make you cry."

She smiled. "I was kind of kidding about that part. I've become a pretty tough cookie. I probably won't cry." Even though she smiled as she said the words, their meaning tore at my insides, imagining a series of hurts that toughened her. I hated that I was one of them.

Pulling the tea kettle off the stove, she poured water over the teabags in the two mugs. I took mine and we went back to her patio, where she turned on a gas fireplace fitted with fake logs that flamed up in front of the couch.

We sat back down, two feet of distance between us. Better that way so I wouldn't be tempted to reach out and touch her, which I'd already done a few times too many over the course of the night.

"Okay, enough lead-up and anticipation. Tell me what you have to say." She faced me, wide-eyed and holding her tea mug between the sleeves of a navy-blue sweatshirt she'd put on before we came outside.

I took a deep breath and felt my heart racing despite the cleansing mantra I'd had on repeat through half of dinner: *The sooner you talk to her, the sooner you can kiss her.*

Shrugging, I began. "I've probably spent more time thinking about that one day in high school than any other part of my life. Like that movie, *Sliding Doors*. Did you ever see that? With Gwyneth Paltrow?"

"I kind of remember it. She gets on a subway then gets to see what her life would be like if she hadn't gotten on?" She brushed the hair out of her face with her sweatshirt sleeve, and something about the motion and that her hands were stuffed inside the oversized shirt reminded me even more of the younger Rebecca, wearing a too-big jersey of one of the football players and brushing her always-crazy strands of hair away.

"That movie . . . it kind of haunts me. Like, if I could see what my life would have been like if I'd just manned up and come to school the day after we hung out or talked to you instead of running away like a coward...my life would be so much better now."

"Is your life bad today?" She showed no judgment or implication that my life *should* suck. She just wanted to know how I was doing.

"My life is...fine. How about you?"

"My life is fine too."

Her life should be so much better than fine.

I sat forward on the couch, turned toward her, and poured every-thing—well, almost everything—out.

"I just . . . when I think back on everything that went down, I'm so ashamed. You didn't deserve that."

Becca nodded. "Thank you. I didn't think so either. But why, Blake? Why did you act like you didn't know me—like that day had never happened? I thought we had shared this great time. I thought we had established something—at the very least, a friendship. Then you turned all blank like it was nothing. I felt like such an idiot."

I'd known as much back then, but hearing her say the words was a fresh knife in the gut. "You are the farthest thing from an idiot I've ever met. That night...you floored me. I was completely besotted with you, probably so much more than what you felt. That was a problem for me."

"Why? How was it a problem?"

"Because I worried I was taking advantage of you in a vulnerable situation. I manipulated you into hanging out with me. And then...I couldn't be the guy you needed." I thought back to that night, to how much I'd wanted to sweep her up and never look back. I'd wanted it all and had come so close to taking it.

"What does that even mean? I almost lost my virginity to you. I wanted you. I remember it clearly."

"Exactly. I almost made your first time a car fuck after I convinced you to ditch school because you were having a rough day. I didn't want to be that guy, and I was this close to being exactly that. The more I thought about it, the worse I felt."

"But, Blake, we were friends—or something. What do you mean, you couldn't be that guy? What 'guy' did you think you had to be?"

"I don't know, I just . . . I couldn't. I wasn't evolved. I was a coward, so I ran."

Of course there was more to it, but until I talked to her sister, I couldn't tell her that part. It pissed me off that I had to cover for

Sarah now when this might be the only chance to make Becca understand what happened. But I couldn't betray her family.

Thinking about it brought back a rush of all the feelings I'd had at sixteen—the regret that I didn't call out Sarah earlier, the intense shame at how I'd walked away from her and ignored her for two days. Then two years.

"I freaked out. You'd just lost your dad, and we had such an intense night together, and I wanted to be everything you needed, and I didn't know how."

"So you made the decision for me and just turned away? I didn't even know what I needed, and you decided you did? Without talking to me?" The flush rose in her cheeks, and I could see she was getting angry. I couldn't blame her. I hated the part of myself that hadn't stood up for what I wanted back then.

"I know. I didn't have a plan, and I was a jerk. After that, you wouldn't give me the time of day, which I deserved."

"You're damn right, you deserved it. I trusted you. I shared things with you I hadn't shared with anyone, and you gave me a gift that day—you were there for me. You took me kite flying because you knew I'd feel free of everything on that hilltop. Do you have any idea how excited I was to see you the next day at school? So yea, I didn't want to talk to you after you acted like that day was nothing to you. You left me no choice."

"That day was as far from nothing as you can get. You will never be nothing. That's the problem! You're Rebecca Finley, the girl everyone loved. You were—you are—everything. There was no way that I, Blake Fulton, resident dweeb, would ever be worthy of you. I thought you'd regret everything we shared and did, so I figured I'd run before you could shove me. And once I'd screwed up, and it was clear we were never going to speak again, I did my best to keep my distance. In some twisted way, I thought I was doing it to set you free from me. I didn't want to ruin you or hold you back."

Feeling empty, I slumped back against a pillow. I hoped the explanation was good enough, and I worried it wasn't. But I didn't have more.

She shook her head. "I was only sixteen. I didn't know that was what you were doing. I thought you spent the night with this broken girl and had second thoughts, so you ran as fast as you could in the other direction."

"Not true. Never." I couldn't keep sitting there and not touch her, so I reached for her hand, figuring I had a fifty-fifty chance she would swat it away. "Never could be true."

She didn't let go of my hand, and the feel of her skin did the same things to me now as it had each time I'd come up with reasons to touch her tonight.

It wasn't a glimmer of heat. It was the detonation of a bomb.

I felt a burning zephyr racing through my soul, electricity that I hadn't felt with anyone since her. I held on a little tighter.

"You really hurt me. I didn't deserve that," she said.

"I know. I…fucked it all up…and obviously, I've never forgotten about you. That was why I apologized as soon as I realized you remembered me. I've been waiting years to say it. Because I am. So. Sorry."

Becca stayed silent for a few minutes. She sat shaking her head and blinking at me until finally enough thoughts seemed to be competing for her attention that she practically exploded. "You were…so sweet…and so wrong." Her eyes brimmed with tears. "We could have dated . . ."

In my dumb mind all those years ago, dating Rebecca had seemed like an impossibility. And hearing her say it now took away all the remaining doubt about where I stood. I only saw where I wanted to be. "Do you think maybe this is fate? You don't usually work days, and on the one day you do, you happen to be Sydney's nurse? What are the odds?"

With two feet of space between us on her patio couch, I was two feet too far away. Still holding her hand, I closed the distance, bringing my other hand to the nape of her neck and holding her face inches from mine.

The tip of her tongue slipped out to lick her lips. Then she bit down on the bottom one and looked up at me through her long lashes.

"What are you thinking?" My voice was a rumble in my throat.

"That I don't believe in fate."

I nodded. "Because you don't like to be powerless over your destiny, or because you don't like where fate has taken you so far?"

"I . . . I'm not sure."

Hell, I might as well put it all out there.

"If it's not fate, it's something else, and I believe in whatever it was that led me to you. I don't want to walk away again. I've been wanting to kiss you all night—since the moment we ran into each other, really."

She tilted her head to the side, and a tendril of hair slipped forward. I tucked it behind her ear so I could see her face unobstructed. She didn't say anything at first, and for a moment, I worried she was going to ask me to leave.

She inhaled a deep breath. "Well, that seems like a long time to wait. Then again, it's no fifteen years."

"Goes without saying." My heart thundered in my chest. No woman had made me so wound up, ever.

How the hell does she do this to me? How can I get her to do it forever?

"I guess I don't know how you feel about me—the adult me."

Her eyes hadn't left mine, and I saw smoldering desire in her gaze that matched my own. Her lips parted, her voice a whisper. "I think you know."

What I knew was that I'd lose my mind if I didn't kiss her, touch her, have her.

Pulling her closer, I brushed my lips against hers, softly at first, savoring the feel of my fingertips on her skin and her almost-imperceptible moan when I kissed her harder.

I wanted to go slowly. I did. But this was the girl I'd been in love with for half my life. I had no gears or speeds with her, just full throttle.

She brought her hand up to my jaw and shifted closer, tracing my lips with her tongue. Our soft kisses were quickly replaced by needy, consuming kisses as our tongues tangled, and we lost ourselves and found our way back to the past.

We kissed. And kissed.

Fuck propriety.

CHAPTER TWENTY-TWO

ecca

IT WAS A GREAT KISS—A fifteen-years-overdue, heart-pounding, panty-melting, oxygen-starved kiss. Not that I had any doubts because we'd crossed that item off the bucket list years ago. But whereas our first kiss had been all passion and teen awkwardness, this kiss was powerful, certain, and burning hot.

This man...

Blake pulled me close to him until we were pressed hard against each other. My body remembered his like it was only yesterday when I tried to convince him to be my first.

I knew I didn't have to convince him of anything now. His hand roamed down the length of my side, his fingers wrapping around my waist, and he tightened his grip. His other hand stayed curled around the back of my neck, his thumb brushing lightly under my jaw as our tongues danced and explored the newness and glorious familiarity of each other.

I'd never thought much about the potential uses for my extra-deep Balinese daybed that was my outdoor couch. It just made me happy to load it with colorful pillows and still have ample room to sit with my coffee and Sunday paper.

Now, I understood the point.

Without disturbing a single pillow or parting our lips, Blake shifted so I was on my back and he was hovering over me. He propped himself up on his elbows, so our bodies were barely touching. I missed the connection, and my body craved the weight of him, but he didn't give me what I wanted.

"Ah, Rebecca . . ." His voice savored the syllables of my whole name. I loved hearing it come from his mouth, even though I'd told him to call me Becca. I even loved that he didn't follow rules. "I've dreamed of you."

"I've dreamed of you, too, even when I tried to make myself stop."

He lowered his body slowly onto mine, settling between my legs, where I could feel the hard length of him press against me. It made me crazy, knowing he wanted me. Not that I really needed proof.

"If you've thought about me even a fraction of the times I've dreamed about being with you exactly like this, then you know… I want you completely."

I nodded. Of course I knew. "I wanted you in your cramped Jetta when we were sixteen."

He laughed. "I had no idea how good I had it that night. I mean, I knew I was lucky to be there with you, but I had no idea you were irreplaceable."

His words washed over me, and I realized he'd put into words the feeling I'd had but couldn't articulate. He was irreplaceable. And for a few years, I'd tried. Then, maybe subconsciously knowing it was impossible to find another like him, I'd given up.

But I didn't tell him that. I wasn't sure I trusted him with my whole heart yet. He'd been nothing but open and gallant since we'd run into each other, but I still held a piece of myself back, ever wary of getting my heart crushed again.

That didn't stop me from pulling his face toward mine, pressing my lips to his, and kissing him again, deeper, because it felt like there was no end to how much I wanted him. It was a consuming need unlike any I'd ever felt.

Blake pushed up the hem of my T-shirt, running his hands over my waist and up to cup my breasts through the yoga bra I wore. I felt momentarily self-conscious at my lack of sexy lingerie, but one, I hadn't thought the night would go this way, and two, I didn't own sexy lingerie. He would have to be content with the tight, unsexy Lycra top.

Or I could help him remove it before he had a chance to focus on it. So I grasped the bottom of the bra and scooped it up and over my head along with my T-shirt.

Blake gazed down appreciatively. "Rebecca . . . wow. You're fucking beautiful." His fingers traced the outline of each breast, and he followed with feathery kisses.

I felt the blush creep over my cheeks. Compliments made me blush on a good day, but hearing Blake say those words, watching him react to seeing me, I was in full blush mode.

"You've seen me before," I reminded him.

He shook his head. "No. This is different. All day, I kept pushing thoughts away, thoughts of kissing you, of stripping you naked. Partly because I didn't imagine you'd ever let me kiss you, and partly because I didn't want to build it up so much that I'd be paralyzed."

"So?" I cupped his face in my hands. "Does the reality match what you imagined?"

He shook his head and kissed my cheek, then dragged his lips across my skin to where his voice was a growl in my ear. "It's so, so much better." He nipped my earlobe. "Hotter." He sucked on my neck until I moaned. "Fuck, Rebecca. You're so goddamned sexy."

I almost lost my mind. Taking things slow was an impossibility. I undid the buttons on his outer shirt and reached beneath, my hands feeling his hot skin through the fabric.

"Just to make it fair . . ." I pulled both his shirts free of his pants and up a few inches. I took in the contour of his abs and couldn't stop myself from lifting the troublesome clothing higher to take in more of his carved muscles. He pulled his arms free of the outer shirt, and it fell away. With one hand, he pulled his shirt up and over his head, then threw it on the floor.

I took in the hard lines of his body, the sexy *V* that led to his waistband. My hands rushed to feel his chest and shoulders and the way his hot skin shuddered at my touch. It was like coming home to a place I knew, somewhere in the recesses of my mind, had been waiting for me.

"It's important to be fair." He smirked before taking one breast in his mouth and swirling his tongue around my nipple.

I could feel it stiffen under the pressure, and a sigh escaped my lips.

"That's what I want to hear." He moved to the other breast, taking his time to turn my sigh into a moan of pleasure.

"Oh…yes . . ." I wasn't in control of my words or thoughts except for the one—*more*. I wanted to taste every inch of his skin. I wanted it all.

His hips ground against me, and I wrapped my legs around him, pulling him closer. He moved my mess of hair to one side and kissed along my shoulder blade, the hard bulge in his pants pressing into me. I wanted those pants gone. I wanted to see him. I was out of my mind as I ground into him.

Blake kissed me with urgency. Neither one of us was capable of going slowly. We'd had fifteen years of anticipation, and I couldn't wait another second to see him naked, touch him, have him inside me.

I felt drunk and giddy, and I reached for his belt buckle. Unlike in high school, he made no moves to stop me. Instead, he pushed his pants down once I got them undone and knelt between my knees in his boxer briefs.

His hands tugged at the waistband of my jeans, which sat low on my hips, so they pulled down easily without unbuttoning them. He trailed a path up one thigh with his finger, then hooked it in the elastic waist of my boy shorts and tugged them down as well.

I wanted to see the look in his eyes, but the sheer act of him leaning forward and kissing down my stomach, across my hip, and along the top of my thigh made my eyes close and my head loll back on the pillows. He was everything that had been missing from my safe coffee dates and my protected heart. He cracked my defenses just by looking at me.

He looked at me now, smiling the way I loved. "Can I taste you?"

I appreciated the propriety, but shit. *Yes, please.*

I nodded, and he slid a little farther down, first placing a row of feathery kisses along one inner thigh. I reached my hands for his hair and ran them through it, feeling his breath on my center before his tongue licked and swirled, and I bucked up against him.

Holy hell, I'd never felt anything like this. He slipped his finger inside me, curving it to find the perfect spot while his tongue made me mad as he circled the bundle of nerves that drove me wild. I wouldn't make it more than thirty seconds, the way he was moving.

"You taste amazing. I love it."

I barely heard him over my own shouts. "Oh my God, Blake!"

He was so good at it I didn't even care where he learned it. I didn't have the wherewithal to be jealous. I had it too good at that moment. I saw stars. I felt a crash of bright sparks. He pushed me farther, then over the edge while I grasped his hair and moaned his name.

His eyes fixed on mine, and I had no words, so I reached for his face, needing to kiss him and communicate what I couldn't with words. I also had no need for his boxer briefs and worked to get rid of them. He laughed at my insistence and pushed them down until he could step out of them. I reached for his erection, which was gorgeous and thick and wet at the tip.

"I'm not gonna make it very long if you do that," he said, his breath ragged as I stroked him up and down.

"Always underestimating yourself, Blake Fulton," I teased. I stroked him harder and watched his gray eyes grow cloudy.

He hovered over me and finally threw his head back. "Seriously, darlin', you're gonna kill me." He rolled away just long enough to find his wallet in the pocket of his pants and pull out a condom.

"Oh, I'll take care of that." I put out my hand.

He handed it over, and I ripped the foil packet and rolled the condom slowly, slowly down the length of him, enjoying how he pulsed under my hand.

But that was the last moment anything was slow. He practically threw me backward, and his mouth crushed mine with beautiful insistence. His tongue roamed and I fisted his hair, pulling him closer if it was even possible.

When he lowered himself onto me, pressing at my entrance and teasing me again, I felt a moan build at the back of my throat. I had no idea I could come more than once. I knew about multiples, but they were some mythical concept I'd only read about in romance novels.

Nope. They were real.

Blake eased inside me, inch by crazy-hot inch, until he filled me. "I'm going to say it again. High school Blake should be locked in a nuthouse for saying no to this."

I nodded because all words had failed me. I was already building back to another climax, and it took all my concentration to slow myself down and feel him rhythmically thrusting, moving against my core, his breath coming harder as his hips circled over mine. The feel of him moving inside me was almost too much to handle.

The view of him hovering above me was spellbinding. I still couldn't convince my brain that what I saw and felt was real. He rocked his hips, pushing me higher until everything splintered around me, and I heard his moans as he fell apart with me.

Nothing had prepared me for how good it would feel, and I became more and more convinced that for all those years, I hadn't been avoiding other men because I was scarred by Blake. I'd done it because I was waiting for him.

SOME NUMBER OF HOURS LATER, after two more rounds of toe-curling sex on my patio daybed, we lay facing each other under a blanket. The night had gotten a little colder, but neither of us wanted to move inside. Also, I didn't want to invite him up to my room and have him see how many outfits I'd gone through earlier.

Blake encircled me with his arms and wedged one leg between mine. He explained how he cooked gnocchi. We laughed about a billboard we'd seen earlier on our walk. We kissed every couple of minutes because we couldn't help it. The tangle of lips and limbs was exactly right, and I had no desire to move.

"I have a question, and I want you to consider your answer carefully," he said.

"Uh-oh, this sounds serious." I prepared myself with a serious face.

"Nah, not like that. I just want to make sure you think before you answer. Will you go out with me? Not a date where I apologize and dredge up all my past misdeeds. A real date, where I wine and dine you and do dirty things to your body all night long."

"Yes, to the dirty things, but, Blake, I don't date."

"What do you mean, you don't date? Like, you have a policy against it?"

"Basically, yes."

"Why?"

"I just do."

He leaned away from me and looked hard into my eyes. All I could think was that I wanted to go on a date with him, especially if every moment felt like this. If I could look at him and kiss him and talk to him for hours, I wanted to go on a date. But I didn't want to have to get over him again.

In order to change the subject, I rolled away from him and wrapped a gray throw blanket from the other end of the couch around myself. I went to the kitchen to get us more water.

When I came back, Blake was sitting up and watching me. I smiled because I wanted him to know everything was fine. We didn't need to date. We didn't need to get entangled or get our hearts involved. He didn't return my smile.

I noticed that the sky was a bit lighter than it had been. "Wait, is it already almost morning?" I hadn't checked the clock in my kitchen.

"I'm afraid so. And I have a meeting with some folks at eight."

"Well, that makes twice I've stayed up all night with you. Maybe that's our thing."

Finally, I got the smile. "I like that. Maybe it is."

I fought my feelings of not wanting him to leave. I hated what it said about me, that one night with him had turned me back into the needy girl I was in high school, wanting something he probably had no interest in giving.

"I don't have to leave yet. And I don't want to leave at all, just so you know," he said, as though he could read my mind.

I nodded. "Stay as long as you like."

He leaned back and pulled me on top of him. "I changed my mind."

"About what? Now you want to leave?"

He laughed. "No, not about that. I know I said you should think before you answered, but I'm reneging on that. Will you go on a date with me? Don't think. Just answer."

"Blake, I—"

"Nope, don't think. Becca Finley, I'd really like to take you on a romantic date, where I wine and dine you, and we laugh and talk, and I fuck you hard and make love to you soft and give you orgasms all night long. Are you in?"

I had a hard time waiting until he finished before answering. It felt as impulsive as deciding to stay out all night when we were sixteen, but I knew I wanted him. I'd spent too many years mourning the loss of what we could have had to pass up the remote chance we could have it now. "Yes. In."

He kissed my nose. "Excellent. We're going on a date. You will wear your sexy nurse outfit, and I will pick you up at seven on whatever the next night is that you have off—no work the following day."

"That would be Wednesday, and I don't have a sexy nurse outfit. I wear scrubs."

"Fine. Wear whatever you want. Preferably not scrubs."

"I don't want to tell you how many dates I've gone on in scrubs."

"I thought you don't date."

"I don't date guys I might fall in love with. It's self-preservation." The words were out of my mouth before I could stop them. I closed my eyes.

Was there any chance he didn't hear what I'd just said?

"You should date me," was his response, leaving me to interpret what he did or didn't mean in reference to my blurted words.

I was confused, and I hated that unmoored feeling. My heart wanted him, but my brain told me to be careful.

So I kissed him and hoped my brain would mind the store.

Becca

"YOU'RE GOING to need to do better than that," Carla said, clucking her tongue at me when she saw my jeans and black T-shirt ensemble. I'd come to her house looking for some accessories to spice up my outfit.

Instead, I got a lecture.

"You like this man, correct? This is the one you almost banged in the back of a Buick, yes?"

"It was a Jetta. And what's your point?"

"Buick sounds better. Alliteration."

"Your point?" I was beginning to wish Carla had kept her focus on the cats. Instead, she'd stopped in the middle of an oil painting to give me fashion advice before my date with Blake.

"This man read *Pride and Prejudice*, for heaven's sake. *And* watched the movie. He deserves better than this nothing outfit. Do you at least have sexy lingerie on underneath?"

My mind churned through the possible connection between lingerie and Mr. Darcy as I gaped at her and willed my jeans to transform into something acceptable to her. "I'm really regretting sharing the details of our one night in high school."

"Not at all. It's important backstory. I just want to make sure you're prepared for the main event."

"I don't even know what that means." I was also getting tired of people telling me I had horrible fashion sense. As if to drive that point home, Cherry had dropped off a bag of her clothes for me to try on, hoping something would jump out as "perfect Blake seduction attire," as she said in her note. Unfortunately, Carla had been gardening when Cherry dropped the bag off, so there was no hiding its existence.

"Bring me the bag of your sister's clothes. You're not wearing this pathetic getup."

As I slunk back to my room to retrieve the bag, I looked down at my jeans and shirt, certain they weren't actually pathetic.

Were they?

"Ah, now this is more like it," Carla said, rifling through the bag and hanging various dresses and skirts over the backs of chairs. I also noticed she'd managed to scoop coffee grounds into my pot and start the water boiling. "You will wear this skirt," she said, handing me a denim mini skirt that would leave nothing to the imagination.

"Cherry is shorter than me. I'm not sure that thing is street legal."

Carla waved her hand at me as though she wanted me to disappear, though that would defeat the purpose of our little fashion exercise. "Wear that with those cute heeled booties of yours, and that man won't be able to swallow his dinner. You have some pretty lingerie for later?"

"Carla!" If my face wasn't bright red, I'd be shocked. Then, sheepishly, I replied, "And no, I don't."

Fishing deeper into the bag, Carla pulled out several new matching bra and panty combos that Cherry had apparently selected for me as well. "I'm liking this sister of yours," Carla said, raising an eyebrow.

"I don't need that stuff. The skirt is enough for tonight, don't you think?"

"If I thought that, I wouldn't have told you to wear it."

The tea kettle whistled, and Carla turned off the stove. "You make us some coffee, and I'll go to my place and find you some nice accessories for that boring T-shirt. And maybe a cute jacket that cinches at the waist."

While the coffee steeped, I considered the lingerie and ultimately decided against it.

She was back after a few minutes with long strands of necklaces and was still layering them and considering my "look" when Blake knocked on the open doorframe.

"Hey."

When I looked up to see him, my heart did an actual flip in my chest. He looked so good, freshly showered, hair slicked back, handsome angles of his cheekbones on full display, setting off his kissable lips.

If that weren't enough eye candy, he handed me a bundle of tiny yellow roses in a glass jar. "Didn't want you to have to search around for a vase."

"That was so thoughtful. Thank you." His hello kiss nearly melted me into a puddle.

When he looked me over, starting with my bare legs and ending at my lips, I silently thanked my two fashion angels for getting me into the tiny skirt. Carla looked at the scene of us with a satisfied smirk on her face. Then she cleared her throat.

"Sorry. Blake, meet my neighbor Carla."

Blake extended his hand to shake Carla's, and she glared at him. "What's that?" She swatted his hand away and pulled him into a hug that lasted for nearly a minute. "Tryin' to shake my hand . . ." she muttered. "Family doesn't shake hands."

I tried to clarify because the look on Blake's face told me he was confused. "We're not actually related, but we are really good friends."

"This woman . . ." Carla put a hand on her chest and blinked a couple times before letting out a long exhale. "Yes, we are really good friends. The best."

"Well then, it's an honor to meet you, Carla. And you're right. She's quite a woman." He reached for my hand, and Carla nodded her approval, her eyes getting misty.

"Okay, enough, you two. Let me get my coat so we can go." I left the two of them staring at each other in my kitchen and raced over to Carla's house to grab the jacket that made my legs look longer.

And I changed into the lacy lingerie, cursing her as I did it.

lake

BEFORE WE LEFT HER HOUSE, Carla pulled me aside for a chat. Becca had gone over to Carla's to retrieve a jacket or something she'd left there, and Carla pinned me with a stare. If I'd thought Becca could be intimidating, I decided she had nothing on grandmotherly spitfire of a woman who lives next door. "You're gonna be good to her, yes?"

"Absolutely, yes." I was being judged, I knew that. I just didn't know how much Carla knew about our past. "I'll be great to her."

Carla nodded, still assessing my character.

"So, you and Becca have been friends a long time?" I asked.

"Six years. We both rented at first, then four years ago, she bought this place, and I became her tenant. She's been . . . really great to me."

"Well, it's hard to find a good tenant. I'm sure she appreciates you."

"It's not just that." Carla carried the coffee cups over to Becca's sink, but when she turned around, she blinked—just once—but it was enough for me to see she was pushing back tears. "I'm gonna tell you something, just to make sure you know you've got someone truly special in that girl."

She turned to make sure Becca was still gone before continuing. "You know the city lifted rent control on this place four years ago?"

"I know the laws keep changing."

"Well, this place . . . the owner could've jacked up the rent, quadrupled it. Would have meant I'd be out looking for a dirt-cheap place in some crappy neighborhood. That's right around when Miss Becca bought the place. She told me the laws hadn't changed anything, that my rent was protected under rent control, I could live here as long as I wanted."

I wanted to make sure I understood what she was telling me. "Becca bought the house and keeps the rent artificially low so you can stay?"

She nodded. "Now, how many people look at an irritating, cat-loving coffee moocher and do a thing like that? Heart of gold, that one."

I pulled Carla in for another hug. "I can see why she thinks you're worth keeping around. Hope to see you again soon." She hugged me back, then pushed me away.

"Make her happy, will you? She deserves it."

"What do I deserve?" Becca was back, wearing a flattering coat that made her legs look long and lean. It was all I could do to keep my mouth from watering at the sight of her.

"A delicious dinner. Let's go. I'm cooking," I said, taking her hand. Carla winked at me before we headed out the door.

I WAS nervous to show Becca the new restaurant, mainly because it wasn't finished, and I didn't want her to think the place was a dump. It would look great in a few weeks, as long as I busted everyone's balls to keep them on schedule.

"It's still a work in progress, so don't judge the way it looks. A whole team is still working on the design." I held Becca's hand as we walked from my parking spot in the alley behind my restaurant on Oak Street. I felt more nervous showing the restaurant space to her than I had when I'd met with investors I'd had to convince to invest millions in my multi-restaurant concept.

"I'm not a judgy person. I'm super excited to see it." She squeezed my hand.

I could have let us in through the back entrance, but I wanted her to get a sense of the grandeur of the place. It had high clerestory windows above well-used double doors, all salvaged from a church renovation. On either side of the doors, two-foot-high brick walls fanned out and held the plate glass windows that reached to the ceiling. I was still debating about whether to have metal curtain rods with French-style curtains in the windows.

When we rounded the corner and Becca took in the expanse of windows, she gasped. "Oh, I love these. So much great light."

I punched in the code on the lockbox.

"Why is it locked like that?" she asked.

"Until we open, no one's really using these doors. The construction guys and the deliveries come through the back. So...you like what you've seen so far?"

"I love it. The windows are gorgeous, and the oak on those doors is incredible."

I was impressed that she knew it was oak.

At my raised eyebrow, she said, "Yeah, I know my wood." Then she turned pink with embarrassment, and I pulled her tight against my chest.

"Is that so? Because there's some nice wood elsewhere that you might want to examine." I brushed a few strands of hair off her face and smiled. She wore booties with high heels and a denim miniskirt that had been driving me crazy since I picked her up. She'd hidden those gorgeous legs the other times I'd seen her, but tonight, I couldn't stop staring.

"I'm familiar, and you're right—it's very nice . . . very impressive . . . wood."

As if on cue, my cock sprang to life, begging me to pull her closer. I nipped at her neck and almost melted when I heard her moan. "We might have to talk about that some more."

"You're the boss," she whispered into my ear, her gravelly voice sending another shock wave through me. I might not make it through dinner.

She tilted her head back and brushed her mouth against my lips in that way I loved before sinking in for more. I pushed my hands into her hair and sucked on her luscious bottom lip before finding her tongue with mine.

The scent of plumeria from her shampoo washed over me as our tongues tangled and I savored the sweet taste of her. Being with her made it hard to stay focused on anything else, and for a few minutes, I forgot we were still standing in the doorway of the restaurant with a crew of workers sanding and hammering in front of us.

Reluctantly, I pulled away from her and grasped her hand again before pulling her into the restaurant. All six guys, who I'd been convinced had no interest in me or my activities in the doorway, broke into a round of applause and whistles. I immediately felt protective of Becca, not wanting her to feel on display, but she shook off the attention, giving them a wave and a curtsey before walking through the space.

"Ooh, this is cool." She eyed the wrought iron staircase that circled up to the second floor.

"Way to open a restaurant, boss." Burt, my construction foreman, wore a shit-eating grin on his weathered face. He rubbed a hand over his shaved head and flashed me a thumbs-up."Okay, enough. Guys, this is Becca, and Becca, I'm not going to introduce you to each of these oafs because I can't keep them straight myself."

"Haha, you know you love us because we're on budget and on time," Burt said. "No one else in the business can say that with a straight face."

He was right. I'd worked with them on three other projects, and I'd never work with anyone else. "Fine. I'll buy you guys a six-pack at quitting time."

A loud grumble rose among them.

"Fine, a twelve-pack, but then no one's driving."

I ushered Becca past them into the kitchen, which was mercifully empty. "So, that's the dining room." I pointed behind me and grabbed her hand again. I needed to be touching her. Always. Preferably in multiple places.

Looking around the kitchen, I saw all kinds of ways I could take her—up against the walk-in fridge, behind the flattop grill, on top of the butcher-block island, which I'd always envisioned as a great *mise en place* setup area, but which now had so much more potential.

She peeked back through the open-plan window of the kitchen. "I didn't get to see much of that. Are you going in the French direction with the curtains and the globe lamps?" She pointed at the lighting fixtures in boxes on the floor.

"Kind of a bistro feel, yeah. I'd paint over the exposed wood and probably take out the staircase in the middle of the room, open it up. You like?"

"I do, mostly." She met my gaze for a second before looking around the dining space again. "And what are you thinking for the booths? Chesterfield sofa leather or a more modern take?"

"The brown leather. You know your design," I said, impressed. I'd seen signs of her visual flare around her house, but she'd made a point of telling me she was only into sewing as a hobby, so I wasn't sure she saw herself doing more with her talent. "Now let's talk about 'mostly.' What don't you like about the French bistro idea?"

The flush hit her cheeks, and she shook her head and waved her hands as if to erase the comment. "No, nothing. I didn't mean I don't like it."

"And there's the double negative. Do you like the bistro look for here, or do you think it doesn't work?"

She shrugged and looked a little tortured. "Ack, I didn't mean to dig myself a ditch. I guess the building just struck me a certain way when I saw those gorgeous windows and the materials. I love when a finish people typically think of as belonging outside is used indoors—like the brick and unfinished wood and stone you have. It seems a shame to cover them up. Are you planning to serve French food?"

"It's a fusion tasting menu. Some French, some molecular gastronomy."

"So why pigeonhole yourself with design? It's a great space, and the staircase is such a set-piece. You could work everything around it if you decided to keep it."

I squinted, trying to see her vision for the space, but design was my weak spot. "You're good at this."

"I don't know about that. I just know what I like and what I think looks good together, colors, fabrics, materials. Like I love the fact that you have the brick accent from outside carried through the dining room." She pointed at the low brick wall that would eventually hold a countertop and allow people to look into the open kitchen and watch the chefs.

"I'm pretty sure that's design," I said. "And you're very good at it. I should hire you to whip this place into shape."

"Don't you already have a designer? Who's bossing these guys around and telling them how stuff should look?" she asked.

"That would be me, and I've got my hands very full trying to design the menu. I always do this—try to find someone who can manage the project, then I either run out of time or get frustrated when I can't find someone who gets my vision, and I give up and try to juggle everything myself. Each time, when I'm running around like a headless chicken, I tell myself it's the last time I'm going to do it that way, then . . ."

"You do it again. I get that. I'm kind of the same way. Lone wolf, easier to do things myself than try to explain them to someone else. But when I'm up in the middle of the night, ripping the shutters off their hinges because I hate them and the streetlights pouring in my windows, I end up on the computer, raiding home supply places for materials so I can fix the problem."

"So you know." I was serious. I really would hire her. "What do you say? You want a part-time job?"

She was already nodding. "I'd love to help. But not as a job, just for fun. That way, you won't be able to fire me when the whole thing goes to shit and you hate everything I've done. I'll put together a Pinterest board, and you can get some ideas."

"Pinterest? Cool. That would be great." I pulled her away from the open space and toward the walk-in fridge. It had space to do all kinds of things back there, though I wasn't about to strip her clothes off with six guys working a few feet away. But I was sure as hell going to kiss the fuck out of her by the prep station.

I MADE good on my offer of a six-pack, mostly because I liked offering tiny perks to the guys who did good work for me day in, day out. I brought them lunch on the regular, and I trusted they weren't cutting corners, so I did my best not to micromanage their work. That was Burt's job, and he'd never let me down. As far as the beer, I wasn't trying to cheap out, but I meant what I said about drinking and driving, and after two beers apiece, I wasn't so sure about them on the road. Plus, if I were being honest, I wanted them gone sooner rather than later so Becca and I could have the place to ourselves.

Fortunately, the kitchen was almost entirely finished, so we were well set up to cook a great dinner. I'd left her behind under the guise of giving her time to make notes on the kinds of fabrics she might like to use and measuring various areas of the dining room. In reality, I wanted to make my grocery run without her so I could surprise her with the menu.

"What are we cooking?" she asked when I started unloading the bags I'd stowed in the walk-in.

"We, you ask? No, no, my lovely, hot, long-legged maiden. There will be no 'we' cooking tonight. There will be me cooking for you and you lounging around, drinking wine, and telling me that everything smells delicious."

She smiled, but her eyes gleamed. "And what if I think it smells horrible?"

I struck my chest in mock shock. "First of all, not gonna happen. And second, did you really just insult my cooking before I've even gotten started?"

I made a playful lunge for her, but I didn't hesitate to attack her fully. She squealed as I grabbed her and flipped her around, pulling her back against my chest. Then I nuzzled her neck the way I knew made her crazy, and she relaxed in my grasp. Slowly, I ran my hands up her stomach to cup her breasts. She turned her head to meet my lips, and I dove into the kiss, licking and sucking her lips, claiming them for my own.

My hands moved higher, massaging her breasts and moving to her hard nipples, which strained against the fabric of her shirt. I dipped my head toward her shoulder and planted a row of soft kisses along her collarbone. She moaned softly and kissed my cheek, then she turned in my arms, facing me, and kissed me harder.

I lifted her on top of the butcher block, and she circled her legs around me, pulling me in so I couldn't escape. Not that I wanted to. Ever.

"Apparently, I'm very sensitive about my cooking." I ran my hands down the length of her thigh and back up again, under the hem of her skirt. I rubbed circles on her skin with my thumbs, reaching higher one inch at a time.

"I apologize," she said, breathless. "I was kidding . . . but if insulting your cooking gets me the current situation, then I'm afraid you might be serving me some rotten-smelling, gut-blasting . . ." She melted into me, her lips pressing against mine and her hands drawing a trail down my chest to my abs, then lower.

"I'd planned on using my cooking skills to seduce you, but I can't wait that long," I whispered against her mouth. There was no end to how much I wanted her.

"Water takes forever to boil. Too. Long." She arched as I moved my thumbs higher, feeling more of her soft skin, edging closer to the apex of her thighs. And when I did, I felt lace.

Fuck me, if ever anything was sexier than Becca Finley wearing a skirt, it was her with the skirt pushed up around her hips as she leaned back on my brand-new butcher block, propped on her elbows, with a whisper of soft white lace just inches from my face.

I took in the sight of her because I wanted it burned into my brain. I knew she had PTSD about our past, but so did I, my version being that each moment I was with her might be the last. So I took careful mental notes. The vision of her, chest heaving gently as I hooked my thumbs in the lace panties and pulled them down, was something I wanted to remember forever.

More than anything, I wanted to remember the sound of her sigh as I ran my hand along the soft flesh on the inside of her thigh and the way her lips tasted when I leaned over and captured her mouth with no intention of ending the kiss anytime soon.

I still didn't fully believe I deserved her, but I was going to do my damnedest to give her every reason to want me. I had a few cooking skills to fall back on, but first, I was going to let her orgasms do the talking. I pulled her in, so her body was flush against mine. She wrapped her legs around me and pressed her breasts against my chest. Our tongues danced, and our bodies connected, and everything felt effortless with her.

It should be noted that industrial kitchens weren't well designed for sex lying down. All the surfaces were hard, and most of them were made of metal. But we made it work.

"HEY." She leaned her elbows on the counter where the steam ovens were preparing spinach and poaching salmon.

I didn't know what kind of food she liked, so I'd gone with a tasting menu idea that I was thinking of using in the new restaurant. A lot of my fellow chefs had gone in that direction, and I'd been wanting to try it. I just didn't know if I could pull it off on the scale I needed to keep the restaurant solvent.

"Hey." I looked up at her sparkling eyes while still managing to keep an eye on the polenta toast triangles under the broiler and an octopus dish I was working on at the sauté station.

"So, you started to tell me before why you're scared to do a tasting menu. Care to elaborate?" She wore the long tunic top she'd paired with the skirt, but the skirt was nowhere to be found.

"I didn't say I was scared."

"Okay, intimidated."

"Maybe that. It's a lot of work, really labor intensive. Like you see here, different flavors, small portions, and when I get to the presentation part, it's like art, with sauces and different flavors that complement each other." I finished the octopus in a pear demiglaze and pan-fried some scallops I wanted to serve with pea shoots and a guava puree. It was a little hard to concentrate on cooking when I wanted to concentrate on her, but I persevered in the name of seductive menu planning.

"It seems like a lot of work. Why won't you let me help? It'll be more fun if we're cooking together, as long as you don't mind that I'm a dunce in the kitchen."

"I doubt you're a dunce."

She'd asked to help a couple of times, and this time, I handed her an apron and put her to work making a ricotta crumble to go with the polenta and the figs. She followed my instructions and added a few of her own flourishes to the plate, using some herbs and lemon zest. I tried not to feel guilty that I would probably steal her idea and add lemon zest to the dish from then on.

"This is photo worthy." She snapped a picture.

"Here, taste the octopus and see if it needs something." I sliced off a piece, making sure it was coated in the glaze. I watched her as she chewed, and when her face lit up as she savored the bite, I felt like I'd scaled Everest. I'd always cooked for lots of people, but I'd never cared more about what one person thought of my food.

"Blake, this is amazing," she said. "When's everything going to be done? I'm dying to try it all."

"We're pretty good now. Just need to plate everything and garnish. You're gonna help me with that."

I'd shown her how I set up my mise en place, the garnishes and seasonings every chef set up differently before working a shift to make sure the most important things were handy. "Flaked sea salt, Himalayan salt with a grinder, chopped basil, chopped Italian parsley, chutney, lemon rind . . ." I'd pointed out everything, so when we started plating the food, I had Rebecca serve as my sous chef and pointed out which garnishes went on which dishes until we had seven tiny plates, each with one perfect dish, dotted and swirled with sauces and spices and a few edible flowers.

"These are too pretty to eat," Becca said.

"That's the sign of a good tasting menu," I said. "Let's eat and talk."

We juggled the multiple plates to the newly installed countertop overlooking the kitchen. I was glad I'd found the stone slab we'd honed to fit in the space, and this was the perfect way to break it in.

"What kind of material is this?" Becca tapped the dark stone.

"It's bluestone. I needed something that wouldn't stain and could take a beating."

"I like it." She tried the polenta dish then took a bite of a scallop, humming her pleasure with each bite. "I can see why this would be a lot of work to do for multiple tables and multiple seatings."

"It is, but I need to keep it interesting, or I'll stagnate. The menu I'm planning for this place will keep me on my toes, and if I get bored with the menu, I'll rotate it out for a new one. That's the beauty."

"Do you plan to cook here every day or just be the boss man and hire a bunch of chefs?" She twirled a strand of spaghetti squash pasta on her fork and dipped it in the garlic butter.

I stabbed a bite of octopus and popped it in my mouth. "Both. I'll cook as much as I can, but I'll need to hand stuff off too. I won't always be able to be here." I wondered if she asked because she was hoping I would have free time to see her.

No, I was getting ahead of myself. She was probably just making conversation.

We were working our way through the food, and we'd polished off most of the white wine I'd opened while we were cooking, but something nagged at me. I didn't want to ruin the night with my question, but it kept eating at me, so I had to ask.

"Hey, can I ask you something?" I tried to sound casual, but I could hear the strain in my voice.

She looked concerned. "Sure. I mean, you can ask, but . . ."

"I know, you might not answer." We'd been down that road before. "When you said you don't date, is that because you don't enjoy dating or because you're not interested in a relationship or . . . what?"

She finished chewing a bite of scallop and took a sip of wine before answering. She turned to face me on her barstool. "I don't like the way my heart feels when relationships end, so I keep things casual. Coffee, maybe a hike. Easy. Nothing ventured, nothing lost."

"Isn't the expression 'nothing ventured, nothing gained'?" I treaded closer to what I needed to know, and I wondered if she'd answer.

Her expression was serious, and she didn't look away from my gaze. "I changed it."

"Okay . . . I have another question. Would you consider making an exception to your rule if it wasn't dating but . . . venturing?"

"Are you asking me to venture with you?" She smirked, and I loved it.

"Abso-fucking-lutely."

She nodded. "On one condition. I want you to take me at the top of that staircase."

She pointed with her fork, then yelped when I pulled her into my arms and launched up the stairs two at a time.

CHAPTER TWENTY-FIVE

Becca

IF I'D DOUBTED that Howard had herding in his blood, I was convinced within five minutes of meeting the adorable tan-and-white corgi. When Blake and I walked through the door of his apartment, Howard's tall ears perked up, and he sprang from the dog bed, which was tucked into a corner of a navy-blue couch.

I scratched him behind the ears, and his tail wagged. After a couple minutes of that, he started nudging me with his nose.

"That's his way of saying he likes you, like *really* likes you," Blake said in warning right before Howard's enthusiasm manifested in him trying to hump my leg. "Okay, you don't get to have her, buddy, sorry." Blake pulled him away, scooping him into his arms.

He carried Howard like a baby back to his bed and placed him in it. If I'd had any doubts about whether Blake Fulton was the hottest man I'd ever met, seeing him with his dog pushed him into criminally hot territory. He pulled a tiny bag from his pocket and extracted a piece of octopus he'd saved from our dinner. Howard nipped it from his fingers and swallowed it in an instant.

"I'm not sure he even tasted that on its way down. Does he know how good he has it?" I asked.

Blake shrugged. "He'd be just as happy with a rawhide chew, but I don't cook those."

I started to walk to the window where I could see the sparkling lights of an incredible view, but Howard was having none of it. He circled my legs and guided me back to where Blake stood, effectively herding us into an embrace. I wasn't going to argue with his nature.

Blake kissed my forehead then whistled for Howard to follow him to the kitchen, where he filled his food and water bowls. Howard got busy eating, and I made my way back to the window.

Wow. "I know you said you had a view, but this is a *view.*" I looked through the bay window of Blake's top-floor apartment in Pacific Heights. I could see the Bay Bridge and a sweeping view of the East Bay, from the campanile on the UC Berkeley campus up to the Berkeley Hills, where Finn lived.

He came over and put his arms around me, and we stared out at it together.

"Yeah, I never get tired of it. Probably why I'll never move."

"Yeah? How long have you been here?"

"Two years. I had a smaller place in Bernal Heights, which was awesome when I wanted to hike. I had hills right outside my door. But I only had a tiny view from that place, and I had to go out onto the fire escape off the kitchen to see it."

"This one's a keeper."

"I agree."

From the reflection in the glass, I could see he wasn't looking at the view anymore. He swept the hair off my neck and lowered his lips to my skin, lightly sucking and licking his way to my jaw, where his breath made my insides twist with wanting.

I started to turn around, but he leaned into my back, pressing me harder against the glass. He moved my hair and began the same delicious assault on the other side of my neck. My head fell back against his chest. My body was giving me firm instructions, *Go with all of it. Say yes to everything.*

I still didn't fully trust Blake. I had a deep worry that something would change, and the picture he was painting of the two of us would get smeared and ruined. But for a moment, I couldn't tear myself away. Being with him felt like coming home to a place I'd fantasized about for years, even as I'd tried to push the dreams away. I'd known reality couldn't possibly measure up to the fantasy.

But now . . . as Blake pushed my skirt up to my waist, ran his hands up my inner thighs, and tugged on the lace of my panties, I had to come to terms with the truth—the reality was even better than the fantasy. My brain still felt wary of him, but my heart was all in. I decided to let my heart have its fun. I would have a talk with it later.

"C'mere." He pulled my sweater over my head and ran his tongue over the curve of my shoulder before pulling my hips back, so my forearms leaned on the window.

He slid my panties down, inch by inch, leaving goosebumps on my legs as he ran a single finger up to the apex of my thighs. His thumb circled the sensitive nub while his finger glided inside me, curling it to hit all the right spots. I arched my back, grinding against him and loving how hard he got for me.

"You feel so good. I can't stand it," I panted.

"Oh, baby, we're just getting started. There's so much more good I want you to feel."

He must've had a condom in his pocket because it took him about three seconds to drop his pants and roll the condom on. Then he eased inside me, an inch at a time, his body hard against my back and my cheek chilled by the cool glass.

It felt like we were making up for fifteen lost years of sex in one night, and I was all in. As he thrusted inside me and dipped his hands into the cups of my bra, I took everything he had to give. When the building rush of pleasure took me over the top, I felt his lips on the sensitive spot below my ear, like he knew how to destroy me in the best possible way.

And when he came hard, pounding his release into me, I caught a glimpse of his face in the glass and did my best to commit it to memory because I never wanted to forget how he looked at that moment. He looked the way I felt.

BLAKE SHOWED me the rest of his apartment—a decked-out kitchen, study, three bedrooms, and a loft—and ended the tour in his bedroom, where a king-sized bed took up most of the room.

My heart started pounding, and I tried to think of what to say to him if he invited me to spend the night. If I didn't do dates, I definitely didn't do sleepovers. Better not to let him broach the subject and tell him I had an early shift in the morning.

But he'd asked me to dinner on a night when I didn't have to work the next day. *Did he plan for a sleepover even back then?* All the familiar impulses were telling me to grab my purse and run. Until a new impulse snuck in—*what if I . . . stayed?*

"Hey, I hope it goes without saying I'd like you to stay," he said, his smile suddenly shy.

It was cute, and it made me feel even more conflicted. If I was honest with myself, the last place I wanted to be was home by myself. I wanted to be with Blake. I wanted to sleep tangled up in him and wake up with my head on his chest.

I couldn't say how long I stood there with an expression on my face that probably looked way too much like a grimace for someone who'd just had her umpteenth orgasm of the night.

Blake took my hand. "Becca? You okay?"

"I'm just having a hard time adjusting," I said. "I've tried so hard to forget you. I wanted nothing more than to erase you from my mind and heart, like I thought you did to me all those years ago. But now . . . I feel conflicted."

His expression told me he didn't like hearing that I wanted to forget him, even as he held me in his arms. "You still want to erase me?"

"No. But I don't totally trust you. Not yet. I hope you can under-stand that. You broke my heart once, and a part of me is going to hold back because I can't let you do it again."

He sat down on the white fluff of a down comforter and put his head in his hands. When he glanced up, he looked miserable. "I know. I fucked it up, and I don't know how to make you trust me again. But I want to."

"Thanks. I want it, too, but I'm not there."

I could envision it, but I needed to be sure.

"Okay. Take your time. I understand."

I sat next to him on the bed. *Wow,* it really was soft. "I'd like to stay. That's what I know right now."

He leaned back on the bed until he was fully reclined and pulled me toward him. I lay with my head on his chest and his arm tight around me. It felt good to know what I wanted.

CHAPTER TWENTY-SIX

It had been a great morning. My shift ended right at seven, and I handed off all the patients to the day nurse. The two women I'd helped through labor hadn't had any complications, and both had delivered before my end of shift.

I liked it when I could come in at the early stages of labor and see a patient through to delivery. It was sometimes frustrating to bond with a patient over a twelve-hour shift only to have her deliver after I left and move to the postpartum wing before I came back. Some shifts went that way, and others played out like they just had. I'd gotten lucky.

I'd also paid a visit to the head of the nursing staff when she got to the hospital to ask about changing my schedule. The night shifts had always been my thing, but maybe it couldn't hurt to incorporate some day shifts and take a few more nights off each week. She told me I could have whatever schedule I wanted.

After ten years, I had enough seniority to choose my schedule. It felt good to hear that, even if I ended up sticking with what I had. I just liked having options, and I told myself the request had nothing to do with wanting to spend more time with Blake, although Myself respectfully replied, *Bullshit*.

I had about an hour at my house to work on the Pinterest boards for Blake's restaurant. I'd promised to do them, but I was pretty sure he was set on the design he already had. Still, he'd been nice enough to show interest in my ideas, so I worked hard to give him a vision of what had struck me when I first saw the space.

After that, I stopped by the Berkeley rec center and swam laps for forty-five minutes, then walked the few blocks uphill to meet Isla for coffee and a hike. I knew I would run out of gas in a couple of hours, but I was starting to like doing things during the day.

"Finally! I was beginning to worry you really were part vampire. I'm happy for you. You must really like him," Isla said when I told her I was thinking about working more days.

I'd arrived at Cafe Strada before her, so I'd bought our lattes and met her outside so we could walk up to the fire trail above campus.

"This has nothing to do with Blake." I walked ahead of her up Bancroft Avenue so she couldn't see my face. The problem was Isla didn't need to see my face to know I was lying.

"Um, okay."

"Fine, I do like him." I couldn't keep the grin off my face.

She'd been having trouble with one of her Oakland vendors, which meant more time away from baking bread and dealing with brush fires, but the silver lining was that at least once a week, lately, we'd been able to get out for a hike.

I was curious about what was happening with Isla and Tom, but I also knew she'd need to be the one to bring it up. She had a lot of pride, and if she didn't feel like talking about something, it would only aggravate her if I pressed the issue. I'd wait her out.

"You should meet him. Maybe he can hire you to do the bread for the restaurant he's opening," I said.

"Ha. Well, I'm all for meeting him, but I'm not sure we're destined to be working together."

"Why's that?" I wondered if she held something against him the way Sarah seemed to.

She laughed. "Because I don't bake for Blake Fulton's type of restaurants." She must not have sensed my utter confusion because she didn't explain. She reached for her coffee, which I'd forgotten I was still holding.

I held it away from her.

"Hey!" she protested.

Nope. I would withhold her caffeine until she explained. "What does that mean, 'Blake Fulton's type of restaurants'? Are we talking about the same guy? He's a chef, and I'm pretty sure this is his first restaurant. He's nervous about it. It's actually adorable."

She looked at me like I was daft. "Did he tell you this was his first restaurant?"

"No, but . . . I guess I'm an idiot for not googling him."

"Seriously. Don't you google all the men you date?"

"Um, no. And when Blake told me about the restaurant, it seemed like a huge deal to him. He didn't mention other ones. But even so, why would he not consider you for his restaurant? You said it like he's the king of bread or something."

"Ooh, that would be a great name for a bakery, The King of Bread."

"Island! Talk to me. You're freaking me out."

She waved me off. "It's not something you'd be expected to know. You're not in the food scene. But he's a big player. He's part owner of the Marin Restaurant Group. They have about seventeen restaurants all over the world, and this is the first one he's opened in the Bay Area, so it's kind of a big deal since it's his home turf. I'm sure a lot of artisanal bakers are trying to get the contract for that place. That's all I was saying."

I tried to think back to what he'd actually said. I could picture the way his eyes crinkled when he smiled and talked about being a chef. I could remember him talking about celebrity chefs and realizing that cooking could be a bigger career than he'd thought. *Had he mentioned multiple restaurants? Was I too busy gazing at his chiseled face and noticing that he had strong forearms to hear what he was saying?*

"Seventeen restaurants?" I asked to be sure I'd heard right.

She looked sheepish. "Can I have my coffee now?"

I realized I was still holding it over my head. I handed it to her.

"Are we good? Or are you going to refuse to speak to him for another fifteen years?"

"Okay, yes, it was fifteen years, but it's not as if he was calling me, begging to talk during all that time. And let's not forget that he broke my heart. But I feel dumb for not knowing he was such a big deal in the restaurant world. That's what I get for never googling him. Plus, he downplays. He has all these talents, and he dials everything down. So maybe I just assumed he only had the one restaurant because that's the one he's been talking about."

We'd reached the trailhead off Centennial Drive and started hiking through the eucalyptus and wild blackberry bushes. I loved the smell on the cool dirt path. It reminded me of summer camp. We'd had a good rainy season, and a small stream ran through the underbrush.

She laughed. "You two are perfect for each other. in your head."

I eyed her coffee as we chugged up the trail, considering taking it away. "Of course it is. I'm worried I'm making another mistake with him. I know it was fifteen years ago, but it hurt. He hurt me. And sometimes it still hurts when I think about it. Can you blame me for being a little leery?

"Why, because he did the wrong thing when he was a hormonal teenage boy without a clue?"

"No, because I'm convinced he's gonna do it again," I said. Once burned, always terrified of matches.

Isla stopped walking and held out a hand to stop me. "Okay, I'm only going to say this once, so you'd better damn well listen. I've watched you hide on the night shift and go on your stupid coffee dates for years now, and it's been fine because none of the guys you met seemed so special. But now you have the guy. He may be your one, and you're still living in the past and making up excuses instead of allowing yourself to be happy. You deserve to be happy, and he sounds like a good guy. So go to therapy, or do whatever you have to do to get over your trust issues. They. Are. All. In. Your. Head."

I didn't respond because, for once, I had no comeback. I'd never been to therapy, and I'd never examined my lack of trust. I'd just accepted it. I rebelled against anything that didn't seem logical, but I accepted *that*?

"It's hard to look in the mirror sometimes," Isla said.

"Yeah. Kind of explains the scrubs and ponytail thing I've got going most of the time too."

"Are we good?" She ran a hand through her honey-colored hair.

I nodded. "We're good. Let's keep going."

We kept hiking, and I stole a look at Isla's hair, which had grown past her shoulders and had a controlled bounce and curl to it that my crazy waves had no prayer of pulling off.

I decided to change the subject because talking about my issues while walking uphill was making me extra tired. "I'll bet you came out of the womb with perfect hair. I haven't seen your baby pictures, but I'm gonna ask Mom next time I see her. You probably even had a perfect pink bow at birth."

Her hand went back to her hair. She smoothed it out and laughed. "You're hilarious. I go to one of those blow-dry places. They do all the work. I just swipe my credit card."

"Seriously? How do I not know about this?"

"It doesn't work if you're in a pool five days a week."

"Ah, good point. So if I want good hair, I have to, like, spend money on it?"

She laughed again. "Probably. Or at least a little bit of time. But hey." She patted me on the head like a dog. "Before I left for college, I remember you spending tons of time on your hair and makeup. It's like riding a bike."

"I was fourteen. That's a very rusty bike." It felt good to breathe a little deeper as we went uphill, but I needed to get her talking before I fell asleep on her and felt worlds of guilt. "Tell me what's up with Tom."

"Still wallowing in purgatory. Haven't talked to him."

"What are you waiting for?"

"I dunno, but I'll know it when I see it. Right now, I know I'm thirty-four, and I want more from a relationship than nice dinners out and average sex."

Isla never hesitated once she'd decided on a way forward. I admired that about her. "Okay, well, good. I guess that's the first step."

She started hiking faster, and I had to pick up my pace to keep up. "Uh huh. And I'll let you know when I figure it out."

"You want to talk more about it?"

"Nope."

We'd reached the part of the trail where we either had to turn around, go out onto the road, or walk up a super steep offshoot that took us to the upper part of the trail. "You want to walk up the connector?" That was what we called it.

She shook her head. "I want to run it." Then she left me in her dust.

CHAPTER TWENTY-SEVEN

lake

OVER THE NEXT THREE WEEKS, Becca and I spent almost every waking hour together when we weren't working. Her night shifts were a little challenging to work around, but she'd started to pick up more day shifts, which made it easier to coordinate our schedules.

Since I'd handed off my other restaurants to the head chefs and managers who ran them day-to-day, I was mostly free to focus on the new venture, and because it wasn't open yet, my hours were flexible—and also all-consuming, the closer we got to opening night.

I wanted the new restaurant to be a success because I had investors with a lot riding on it, and I wanted to do San Francisco proud with a landmark restaurant. But for the first time since I'd gotten my initial job as a line cook, I didn't just want positive write-ups and a booked calendar. Because I wanted her more.

It was weird to think that way. I'd dated plenty over the years, and it had been handy to have girlfriends to bring to other chefs' openings or to dinners with investors. But it always felt like a business proposition—I would impress the chefs or investors by showing off a pretty woman on my arm. She would get a nice dinner out of it. The sex would be a bonus.

It hadn't ever felt like this. I never wanted to say fuck it to the perfectionism of getting the menu exactly right if it meant getting to spend an extra hour eating cheesecake and watching reality TV with Becca. She was the one. I'd blown an opportunity to be with her when I was sixteen, but I would be damned if I made that mistake twice.

I had to make sure she knew that. Otherwise, she would never fully trust me. So I worked on it, little by little, date by date. I gave her the time she needed to get enough proof to open up the vise that seemed wrapped around her heart.

"You know what we should do?" she asked on a Tuesday when we both had the day off. "We should have a San Francisco day and do all the touristy things no one who actually lives in San Francisco ever does."

"I'm game. I've never been to Ghirardelli Square or ridden a cable car."

"Exactly. Stuff like that," she said.

So we rented bikes and rode along the water, passing all the working piers until we got to Pier 39, the ultimate tourist spot. Normally, I avoided places like that because they were tourist traps that sold overpriced San Francisco memorabilia. But Becca and I pretended to be tourists, taking goofy selfies of each other on the moon bounce and eating ice cream at ten in the morning because we could.

We goaded a silver-painted busker pretending to be a statue into whistling and moving like a robot. Then he chased after Becca, whistling at her until she jumped into my arms and wrapped her legs around me. I tipped him a little extra after that.

We ate clam chowder in a bread bowl and looked at lobsters in the tanks at Fisherman's Wharf. And we went to Ghirardelli Square and bought chocolate and watched little kids splashing in a freezing fountain.

Anything that was sort of fun to do with anyone else was incredibly fun with her.

"You know what I suddenly have a craving for?" Becca asked when we left the Tactile Dome at the Exploratorium—full disclosure, we'd been kicked out. Apparently, the guards at the museum didn't like it when adults used the darkness as an excuse to make out.

"What? French fusion food? I could cook . . ." The truth was I really ought to have been spending more time working on the menus for the new place. I had a meeting with two of the investors in a few days, and they'd want to have a tasting of the hallmark dishes.

"I love your cooking, and I'll never say no to that, but I was thinking you should put your feet up instead, and we can get Zachary's."

She didn't have to twist my arm. Zachary's was my favorite pizza place. They did a Chicago-style deep-dish pie stuffed with toppings under a second layer of crust with seasoned chopped tomatoes as a top layer. "Zachary's. Yes. Now." The suggestion had reduced me to caveman capabilities.

Becca had taken BART into the city, but instead of taking the train together, we drove back to Berkeley so I'd have a car at her house. The past few weeks had been a study in coordinating modes of transportation back and forth from the city to her Rockridge neighborhood. We'd been pretty good about spending equal time at both houses, and my neighbor had been great about offering up sleepovers for Howard when I wasn't there.

But I missed the little guy when I was at Becca's and felt bad about shoving him off a couple of nights a week. Plus, commuting was starting to eat into the time I should have been spending on work. I'd pretty much left the restaurant construction in Burt's hands, which was fine because I trusted him, but my normal once-a-day visits had decreased to once or twice a week, and that didn't bode well if I needed them to make any design changes.

We drove over the Bay Bridge, leaving the city, which meant we were on the lower level of the huge piece of metalwork that spanned the water between the Embarcadero neighborhood and West Oakland.

"I always feel a little sad going in this direction," Becca said.

"You mean because we're on the bottom level? Can't see the spires?"

"Partly that. I always thought it seemed fair to pay a toll on the ride into San Francisco because it's the better view, even though I know that's not the reason they do it." She craned her neck as though she'd be able to somehow see the best part of the bridge from where we were.

"It's a good theory though."

"Yeah. Anyway, I used to feel sad because going to San Francisco was always a fun adventure. I got so excited going in that direction. But driving home meant the adventure was over. It was like leaving the Disneyland parking lot after watching the parade on Main Street. Did you ever do that?" she asked.

I nodded. "Not since I was a kid. But I remember the feeling." I stole a look at her before returning my eyes to the road. "Do you feel sad now?" I put my hand on her knee.

"No. I don't ever feel sad when I'm with you."

From our spot just west of Treasure Island, I could see part of the second half of the bridge where it curved. She was still looking out the window, eyes riveted on that part of the bridge. But if she'd been looking at my face, she'd have seen my big smile.

<hr>

"So I have a question for you," she said after our pizza had been served.

We'd agreed on a spinach and mushroom pie and had to wait a few minutes for the steaming slices to cool.

"Shoot."

"Did you try to downplay the fact that you're a big, impressive restaurant owner?"

My expression must have betrayed my shock at the question because Becca laughed. "Okay, let me break all that down. First, no, I'm not hiding anything from you. I guess I assumed you probably googled me or something before you agreed to go out with me. And if I forget to tell you stuff, it's just because my mind is a sieve lately with trying to juggle so many balls and the opening coming up in two weeks. Besides, where did you get the idea that I'm an impressive restaurant owner?"

"Isla. My sister."

"The bread maven." She'd told me about her sister, but I had yet to meet her.

She smiled. "I think Isla would like being called a maven. Anyway, she knows the restaurant scene, and she said you're a big deal."

"I'm not a big deal. As celebrity chefs go, I'm a very small deal. But I work my ass off, and I love it, and I don't plan to slow down. So there's that."

"Will you tell me about it? Like, all of it—the whole story. How you started, each job, each restaurant, each dish you learned to cook. Is that invasive?"

I loved that she was so interested. "Sure, what do you want to know? I told you about my ignominious beginnings as a law school reject trying to piss off my dad. The rest is just a lot of good food and hard work."

She dug into her pizza, slicing off a chunk and putting it in her mouth. Only one reaction to Zachary's pizza was correct, and I saw it in the satisfied way she savored that first bite. It was that good. She took a sip of beer and studied me before responding. "I guess, just tell me how you felt before your first restaurant opened. And which one was it?"

"I've opened four of my own, and the restaurant group I'm part of also owns thirteen others. I've been involved with those openings as well. But I assume you're asking about my restaurant."

She pointed her fork at me. "Bingo."

"Yeah, I was a fucking nervous wreck. I probably made ten menu changes the day before we opened, and it was a shitshow of firing my assistant chef at the last minute and hiring extra line cooks we didn't have room for and botching the seating for opening night. If something could go wrong, it did that night."

She grimaced. "Yikes, that doesn't sound good." She took another bite of pizza.

"Oh, it was so good. Awful because a food critic blasted me and my menu, and about half the people who came that night ended up with the wrong meals and lots of wine and desserts on the house, but we had the best fucking time in the kitchen that night. We stayed up until three making extra dishes, tweaking the menu, and drinking half the wine in our cellar. It was probably my favorite night in a restaurant ever."

Becca gave me the look I'd started to recognize as admiration mixed with concern that I might actually be crazy. She put her fork down, folded her hands under her chin, and gazed at me.

"What?" I asked.

"I have an idea for after dinner."

I wondered if it had anything to do with my opening-night story. "Let's hear it."

She leaned in with a gleam in her green eyes that reminded me for a split second of our one night together in high school. "Do you remember how we hopped the fence at Lake Anza that one time?" she whispered, as though anyone who overheard would have any idea what we'd almost done. But I knew instantly.

"Of course I remember, and I think it's a great idea." I flagged the waiter and asked for a box. We could eat our pizza later. When the woman I couldn't get enough of suggested skinny dipping, it wasn't time to look at the dessert menu.

We'd each finished one slice of pizza, so at least we weren't hangry. Our waiter brought the check, and I threw down a few bills, scooped up the pizza box, and pulled Becca's hand into mine.

I tucked her under my arm as we walked to my car and thought, for maybe the forty-thousandth time, that I couldn't possibly deserve this woman. I probably didn't. That was the beauty of love. It didn't tally up an exact tit-for-tat list of qualifications in two people and decide whether the scales were balanced. It just let hearts decide. And mine had decided on hers fifteen years earlier. I just hoped she could trust hers enough to trust me.

The drive up to Lake Anza took us along Skyline Boulevard to Grizzly Peak, where the views of the city were blotted out by a layer of fog that had settled in, as it often did. But I wasn't there for the view.

"No one's here," she confirmed, looking around the parking lot. "Lucky."

I didn't know how many people would bother to hang out in the parking lot outside a fenced-off lake, but I would take luck anytime. "You think we can get over that fence?"

"We did in high school," she said as though that settled it.

It was easier than it looked. Becca grabbed my hand, and we wandered down the tiny patch of beach to where the water lapped at the sand.

Becca toed her shoes off and dipped her feet in the water. "Yikes, it's freezing."

I wondered if that might dissuade her and was about to say we didn't have to go through with it when she pulled off the tight pink long-sleeved shirt that had been driving me crazy all day. Then she edged down her jeans, and I saw that she was commando.

"Holy shit." I pulled her flush against my body, crushing her lips to mine. She was going to kill me, and I was going to die willingly at her gorgeous feet. Her hands pushed my shirt up, and I didn't waste a second throwing it off and stripping the rest of the way down. She unclasped her bra and threw it on the pile of clothes.

"Ready?" she asked, interlacing her fingers with mine.

She looked at me, and I took in the light that radiated from her when she was excited about something.

"Rebecca . . . I love you." The words tumbled out apropos of nothing she's said, but I didn't care.

Her face grew serious for a moment, and she met my eyes, hers still blazing with intensity. "Blake . . ."

"You don't have to say it back. I know you're working on trusting me. I'm not trying to pressure you—"

She stopped me with a finger against my lips. "I don't feel pressured. I feel lucky. If you love me, I feel exceptionally lucky."

Fucking hell, she thinks she's the lucky one?

"It's gonna be cold, but I've got you. Ready?" I scooped her into my arms and charged into the water. I ran as far as I could before the depth of the water caught my legs, and we just plunged.

Becca yelped at the cold. "Yikes! It's fucking freezing." Then she exploded with laughter. "It's so good!"

It was. So good.

CHAPTER TWENTY-EIGHT

Becca

"You should know about the curse of the family dinner. I just want you to go in with your eyes open," I told Blake when we met at the restaurant so we could walk down Hayes Street to Isla's house.

I'd just finished back-to-back shifts, and he'd been at the restaurant nonstop. I couldn't believe how much I missed him in that short time apart. But I did, and I was starting to accept that I couldn't live without him. Instead of feeling freaked out by that idea, I felt ridiculously happy.

He laughed, but he stopped when he saw I was serious. "Okay, tell me about this curse."

"You think I'm kidding, but no one who's ever brought a date to our family dinner is still dating that person—except for Finn, and they were already engaged. Something about my family must ruin any chance for future happiness."

He held up a finger. "But there is an exception. Finn. It can't be a curse if there's an exception."

"And this is why I hang out with you, eternal optimist. Okay, then. I just wanted you to go in fully prepared."

"Always, because I can't stop looking at you," he said.

This guy. How did I get so lucky? I stopped walking. "Blake . . ."

He looked to see why, and I explained by putting my arms around his neck and leaning toward his ear.

"I love you so much. I'm sure it isn't news to you, but I wanted you to hear me say it."

He closed his eyes for a long blink, and then he was kissing me. Tenderly, slowly, and with heat that almost melted me into a puddle.

"You're my one," he whispered. "I love you too."

We took the rest of the walk slowly, ambling and stopping every so often to kiss. It was fine. I had a tendency to be late.

I knew there would be more than a couple of raised eyebrows when I showed up for our sibling dinner with Blake in tow. The last time any of us had brought a plus-one to a family dinner had been when Tatum was first dating Jared more than two years ago.

She'd started working at Yahoo after college, and within weeks, she'd had three different guys asking her out. Of course she did. She was nerdy, gorgeous, and nice to everyone she met. She chose Jared, the one with the Ivy League degree and two start-ups under his belt by age twenty-four. I knew it was hard for Tatum sometimes because she was super brainy and most guys couldn't keep up. She only went for smart, accomplished men who had a minute chance of keeping up with her. And still, most of them couldn't.

At that point in our lives, Finn had still lived in Los Angeles, and our family dinners had been more like haphazard girls' nights at one of our apartments. We had no idea we were starting a tradition that would last for years. We were a hen club of sisters, and we used the time together to talk about our relationships, to bitch freely about the men who were driving us mad, both for great and awful reasons. More than a couple of breakups were decided at those dinners.

All the more reason why bringing guys along was discouraged. "How can we talk about him if he's right here?" Sarah asked jokingly when Tatum announced she was bringing a guest.

"You can talk about him after he leaves. I told him I'm sleeping over because I need to be in the city in the morning. It'll be perfect. I want to know what you think of him. He's super smart and accomplished, but I think that's blinding me to everything else about him."

"Blindfolds can be fun." Cherry winked. She knew Tatum would flee from any implication of "bedroom talk," as she referred to it. Like the ninety-year-old nun she was.

"Haha. You're all so funny. I can't believe I'm the only adult in the room," Tatum said.

"You're not. You're just the only puritan in the room, and with Becca's re-virgining streak going strong, that's saying a lot," Cherry said.

"Hey," I said. "Don't drag me into this. I'm not re-virgining. I'm just not doing relationships. There's a huge difference," I'd said.

"Well, for the love of vegan sausages, I hope he's huge."

Tatum left the room.

"She's just too fun to rile up," I said. "I barely feel bad about it."

"Neither do I," Cherry said. "I'll bet this Silicon Valley dude has a huge dick, and Tatum's scared to death of it."

"Should we ask him?" Isla asked. "I can ply him with bread until he cracks."

We didn't have time to come up with other methods of torture because someone knocked at Isla's door, and Tatum ran to answer it, returning a couple of minutes later with her hair slightly mussed and her lipstick gone. I, for one, was happy to see her like that.

The evening had started out well enough. Jared brought flowers and a bottle of wine and complimented Isla's cooking. Then he started picking out flaws in our youngest sister, first jokingly, then with more pointed intention.

"She likes to buy jackets and return them after a week." He laughed at Tatum like she was a cute, silly girl who couldn't make a decision about her clothes.

"Actually, I buy a lot of stuff online because I don't have time to go into a store, and if it doesn't look good, I return it. That's normal." She didn't sound offended, but I knew Tatum well enough to wonder why she felt the need to defend her actions. She never cared what anyone thought, and of any of us, she made the most rational decisions. None of us would ever question her decision to buy and return a jacket.

"Oh, you know you're an impulse shopper. I think it's fun," he said. "I'm just too much of a workaholic to need anything besides jeans and hoodies to wear to campus. And I sleep naked, so there's a money-saver, right, honey?" He poked Tatum, who turned as pink as her glass of rosé. Jared looked from one of us to the other, pushing his hands up. "What, no one's gonna touch that? Good thing my brothers aren't here, they'd be asking for a visual."

I could see Isla glaring at him through the steam from her pot of chicken chili on the stove. I wondered if Jared would make it to dessert before one of us murdered him.

"I'd hardly call buying a ski jacket impulse shopping when I have plans to ski in two months," Tatum said. "But you're right. Buying four different jackets before I found the right one might be overkill."

"See?" he said to all of us, victorious.

I wondered why Tatum had capitulated. Trying out four jackets was not excessive. Cherry and I exchanged a glance, and we barely had to make eye contact to communicate that he wasn't good enough for our sister. It didn't matter how many stock options he was set to cash in or how much nerd cred he had. No amount of money or prestige could make up for how he was belittling our most accomplished sister for trying on jackets.

Isla offered him a piece of her sourdough, and he waved it off. "Carbs? I don't think so. I'm strictly paleo," he said, seemingly oblivious to the fact that bread was Isla's business.

Jared wrapped an arm around Tatum and pulled her to him with unnecessary force. Then he bent and kissed her forehead with an audible sucking sound.

Ew. Yeah, he did that.

From that point on, the dinner became a contest of wills. My sisters and I banded together to compete over whether we could scare Jared off before Tatum sent him packing. She won, breaking up with him later that night. None of us had brought a male guest to our family dinners from that time forward. No one dared. If one of us did like someone enough to hope for a future, the last gauntlet we put him through was the sisterhood. Then again, if a man survived it, he was a keeper.

I felt confident about Blake.

And really, the curse was bullshit. I did have the memory of the four of us quizzing one of Isla's boyfriends on the ethics of artificial intelligence until he'd painted himself into a corner. I also remembered Isla asking him not to call her again before she escorted his pompous ass out the door of her house, which he called a charming lean-to, before explaining that "real" money was needed to buy in the city.

"I spent real money, the kind I earned with carbs," she told him as he backed away from her house, gesturing that he meant no offense. It didn't matter. Just existing was an offense at that point.

Having our family dinner at Isla's felt like a throwback to the old days, and she'd practically had to arm wrestle Finn to get him to deviate from his weekly hosting habit. But when I'd dangled the probability that Blake would be there, Finn was easily persuaded. As an economist, he liked probability, and he wasn't about to pass up the chance to experience the first plus-one at a family dinner. It had made life so much easier, since we were already in the city for Blake's restaurant meeting. If we'd had to fight traffic back to Berkeley, we never would have made dinner on time.

We hiked up a couple of good-sized hills before Isla's place came into view.

"I love this area," Blake said. "These old houses have so much charm."

Isla was sitting on her porch, so she heard the compliment. I could tell he'd scored points with her before we'd even hiked up the front steps because she was grinning, and that only happened with people she liked. She held a dough scraper, which most people would find unusual, but Blake took it as a compliment.

"She stopped mid-bake to greet us. You must really be her favorite sister," Blake said.

Isla's genuine smile told me she liked him already. She stood to greet him.

"Is this the famous Isla? I've heard stories about your bread that make me weep. Becca also says you're a nice person, which is almost as important as a good bake in my book. Speaking of books . . ." He held out the French pastry cookbook he'd bought her as a thank you for hosting.

Isla loved him already, and I'd already fallen hard. He'd melted all my resistance, and my inner skeptic had finally given up the fight. It felt good.

He extended his hand, but Isla pulled him into a tight hug. "No handshaking. You and Becs go way back. That's as good as family to me."

When she let him go, Blake looked surprised at her effusiveness. "Keep saying sweet things about my bread, and I'll be in your corner forever." Then she shook her head and amended her statement. "Well, only if you're good to my sister. If not, I'll stuff you in a bread oven."

She'd gotten a contract to sell her bread at every Whole Foods in the country and had paid for her three-bedroom classic with a view of the Haight from her success. I could already see the wheels turning in Blake's head, trying to figure out how to court Isla for his restaurants.

"He's good to me. The best," I told Isla, but I knew she could already see it.

She pointed her dough scraper at Blake. "I hear you have restaurant plans. We should talk."

"That's music to my ears." Blake followed her into the house.

The house had the raucous feel of a party, and before we'd even gotten past the entryway, we were swarmed by sisters. Cherry and Tatum appeared with full glasses of wine, which they pressed into our hands while taking our coats and throwing them on a chair by the door. "We could have thrown our coats in a pile, but thanks." I introduced Blake to them and tried to get him through the maze of family greetings in one piece.

But one voice stood out among the rest. "There she is." My mom grinned like a school kid who'd gotten an A. She was practically jumping in the running shoes she wore with everything—including the navy-blue maxi dress that looked great on her.

I hugged her. "I love this dress, Mom. It's so pretty on you," I said.

"And pigs just be flying around with fairy wings because my sister noticed fashion." Cherry hung an arm over my mom's shoulders and looked me up and down. She gestured to my outfit. "And you did well yourself. The scarf is killer. I might have to steal a few of these from your house when you're not looking."

"Thanks, Cher. You're a good teacher," I said.

"Oh, enough with the mutual admiration club. I want to get to know Blake." My mom linked her arm through his and walked him into Isla's living room. "I hear you like to cook."

He looked back at me as she led him away, and I mouthed "sorry," but he smiled, and his dimple reminded me that he was there for me—because he wanted to have something real with me. Talking to my mom didn't freak him out because he wanted to be with me, whatever that entailed.

Dinner was easy. After the first half hour, I relaxed as it became clear that my family was crazy about Blake. It didn't take long before the Jared story needed to be told, and even though Finn and Annie hadn't been there for it, they'd heard it enough times that they both jumped in to narrate portions of it, as did Sarah.

AFTER DINNER, we all moved to the living room, and I braced myself for what would no doubt turn into a game night. I'd warned Blake ahead of time, but even so, there was no telling whether things would go in a classic charades direction or in a raunchy Cards Against Humanity direction.

If Finn and Annie were hosting, the odds favored classic games. But at Isla's house, we were at her mercy, and it all depended on her mood.

"Okay, okay," she said, bringing in a blue box. "Ordinarily, I might choose the most offensive game I could find and watch Mom squirm as we all say rude, foul things, but I don't want Blake to run away screaming after just one night."

Blake raised a hand. "No, no, please don't hold out being foul on my account."

"She's not. Isla just loves Pictionary and will take any excuse to make us play it," Tatum said.

"So I thought we'd play Pictionary," Isla said. "In honor of our guest tonight."

"Oh, you're so full of shit." Finn threw a balled-up napkin at her, but I knew he shared her love for games that involved drawing, so he wasn't one to talk.

Isla dragged out two easels with blank white paper hanging on them and divided us into teams. The game got underway, and after four rounds, we realized the teams needed to be reorganized. Our team hadn't been able to draw or guess anything, and Isla and Finn's team had wiped the floor with us.

"I think we need to separate those two," I said.

"Fine," Isla said. "Someone else make the teams. I don't care. I just want to play."

"Can we take a break to refill our drinks?" Cherry held up her empty glass. "Anyone else? I'll make another pitcher of sangria if anyone wants."

"I'm in," I said, and Tatum got up to help her in the kitchen.

Blake leaned toward me, his lips grazing my cheek and sending chills down my spine. "Where's the bathroom?"

I pointed him to the door in the hallway on the right.

"Will you do that again when you come back?" I asked.

He leaned in again, and the heat from his breath made my eyes close as I savored his lips on my cheek.

"Oh, get a room, guys," Isla said from the doorway behind us.

No one else was paying attention, and I didn't know how long she'd been standing there. But when I turned, she winked at me.

Blake ran his finger down the length of my arm, and his eyes met mine. As was becoming usual, I stared into their depths and wanted more of him, which made me want to drag him off to one of Isla's extra bedrooms. *Who'd notice if we were missing for a few minutes? Or an hour?*

But Blake squeezed my hand and stood. His unspoken words said we would have plenty of time later for everything I had in mind. Then he passed behind me to find the bathroom.

Isla came and sat on a stuffed pouf that looked like a furry snow animal.

"Thanks for inviting him. I think it's going well so far," I said.

"See? The family dinner curse is a myth."

"Totally."

I was so distracted by my chaotic family that I didn't notice that Blake hadn't come back right away. But after another few minutes, I started to get concerned. I knew it was probably my overactive imagination. He was probably on a phone call or checking emails outside the ever-present stare of my zealous family. I didn't want to disturb him in the bathroom, but on the chance he'd gotten turned around in the apartment or wasn't feeling well, I went off in search of him.

The door to the bathroom was ajar, so he'd obviously finished up in there. Then I heard muffled voices farther down the hall. At first, I thought I was right that Blake was on a phone call. I knew he had a lot to iron out before the restaurant could open. But then I heard a second voice. *Was he on speakerphone?*

I didn't want to pry, but something made me continue down the hall. The door at the end of the hallway wasn't closed, so it didn't take any detective work to see that Blake wasn't on the phone at all. He was having a conversation with someone whose voice was very familiar—Sarah.

I stood there for a moment before either of them saw me, trying to piece together why the two of them would be talking—no, arguing—when they'd only met that evening and had barely interacted all night. Then their words started to wash over me, and certain ones stood out.

"You should have told her . . ." Blake said. "I hated having to lie for you."

"She wouldn't have understood," Sarah said.

Even though I didn't want to hear any more and a rush of blood began pounding in my ears, I couldn't turn away. I leaned against the doorway, feeling lightheaded. And stupid.

Were they...? Had they...?

Blake looked up first and stopped speaking.

Sarah was still protesting, "I still think it's better if you keep it to yourself. She never needs to know." Then she turned to see why Blake was staring toward the doorway. "Shit."

She was right about that.

Whatever it was, whatever they were trying to hide from me, it made me feel like shit, and I didn't need any more of that in my life—especially not from Blake.

He rushed to my side. "Rebecca . . ."

He pulled me toward him, but I was stiff. Frozen. I felt like my heart was beating outside my body. It had to be because I was dead.

How could I be so stupid? Again. Every fiber of my being told me not to trust him. We had history, and I should have learned from it. Starting to trust Blake after all those years and feeling what I'd felt with him was just another betrayal in the making.

Blake loosened his grip and looked at my face. I didn't know what he saw because I barely noticed him. "Rebecca, are you okay?"

"Don't . . . call me that," I managed to say.

"What did you hear?" Sarah asked.

I shook my head. "That's not even the point. I heard enough."

"How long was she standing there?" she asked Blake.

That shook me out of my fugue state. "Quit talking about me like I'm not here. It seems like you've done that enough already."

"Becs . . ." She took a step toward me.

I put up a hand to stop her. "No. Stop. Just . . . stay away from me, both of you."

I tried to pull out of Blake's grasp, but he didn't let go. It was probably a good thing because I didn't feel too steady on my feet. "Becca, it's not what you think."

I jerked my head up and glared at him. "Oh, really? What do I think? Since you know me so well, obviously you know what I think. Did that make it easier to lie to me? Are you two . . . hooking up or something? What?"

Blake's expression went from anguished to confused to betrayed. I was still too shocked to sort through the how or why of his morphing looks. "Oh my God, do you honestly think…?"

"Becs, no, it's not that at all. This is about high school. Really old stuff."

That made no sense. They didn't know each other in high school. I barely knew Blake, and Sarah didn't know him at all. She only knew what I told her about him after we ditched school, after our one night together. "Did you . . . in high school, were you fucking her then?" I asked Blake. "Is that why you ghosted me?"

"No!" they both said simultaneously.

"How could you think that?" Sarah asked.

I didn't really, but they were acting so weird, I didn't know what to think. I felt stripped bare. I felt…sixteen again.

My anger kept mounting, and I didn't care how loudly I was shouting. If I had, I might have noticed that all the fun dinner party sounds from the living room had stopped. But I only saw Blake and Sarah and heard my own voice as I shouted at them. "I don't know what to think! I come to dinner with the guy I'm in love with—the one I thought I was meant to be with because we shared something back in high school that's had a hold on me for half my life—and now I find you two whispering here. About me. Talking about lies and things I never knew or understood. What the hell am I supposed to think?"

Blake somehow guided me to the daybed against one wall, which saved me from having to hold onto him to stay upright. As soon as I was sitting, I scooted as far away from him as I could, pulling my knees to my chest and pressing my back to the wall. Blake looked at Sarah and nodded.

"Would one of you please use your words? Just tell me. I'm not fragile. I won't break."

Sarah sat down on the edge of the bed, swiveling to face me. "Before I tell you, I want you to know that what I did . . . I thought it was the best thing for you. I truly did."

I couldn't speak. I was confused. *If she slept with Blake in high school, how did she figure that it was the best thing for me?* It made no sense. I waited for one of them to explain.

"When you came home the morning after you two stayed out all night, you and I talked about Blake. Do you remember? You told me about all the things you guys did together. You told me about your virginity pact. You were . . . you were nuts about this guy, and I'd never heard of him before. In two years of hearing you talk about your high school friends, not once did I ever hear the name Blake Fulton. And suddenly, you were obsessed."

I remembered how it felt back then. It felt a lot like how I'd been feeling the past few weeks with Blake. I met Sarah's eyes and waited for her to continue. She bit her bottom lip, and I knew she had more to say, things she didn't want to tell me.

"Just say it. What are you trying not to tell me?"

"I tracked Blake down at his house. I was being a protective older sister. I thought I was doing the right thing."

Blake looked at the floor. I could see from his sad, resigned expression that he knew how Sarah's story would go, but he wouldn't look at me.

"We talked. Or really, I talked. I told him to leave you alone, to lose your number, forget he ever knew you. I explained that you were in a vulnerable place, with our dad having recently died, and that you needed time to sort yourself out and get back on track without the distraction of a guy who encouraged you to ditch school and stay out all night."

Fine, she was my older sister. *But how dare she? And how could she not ever tell me?* I turned to Blake. "Didn't you tell her, explain that it wasn't like she thought?"

"I tried," he said quietly. His weakened voice reminded me of the high school Blake, less sure of himself and probably completely terrified of my older sister putting him in his place.

Sarah patted my arm, but I stayed crunched up in my protective ball. I wasn't ready for tender gestures. I wasn't ready to be okay with her explanation. It wasn't even an apology. *After costing me a relationship back then that could have been . . . everything, how did she even feel okay about it? Was she even sorry?*

"Becs, please don't be upset. It was a long time ago. We'd just lost Dad, and Mom was tied up in her own grief. In my mind, I was taking care of you and trying to keep you from getting hurt.

You'd gone off the rails. I was worried. And then this dude comes along and convinces you to leave school and keeps you out all night. I was worried about you getting knocked up or messed up, and I believed I was doing the right thing."

I pointed a finger in her face. "You had no right to get involved."

"I know that now, but back then . . ."

"All these years, you never told me." I couldn't believe her. I couldn't believe any of it. Once again, I was the dumb groundhog who'd stuck my head up in the daylight and didn't notice the farmer with the shovel standing there, ready to whack me on the head. "Just . . . not now, Sarah. I can't deal with this all right now, okay? Back. Away."

I glared at her until she backed away from me, moving to the opposite side of the room.

"I'm going to leave now. Please don't call me. I need to not see or hear from you for a while."

She nodded, and I could see the buds of tears forming in the corners of her eyes. She felt bad. Fine. I didn't care. I felt worse.

"And just so you know . . . me throwing up on your dress and ruining your prom, that was karma."

Great, I'm resorting to being sixteen again.

Somehow, I had the wherewithal to get up off the daybed and walk back to the living room, where I was met with silence and forced smiles. "I'm really tired. I think I'm gonna head home. Sorry to be a buzzkill." I moved like I was walking through mud, making my way to the entryway to grab my coat.

I was slightly aware of Blake following me, saying courteous goodbyes to my family members, and thanking Isla before picking up his own coat. I barely registered that he walked out with me, and I didn't plan to let him take me home. I had my own Uber account, and I was going to use it.

When we got to the sidewalk, he put a hand on my shoulder. "Rebecca..."

I didn't tell him again not to call me that. The truth was, I liked it when he called me by my given name. When I turned to look at him, I saw the anguish in his face. And the regret. Good. At least he knew when he was wrong.

"Can we talk about this? I'd like to explain." He slid his hand down my arm, reaching for my hand. His fingers left a trail of heat that I could feel through my shirt.

"I feel like you're always explaining. I don't know what to believe anymore."

He'd said barely anything inside, just let Sarah do the talking. I wanted to know why he went along with her, even now, when we had a real chance at something good. *Why base it on a lie?* But I suddenly felt exhausted. I knew my mind was too scrambled to discern truth from lies, and I needed to be alone. I couldn't take the distraction of Blake's eyes or the fire that threatened to consume me each time he touched my skin.

"Can we go somewhere and talk? I'll tell you everything. I promise."

I pulled away and took out my phone to call a ride for myself. "I can't do this with you right now . . . I feel depleted. I feel deceived. I thought we were building something, but you left out a whole chunk of very important information that I needed to make sense of everything."

"I know." He rubbed a hand over his face. He looked pained, and I knew it hurt that I was pushing him away. I didn't care because right now, I needed to take care of myself. "I wanted to tell you the truth, but I was mindful of your relationship with your sister. I didn't want to betray something between the two of you if she wasn't ready for you to know."

"That's valiant of you to care so much about her needs, but what about me? I'm the one you said you cared about, and I'm the one you had no problem lying to. Maybe it was easy because you've been doing it all along. That's the basis of us." I didn't truly believe that, but I felt confused and hurt. I should have been his priority, not my sister. In a way, it felt like he chose me over her.

A Toyota looped around the corner and stopped in front of us.

"I need to go." I pulled the Uber door open.

Blake didn't argue or try to stop me. He knew me well enough to respect my wishes and know he shouldn't push. I needed to be alone and sort through all the information. But the sixteen-year-old in me wished he would chase after me.

CHAPTER TWENTY-NINE

Blake

Fifteen Years Earlier

I was surprised by the insistent knocking at my front door. It was a Sunday morning, and people rarely knocked on my door. We had a doorbell, for one thing. And also, it was really early in the morning.

My dad was still asleep, and I wasn't particularly concerned about the possibility of a serial murderer announcing himself in broad daylight with a knock, so I flung the door open. I was still in boxers and the British Invasion T-shirt I'd worn to bed. I didn't recognize the irritated face staring back at me when I opened the door, although something about her eyes was familiar, the green rimmed with gray.

Her hair was sandy brown and pulled into a high ponytail, and the glare on her face was real. "Blake?"

"Yeah. It's my house, so . . ."

"Funny. I'm Sarah, Rebecca's sister."

Oh. I started to see the resemblance, but where Rebecca exuded energy and her tousled light brown hair glowed, her sister had a more grounded, methodical presence. And a lot more makeup— green eye shadow and fuchsia lipstick. Her whole vibe terrified me.

"Nice to meet you." I hoped lamely that Rebecca had raved about me so much that her sister had to come in person to see what all the fuss was about. *Right.*

"Listen, I'm sure my sister told you, but our family has been through a lot. She was really close to our dad, and she's been having a rough time."

"Yes. We talked about it. I think . . . I hope I helped her a little bit." I was still feeling good about the day and night we'd spent together. It had only been twenty-four hours since I'd dropped her at home, and I hadn't called her yet, but I was planning on it later in the day.

Sarah's expression confused me. I was telling her that I was a good guy, that I was trying to be there for her sister. Instead, she shook her head. "You think you helped her? Encouraging her to ditch school? Keeping her out all night? Doing God knows what with her when she was lying to her family about where she was? She already has three detentions. You're not helping."

I confessed to nothing. For all I knew, Sarah was just fishing for information, and I wasn't going to be the one to get her into trouble. But she knew an awful lot. I crossed my arms over my chest, hoping I somehow looked bigger or more intimidating.

But Sarah was nearly my height, and she was two years older. She looked at me like I was a fly she could squish with her thumb.

Holding my ground, I tried to make her see it from Rebecca's perspective. "She was miserable at school, and no one was paying any attention. I still think it was good for her to get out a little bit. You should have seen her. We had fun. She seemed happy," I said quietly. I wanted her to understand that I cared about Rebecca and wasn't just some jerk who was joyriding with her to get my rocks off.

"Well, you're a fucking loser if you think that. She needs to quit acting like a rebellious, out-of-control drama queen and get on with her life. Like we all have to do."

"She's hardly a drama queen." It was the wrong thing to say, but I hated hearing anyone disparage Rebecca now that I'd gotten to know her a little bit—now that she'd dug into my heart and I'd felt like a lost puppy without her.

"You don't even know her." Sarah put her hands on her hips and challenged me with her gaze.

I wanted to tell her that she didn't know Rebecca if she thought her sister was being dramatic for grieving the loss of her dad. And over the time we'd spent together, she'd seemed to be feeling so much better. "I can be good for her. If you'd just see that I—"

"What, want to get in her pants so you don't have to be the last virgin in the class of 2007?"

She told Sarah about our pact?

"That's not what it was, not at all. And besides...nothing happened."

"Of course it didn't. My sister's too smart to stoop to a pity fuck. Just…stay away from her. Leave her alone, and let her family take care of her."

"Are you actually threatening me?" I wasn't a big guy or someone who got into fights, but I didn't like to be pushed around, and Sarah was a bitch. I wanted so badly to tell her to go fuck herself, but I didn't want to get myself into even more trouble with her, purely for Rebecca's sake. But she was wrong, so wrong about her sister, and wrong about me. I had to defend myself. "Look, we don't know each other. But believe me when I say that I really care about your sister. I really like her, and I want to be there for her. I know how hard it is to lose a parent—"

She looked at me like I was nuts. "You think you know her? You spent one day with her. You don't know a person after one day. And of course you like her. Everyone does."

"So, what are you saying? You want me to never talk to her again? We can't even be friends?"

Sarah looked at me like that was the stupidest question she'd ever heard. "I'm telling you to forget she ever existed. Leave her alone."

The words pierced me in the gut because a part of me was starting to believe she was right. Or if she wasn't, how was I going to know? My mom was gone, and my dad wasn't in a position to deal with my love life. Maybe Sarah knew what she was talking about.

"What if I don't want to?" I could hear the fight leave my voice, just a tiny crack in my certainty that I knew better, but it was enough.

"I don't care what you want. This isn't about you. I'm protecting my sister, and you are not who she needs in her life. Lose her number."

Talk about a drama queen. But I had much bigger problems on my hands because I didn't want to do anything she'd just told me to do.

Sarah clearly felt like the conversation was over because she turned on her heel and took the porch steps two at a time. Before I'd even formulated my next thought, she was down our front walkway and getting into her car.

"Fuck that," I said as she drove away, initially determined to ignore her. But the doubt had already crept in. *What if Sarah knew something about Rebecca that I didn't?*

After all, I was the dweeb and she was the popular girl. It was never going to work out between us. I'd thought we connected, but maybe I was wrong.

What if I'm just unworthy of her?

So I made a decision. I would let Rebecca's real friends and her family be there for her. I would give her space for a little while and obey her sister's wishes. I would let our fate be her decision. After that, if she approached me, if she told me she wanted to hang out, I wouldn't think twice.

But she never did.

CHAPTER THIRTY

lake

I LET the wrong things get in my head.

In other words, I completely fucked the whole thing up because I was sixteen, and I had nominal experience being a boyfriend or even a quickie hookup. And I was scared shitless after getting yelled at. I'll never forget the words ringing in my ear, "Leave her alone, and let her real friends take care of her." I didn't have to hear it twice.

I was ill-equipped mentally and emotionally to understand what to do next, so I beat a hasty retreat so I could think. That turned out to be a terrible idea. Thinking had a tendency to consume me, and back then, it was a black hole.

Instead of having confidence in what I thought Rebecca felt for me, I got paranoid and worried.

Talk about socially incompatible. What if I'm just a convenient stand-in for someone better? How will I feel when the inevitable happens, and she comes to her senses and dumps me for the next star athlete?

Unsure I wanted to take a risk that things might work out for a week or a month or—serious wishful thinking—longer, I listened to the voice that said we were doomed from the beginning.

Wanting to be a little bit cooler than I was, I thought it was better to be the one to bolt, better to leave than be left. The words came to me as though I'd carried them around for years as my personal motto, but I swore I'd never had reason to even conceive of a motto.

I flat-out ghosted her, ignored the few friendly texts she sent, and hid like a hermit because I was afraid of my other options.

It wasn't excusable, but it was the explanation I had.

She was in a really vulnerable place, getting over intense sadness after losing her dad, and I'd taken advantage of it when I invited her to leave campus with me. I told myself I was doing it to help her, but at some point, I'd lost the thread. *Was I trying to help her or help myself? Was I just an asshole posing as a concerned good guy?*

And because I didn't have a definitive answer, I assumed the worst about myself. *Is there anything more potent than teenage self-loathing?*

When I went home that night, I didn't feel victorious for having made inroads with her. I didn't feel gratitude that I'd been able to make her smile—several times—when her day had been going in the opposite direction. I felt horribly guilty. I'd used her vulnerable moment for my own gain. I'd taken advantage of her sadness to try to get her to like me. I was an awful person. And in a nod to being the worst kind of person, I took it one step further. I ran.

Okay, I didn't literally run. I had no place to go. More accurately, I hid. I hid in plain sight at school, which meant that I showed up every day and went to class. The worst part was that she was nice about it at first.

After I bailed on school and hid in my room for two days, I showed up on campus and saw her coming toward me with a smile on her face. She was happy to see me, even though I hadn't returned her calls.

"Blake," she said, approaching me in the hallway.

Other kids looked at us, but she didn't seem to notice them. I was hyperaware that I didn't belong with her.

"How are you?" I looked past her, desperate for any excuse to bolt. I didn't know how to talk to her—how to be with her—when we were outside of the bubble we'd been in on Tuesday night.

"I'm . . . um, fine. Are you okay?" she asked.

"Yup, all good." And maybe I wanted to prove that I wasn't worthy of her, because I refused to smile at her, refused to look her in the eye. "Anyway, I should get to class. Take care, okay?"

"Sure." She looked confused and hurt.

I hated being the one to put that expression on her face, but she deserved better, and I was right there proving it.

Later, she would substitute that look for anger if I happened to pass by her, but I did my best to prevent that from happening. Rebecca and I didn't have any classes in common, so it was no problem to avoid seeing her during that part of my day.

Then I just had to worry about getting through lunch and walking between classes. Before the one night we'd spent together, I'd seen her all the time. I'd made a point of it. The levity in her personality had made me feel good, even though I knew she wasn't directing her goodwill toward me. Because I knew where her locker was, I'd made it part of my route between my own locker and my classes, even though it generally took me an extra five minutes and more than occasionally made me late. It had always been worth it.

But not anymore. Because I knew where her locker was, I could expertly avoid it, making sure I took the most direct route to my classes. I talked to no one on the way, stopped for nothing. I arrived early and spent whatever extra time I had calming my breathing after the death sprint I did through the hallways. As I said, I wasn't the picture of physical fitness back then.

After school, I'd make a beeline to my car and leave campus. If I was planning to hang out with friends, I made sure to meet them off campus. When I did go to the occasional football game, I sat high up in the stands. And besides, she was busy on the sidelines with the cheer squad. We had zero chance of interacting.

At first, I just needed time to think. I felt horrible that I hadn't called her and even worse about how I acted when she approached me at school. I did plan to apologize, and I never planned to freeze her out completely. I was working on the best way to explain myself, to tell her that my feelings for her went far beyond a one-night stand. At the same time, I didn't want to freak her out. I wrote her a letter, then threw it away. I wrote her a poem. Chucked that too.

I sat outside her house, my car idling for nearly an hour, polluting the goddamned planet because I couldn't decide whether to ring her doorbell or drive away. I drove away because, after an hour of thinking, I still didn't know how to make her understand that I saw her as more than broken. She was the strongest, toughest, most beautiful girl I'd ever met, and it terrified the hell out of me.

People say that when a person meets the love of their life, they just know. *Well, what if that happens when you're sixteen years old and you blow it?*

The bottom line was that I didn't have the confidence back then to believe in love, at least not to believe it was something I could have with her. *I mean, come on. Let's be real. The cheerleader only ends up with the nerd in movies.*

So I decided I was doing her a favor by not putting her in the uncomfortable position of having to reject me. I convinced myself that by hiding for the next two years of high school and avoiding having a single conversation with Rebecca, I was making her life better. Even if it meant making my life so much worse.

By the time our graduation rolled around, I'd become so expertly proficient at anticipating where Rebecca would walk or what direction she would cast a glance that I could always be headed in a different direction. It was almost like I'd developed a sixth sense.

She'd ended up dating one of the baseball players who I'd had a few classes with over the years. He was a decent enough guy, and it made me believe that what I'd predicted had come true: Rebecca was with a guy who fit her better than I did.

Sometimes I would see them walking down a hallway, him with his arm around her or her hugging him around the waist. Those shows of affection didn't bother me that much, but every so often, I would spy them holding hands. That killed me.

I skulked through the rest of high school in the science labs and the debate tournaments, which mercifully kept me busy outside of school, so I didn't have to sit at home every night alone, kicking myself for being an idiot. I only did that most nights.

The good news was that once I went to college, I turned a corner. My body got with the program, and I actually looked like a college guy. I finally filled out the legs of my jeans, and I found the gym on campus. Girls seemed to notice. They also seemed to like the smart guys as much as they liked the jocks.

I hooked up with a new girl every week all through freshman year and had girlfriends off and on for the rest of college. Looking better physically gave me confidence, and I finally felt like I understood what high school must have been like for the jocks and the super social kids. It had been like that for me for one night—and for that night, those guys had nothing on me.

I never forgot about Rebecca, but I learned how to move on.

CHAPTER THIRTY-ONE

Blake

Present Day

Fuck. Or fucked, as the case may be. As in, I was fucked because there was almost no way Becca was going to trust me again, and it had been my own fault for getting myself into the situation.

I'd planned to push Sarah harder about coming clean to Becca, but I hadn't planned to do it at Isla's house after dinner. In fact, I'd avoided being too near Sarah for the entire night, just in case she wanted to try to convince me to leave the past in the past. But she cornered me when I was distracted, checking my texts after leaving the bathroom, and before I'd realized it, she'd escorted me into the back bedroom. Her herding skills rivaled Howard's, and her legs were a lot longer.

Fine, we could have the conversation, I decided. So I told her I wanted Becca to know the real reason I'd blown her off in high school. Pretending to be the asshole I'd claimed to be had been eating at me, and she'd believed it readily. I wasn't sure what bothered me more, lying to her or seeing the ease with which she decided I could be that big of a jerk.

There was no question I was falling harder for her now than I ever had back then, and I couldn't continue anything with her without telling her the truth. Which was what I'd just finished telling Sarah when Becca walked in. I'd pretty much gotten her to agree that she had to come clean with her sister because I couldn't stand Becca believing something that wasn't true.

I could handle her thinking I was the asshole she imagined I was in high school, but I also didn't want her to think I was anything but honest with her now. It killed me that I'd had to lie for Sarah until I could figure out how to sort everything out. And now, I'd probably ruined the best thing that would ever happen to me and alienated the one person I wanted in my life. So yeah, fucked.

"Hey," someone intoned behind me. Sarah joined me on the sidewalk and looked down the street to where I was still staring at the microscopic taillights of Becca's Uber in the distance.

Or maybe I was just imagining things. Like I had been all along. Pretending there was a chance things might work out this time. "Well, that couldn't have gone worse," I said.

"I'm sorry. I was so caught up trying to dig myself out of a pit that I didn't do a very good job of defending you."

"It wasn't your job to defend me. I made a choice. I should have talked to you instead of making up stupid shit about how I was afraid to be her mistake."

"You couldn't have known you'd end up here with her. And I don't mean here at Isla's house. I mean, here with a chance of getting the girl you're in love with. When she mentioned running into you, I should have done the right thing and told her what I did back then."

"I should have told her. But I knew how close you all were back then, and I didn't want to blame you for all the mistakes I made myself."

She blinked slowly and nodded at me. "You're a good man, Blake. I hope you two can make it past this." She patted my arm and frowned at the useless gesture. "I'm really sorry."

I knew she was. Sarah was only looking out for her younger sister's heart back then, and she was doing the same thing now. I nodded. "I'm gonna head back to the restaurant. There's always a beam that needs sanding or some kitchenware that needs to be inspected. That will keep me from thinking about how royally I fucked this up."

She grimaced and shook her head. "I'll talk to her. I need to explain and apologize, and I'll make sure she doesn't freeze you out."

"Thanks. I'll give her some space. But I'm not giving up this time."

Sarah's solemn face edged into the beginnings of a smile. "Good. She's worth it."

"I know." I'd always known. She was right about that. I was also fixated on the part where she'd said I was in love with Becca. She was right about that too.

I WENT BACK to the restaurant. I figured the odds were low to nonexistent that I would sleep anytime soon because all I could think about was Becca and how I'd screwed up my chances with her again.

I drove past the front windows, admiring the oak door as I did every time I saw it. Only this time, Becca's words came back to me. "I know my wood," and I just felt more depressed. The place was dark, as I'd expected it to be, but when I circled around the back and came in from the small parking lot, I saw a light on in a corner of the kitchen.

"Burt?" I didn't see him, but I heard the familiar grunt he made when he was doing manual labor, which wasn't often. That was why he had a team of guys. He mainly supervised and made wise-cracks all day.

His bald head poked around a set of refrigerated metal drawers that hadn't been there that morning when I'd stopped by. "Hey, boss. Just making a few fixes." He stood up and brushed the front of his pants, even though there was no dirt to remove.

I went over to check out the drawers, which I'd been waiting on. They'd been backordered, and I was worried they might cause me to push back the restaurant's opening if I couldn't get the delivery expedited.

"Hold up, you might not . . ." Burt stopped when I rounded the corner to where he was working.

"What the hell?" The drawers weren't drawers. I was looking at a metal table on spindly legs that didn't belong in my kitchen. "Did they send the wrong thing?"

He ran a hand over his sweaty face and closed his eyes. "No, this was user error."

"Meaning? Who'd the user?"

"Me. I made the order online instead of talking to my guy like I normally do. I thought it would be faster. But I input the wrong item number, and the guys installed it this afternoon without realizing it was this piece-of-shit table."

I could tell he felt terrible about the mistake, so there was no use raking him over the coals. But I was sweating my opening night, and this didn't help things. "Is it fixable? I know it's been hard getting the drawers . . ."

He waved a hand, which happened to contain a screwdriver. "No, it's handled. I talked to a friend of a friend, and he was able to jump the line on an order that was supposed to go to another resto."

I couldn't hide my childish grin. "Any idea who I'm screwing over?"

It was his turn to grin. "Spencer Quinn. His hotel on Ashby. He'll be receiving a call tomorrow telling him his refrigerated drawers are on backorder. Might have to push back his opening, but you didn't hear it from me," he said, sharing the glee that came from besting a competitor.

"Hear what?" I quipped.

I looked around the kitchen, where his tool belt hung over the back of a chair. He'd also cracked a beer. When he caught me looking, he seemed chagrined. "I don't drink on the job. You know that. This was extenuating, being after hours and no one was here. At least, I didn't expect anyone."

"It's fine. Are you actually working, or are you just putting a bad juju curse on the weird table?"

"I'm uninstalling it. I didn't want you to see it and freak."

"I wouldn't have freaked . . ." I said.

He shot me a look.

"Okay, I might have freaked. Thank you for looking out for me."

"No problem. We're solid. I want to keep it that way."

From the looks of it, he'd gotten the table unscrewed from its floor braces and the spot where it attached to the other cabinetry. All that remained was to haul it out the back door and send it back where it came from. We did that together and returned to the kitchen.

"You got another one of those?" I asked, pointing to his beer.

"Sure." He pointed to the walk-in, where he'd stashed the remainder of a six-pack. I grabbed one and popped the top with an opener fastened to the wall. The cap made a satisfying clink when it dropped into the metal receptacle underneath.

He leaned against the table and looked me over. Burt was only a few years older than me, but he carried himself with the seriousness and world-weary swagger of someone ten years older than that. He had two ex-wives and three adult kids, and he often said he worked as much as he did because he had to support them all, but I knew he loved it. He pointed a finger at me. "You're supposed to be with your girlfriend tonight. What happened?"

"Just when I think you aren't paying attention, Burt, you surprise the shit out of me."

He sipped the last of his beer and went to the walk-in to grab another one. "I saw her. I saw the two of you together. It doesn't take a genius to know you'd rather be with her right now than sit here talking to me."

I went to the dining room and pulled one of the chairs off the stack against the wall. They'd been delivered two days ago, and I still couldn't decide if I liked them enough to keep them. Becca's comment about the French bistro decor was stuck in my head, and I had a lingering suspicion she was right, as usual.

I flipped the chair around and sat on it backward, leaning against the high back. "I fucked it up. I should've told her the truth about something, and now it's biting me in my stupid ass. Which, by the way, already hurts from sitting on this chair."

"Yeah, they're garbage. I meant to say."

"Wish you'd said."

"I didn't know until they arrived. I brought one back to sit on while I worked, and if you noticed, I preferred the floor."

"Great. One more thing I should've seen coming that I didn't. Do I even have what it takes to open another restaurant?"

He gestured for me to dismount the chair and take a seat on the floor across from him. "Better, right?"

Sadly, the floor was more comfortable. It was probably the only time we'd be able to sit there because, once we opened, it would be off limits—there was probably no place more disgusting than a restaurant floor.

I nodded. "I guess finding new furniture is on my list now."

"Sounded like your girl had some ideas." He leaned against the steam oven.

"She did. I think she's got a great eye. I just hope that after tonight, she's still my girl, but I may have fucked that up royally."

"Tell me."

I gave him the broad strokes of our whole story, and he nodded solemnly until I got to this evening's events.

Then he just said, "Fucking idiot. You had a chance to tell her you were a better guy back then than she thought, and you made it worse for yourself instead."

"Yeah. I'm aware."

"You need to fix it."

"Also aware."

"Hang on, I may have an idea." Burt pushed himself up from the floor, groaning at the effort required to lift his large frame to an upright position. Then he lumbered over and leaned on the countertop, looking into the dark dining room by the light of a hanging industrial bulb his guys had rigged to light the space until the electrical was finished. "Good thing I had my guys hold off on installing those globe lights. Your girl's right. They don't work in here."

"Great. You like hitting a man when he's down?"

Becca had made that point clear when she'd sketched out the alternative design, which I had to admit, took the space in a whole different direction I hadn't considered. And I could see her point.

He grinned. "Relax. You're gonna like my idea."

"Just tell me I don't have to do the lift from *Dirty Dancing* or some corny thing."

He laughed and swigged his beer. "Nah, no heavy lifting. But what I have in mind does involve a movie theme . . ."

"Please tell me I'm not gonna live to regret this. You don't have the most admirable track record when it comes to women."

"Hey! I resent that. I have a great track record . . . until I marry them. But this isn't about me. Trust me, this is a good plan. You got a pen? We're gonna want to write this shit down."

Still not fully certain whether I could trust him, I went to the bare-bones office and grabbed a pen and spiral notebook. When I handed them to him, he immediately started sketching.

After only a minute, I could see a replica of the restaurant's insides taking shape on the page. "Hey, you're a good artist. How did I not know this?"

"Where d'you think I get the drawings for your projects? You think I pay a damn architect?" He snorted and kept sketching in between swigs of beer. "So, tell me about the sister, the one who bossed you around in high school. Is she single? Cute?"

"Not now, Burt."

"I don't mean now. You patch things up with Becca. That's the focus here." He smiled and rubbed a hand over his head as though he were prettying himself up for a date. "But once that's done, we'll talk."

CHAPTER THIRTY-TWO

ecca

I BARELY SLEPT ALL NIGHT. I needed time to think, really think back on what I remembered from high school, and try to understand what had happened.

Sarah called me at the crack of dawn, reasoning that I'd told her to leave me alone last night, but the morning was a reset. She wasn't willing to let me go any longer without really talking things through.

So we talked. She explained. Again. I mean, I couldn't really blame her. From where she'd sat, Blake hadn't looked like a good influence, and she was the oldest of the siblings still living at home. She'd done what she thought was right.

She also told me that Blake had been adamant that she tell me the truth because he wanted me to trust him. "Don't take this out on him. It's not his fault."

I told her that I understood and that she really should have minded her own fucking business. It would take time before I wanted to spend tons of my free time with her. She more or less understood, and her early workday prevented us from talking for hours and hours.

In some ways, knowing Blake intended to follow through with me in some way before my sister threatened him made me feel better about high school Blake. He probably was the guy I thought I knew after spending the night with him, but he didn't have enough of a backbone to stand up to my sister or follow his own mind. For two years.

I remembered him telling me that I was out of his league. I didn't believe it then, and I didn't believe it now, but it made sense that he'd let those feelings get the better of him. It didn't mean I had to like it or help him feel like he'd made some kind of noble sacrifice.

Then there was the man every part of me wanted to be with now. My body wanted him wrapped around me, and my heart wanted him near me. But he hadn't been completely honest when I asked him to explain high school. I didn't know if I could forgive that, even if he'd had second thoughts afterward.

And that was where I stood when Blake knocked on my door. I knew he would. His heart was like mine—it didn't want to stay away. But . . . I hadn't come to a decision on how to be with him. I couldn't be okay with lies.

"Blake, this isn't a good idea. It's too soon," I said before I had a chance to take in the way he looked.

He didn't answer, and my eyes went to his face. He looked like shit. If I hadn't slept well, he hadn't slept at all. He was wearing the same pants and shoes as the night before, but he'd put on a fresh T-shirt. His hair was a wreck, and he hadn't shaved. *Good.*

He looked the way I felt, and it wasn't a new feeling. It was an exact repeat of the way I'd felt in high school, the same level of pain and betrayal.

When I noticed the white bakery box in his hand, I shook my head. "No. You're not going to charm me with cheesecake and make it all fine."

"Can I come in?" he asked.

Almost as though my body was in charge of my brain, I stood out of the way so he could walk past me then followed him into the kitchen. He opened the bakery box on my island counter. Mocha cheesecake.

"Damn it, Blake, I'm so mad at you. You knew I was working on trusting you, and even then, you opted not to tell me the truth."

"I know. You're one hundred percent right. I should have told you. But I want you to understand something. None of what I did tell you about how I felt or my reasons for being afraid back then were a lie. Walking away from you was the worst punishment of my life, and I did it because I believed it was best for you. Even though it made us both miserable, I did it for you."

I thought back to what he'd said, how he didn't want to take advantage of me at a vulnerable time and how he didn't think he was worthy. Those parts of him made me want to melt into his arms and tell him how wrong he was. But the other part . . . I didn't know how to get past it.

"I understand what you're saying, but I don't know how to trust you. How am I supposed to believe anything you tell me when you could be omitting some other little—or huge—detail? You just proved that."

"I know. I can't believe I fucked this up. Twice. At this point, you have no reason to trust me, but I'm asking you to take a leap anyway because it's me. You know me. You know how I feel about you, and I believe you'd feel the same way if you weren't holding yourself back. And I know the past messed with you, and I have so much regret about that. But we can't let the past control us now. We're . . . connected. It's not just physical. It's everything. I know you feel it. We were meant to be together."

His words stabbed at me like tiny swords, daring me to ignore my brain and go with my emotions, but I didn't know how.

"We did just fine for fifteen years without seeing each other." I willed myself to believe it.

"Sure, you seemed really fine with your coffee dates and your no-relationships rule."

He was right, but maybe I was too far gone to find my way to him.

"I can't do this with you again. When you turned your back and avoided me after the night we spent together, it messed with me. I felt broken. My trust, my heart—you broke me. I haven't been able—or willing—to open myself up to anyone since then," I said, even though my resolve was always weak in his presence.

It didn't matter. We stood on opposite sides of my kitchen with two slices of cheesecake on the island between us like the children we were fighting over in a divorce. To be clear, I would take both, and he could have the empty box.

"I accept that. And I've apologized for that. But at some point, don't you think you need to take some responsibility for your own happiness? You're a nurse and a healer, and thanks to you, my restaurant is going to look the way it deserves to look. You own this great house, and you're helping Carla have a place to live. I've never looked at you and thought you were broken. Not then, not now. I know I broke your trust, but you are not broken.

And I love you. I've always loved you. Since before I even knew you."

My eyes filled with tears. "His that even possible?"

"I don't know. It just is."

He picked up my hand and lightly kissed my palm. I'd never considered the idea that it had been as painful for him to walk away as it had been for me. But I believed him. And I knew I loved him. There was no point in pretending otherwise.

I could push him away and be miserable, but what would it accomplish?

"Listen, I know you're holding back a piece of your heart with me, and it's my fault. I take full responsibility for fucking up. But you're not a victim. You can make a choice here to be with me because you love me, or you can get stuck in a cycle of hating me again. But how will that solve anything for either of us?"

He was right. Isla had said the same thing over and over. And I didn't want to be stuck anymore. I'd been living in a state of suspended animation for years, not knowing if I'd ever want to feel again. I'd decided I was okay with that, but that was a lie—my lie. Maybe we all had them.

I wasn't okay blocking my emotions to keep them safe. I never would be. I loved Blake. I needed to stop bracing for impact and looking for reasons to run. "I know you're right."

He looked relieved, but I wasn't done.

"Logically, I know it. But I need to feel it, and I'm not sure how to do that."

"If there's anything I can—"

"It will probably just take time, Blake."

"I can give you that. I'll give you as much as you want or need. And I'll be here whenever you're ready. Because I'm not going anywhere. I can't. I love you too much."

"I know. I love you too. I need to sort out my brain, but we're gonna be okay. Just . . . let me have a nice stern talk with myself. Okay?"

He nodded. I believed he understood what I was asking, and I believed my brain understood. I was asking it to play second fiddle to my heart.

CHAPTER THIRTY-THREE

ecca

I'D SIGNED up to work three shifts in a row, so I hadn't had time to talk to Blake since I'd asked him for time to think. I knew he'd been at the restaurant almost twenty-four, seven, so he was busy with his own stuff.

The day hurled me from one urgent issue to another, leaving me running from room to room and dealing with emergencies. On one hand, it was good because it kept my brain busy and didn't let me dwell on Blake for too long. On the downside, by the day's end, I was no closer to knowing what to think about his decision not to hold back the truth.

I'd intentionally avoided my sisters. I didn't need them meddling and lobbing their opinions into the mix. Maybe what happened in high school deserved to stay there. *So why lie about it now?* If Blake really cared about starting something new with me, he had all the more reason to be honest.

I decided to skip my swim workout and get my water therapy courtesy of my bathtub instead. I'd just bought a new box of bath bombs. Throw in a glass of wine, and I'd have myself a full evening of enjoyment.

I'd only been in the tub for about ten minutes when the feral cats started their mating ritual against the neighbor's fence.

"Of course, perfect timing," I muttered. I couldn't just get one bath's worth of peace.

I sank deeper into the verbena-scented water and debated dunking my head entirely to drown them out. But I didn't want to deal with wet hair. No, I'd just ignore them and try to turn their moaning into white noise.

After a couple of minutes, however, I felt like I was hearing things. Somehow the howling cats started to sound a little like music. Maybe they were picking up on each other's sounds and harmonizing in cat terms.

No. It was definitely music. I knew Carla was out of town because she'd left me a note two days earlier asking me to bring in her newspaper. Besides, she never played loud music. Or rock music, for that matter. And this was *music*.

I strained to hear it, but my windows were closed, and I wasn't about to get out of the bathtub to identify what was probably some kid idling his car on the road out front. When I closed my eyes, I could almost make out what seemed like a familiar refrain. Almost. It wasn't possible to be hearing what I imagined because the longer I listened, the more it sounded like . . . U2. But that was crazy.

Clearly, I was hearing things.

Feral cats rarely sounded like music, and I was sure they were just cats. Maybe the acoustics in my bathroom were rounding out the sound and making it prettier.

Because if I didn't know better, I might think I heard the intro verses of "Stuck in a Moment." And I never listened to that song or that album anymore, which was a shame because it was a really great album. *But was someone really listening to it outside my house, or was I conjuring a reason to think about Blake?* I focused my attention on the melody until I felt certain. It was the song Blake and I had played on repeat in his car back in high school.

Coincidence? I had to know.

With bath suds dripping down my legs, I toweled off and wrapped myself in a white terry robe I kept on the back of my bathroom door. I rarely wore it. I wasn't really a bathrobe kind of gal, and generally I went straight from the shower or tub into a pair of sweats, but the robe was there, and I was in a hurry to find the source of the music.

There was no sign of an idling car in front of my house and no evidence of the source of the music, but standing on my front porch, I confirmed that I was right about the song. Just not the location. It seemed to be coming from behind me. *In my backyard?*

I moved through my house in a daze, still not knowing what I expected to find when I opened the door and stepped out onto my porch.

It was Blake, and the music source seemed to be his phone. I tried to tune out the lyrics because it felt like they applied to me now as much as they did back then. I was stuck. I'd been stuck for years.

What's it going to take to get me unstuck?

Blake didn't notice me as he bent over my paltry square of half-grass, assembling something that contained what looked like tiny plants and flat gray rocks. *Gardening? What the hell?*

"Blake? What are you doing?" I raised my voice to be heard over the music.

He lifted his head and brightened when he saw me, then his eyes clouded. I wasn't smiling. I didn't want him there doing whatever he was doing. If he wanted to talk, we could talk. Making a rock maze on my lawn seemed irrelevant.

He held up a finger and did a little more shuffling of plants and rocks on the lawn. As he did, the song got louder, making it harder to avoid letting the lyrics play with my mind. I knew the song by heart. I didn't need to hear every word to know how it gently encouraged someone who felt stuck in a bad cycle to pull herself out and find a way to move forward.

I knew what those lyrics had meant to me when I was in high school, grieving the loss of my dad. What I didn't know was how to interpret them now. *Was falling for Blake just another mistake, another place I'd gotten temporarily stuck before getting it together and finding my way back to my senses? Or was I stuck because I kept looking for why it could never work for me—for us—not hearing what he was trying to tell me the other night and choosing instead to assume the worst of him because I saw the worst in myself?*

I had no way of knowing as he knelt on my grass, making succulent trails or whatever the hell he was doing. His face was set in a wary mask as he walked toward me. Despite his serious expression, he couldn't dim the playfulness in his eyes. Blake extended his hands out, and as much as I wanted an explanation before I succumbed to his charms, I couldn't help reaching for him. My eyes closed at the warmth his hands brought to every part of me.

Still, I was confused. "What is this?" From where we stood, I saw rocks and some plants, but it didn't make sense. He turned to look and laughed quietly.

"It's nothing from here. Come with me." He dropped one of my hands but kept his grasp on the other, leading me through my living room and up the stairs to the balcony of my bedroom. From there, he stood back and let me look over the railing at what he'd constructed below.

He'd made words out of the rocks and decorated the tableau with sunflowers. It said, "R, WILL YOU GO TO PROM W/ ME?"

It might not have seemed like the kind of thing that would knock me out of my indecision and seal up all the holes in my trust issues, but that arrangement of rocks cracked open my overprotected heart with abandon. I had no idea why he was asking me to the prom using a bunch of rocks, but I didn't care. It was time to stop punishing us both and holding onto past hurt. I was done. I loved Blake. None of the rest of it mattered.

Of course, I still needed some details. "Prom?" I asked, delighted and still dumbstruck at his effort.

"It's my prom-posal," he said as though it explained everything.

"I think we . . . might have missed it by a few years."

"Maybe . . . or maybe not. I'm asking for a do-over. Of everything. Starting with the worst day of my life, when I ignored you instead of gathering you into my arms and holding onto you like I should have. If I'd been a better guy, I'd have kept our pact, I'd have kissed you every chance I got, and I'd have taken you to our prom."

I shook my head. "You're sweet. But I think you were right the other day. I need to stop living in the past."

"Those who don't know history are doomed to repeat it," he said.

I remembered him saying the same thing in Sydney's delivery room. The words hadn't even registered that day because I was still certain he didn't remember who I was. Hearing the words again, I wondered if he was trying to tell me something, even that first day.

"I don't think we're doomed, but I think we should start paying more attention to the present."

"Does that mean you forgive me for not telling you the whole truth about high school?"

"I hate that you lied to me. And if you do it again . . . I don't think I'll be able to forgive you. But yes, I want you more than I want to stand on moral high ground and be mad at you."

"I only heard that part where you said you want me."

"I do. I want you."

"So, will you go with me to prom?"

"Are you serious? You want to crash a high school prom? We'll probably get arrested."

He laughed. "Now that you put it that way, I kind of do want to do that. But what I had in mind is a little different." He handed me a card with a date engraved on it. It was for his restaurant opening.

"Argh, I don't know, Blake. You'll have all your people there . . . it's like a high school reunion—it seems like a good idea to bring a date, and then they're dead weight all night long because you want to talk to other people."

He tilted his head and smirked. "I'm asking because I want you there with me. Don't you get it yet? I always want you with me."

He slid his hands up my arms and under my chin, cupping my face. "Always."

When he bent to kiss me, I really wanted to say yes. I'd never been to a prom, after all, and it would be pretty great to go to one —even a fake one that was really a restaurant opening thirteen years after we were seniors—with Blake as my date.

I didn't quite see how his restaurant opening was the same as a prom. *But why argue?* The gesture was the point. "Yes, Blake. I'd love to be your prom date."

His grin stretched across his face, and he kissed me once on the lips. "Saying I love you doesn't seem like enough to express how much I adore and cherish you. But it will have to be enough until I read the dictionary and come up with something better. I love you, Rebecca Finley."

"I know. And I love you just as much."

Without warning, he threw his hands in the air and shouted to whoever was in range of my balcony, "She said yes!"

Such a goof. *How'd I get so lucky?*

Becca

I OPENED my front door and started talking before Isla had a chance to say a word. "I know, it's a lot for me. Is it too much? Am I going way overboard with this? Just tell me. Don't worry about hurting my feelings."

Isla stood on my porch, dressed in a logo sweatshirt from the bakery and a pair of running tights. She had a weekly long run with a marathon training group, and they met near my house at Lake Merritt. It wasn't unusual for her to stop by afterward if she knew I had the day off, but this time, I made a point of asking her to stop by because I needed a second opinion on my outfit. Isla had the benefit of being a little less fashion-savvy than Cherry, so I knew she'd be honest without worrying about upsetting the fashion gods.

"You look amazing." Her eyes roamed over me from head to four-inch heels that just might be the end of me. They were black-and-white silk fabric with a tie around the ankle. "The shoes are gorgeous, and I hate you just a little for your perfect swimmer arms."

"I don't usually wear such revealing stuff." I felt self-conscious. The dress was pretty, but I'd have been more comfortable with a pair of jeans underneath and a bulky sweater over it.

"I know, and it's ridiculous. If anyone was meant to wear that dress, it's you. Plus, what did you…? Did you do your hair yourself?"

My hand went to my hair, which was smoother than it had ever been, and it fell into organized waves instead of looking like I'd slept on it. "Nope, I went to a blow-dry place in Oakland. Learned from the master."

Isla's hand went to her high ponytail, which somehow looked perfect even after her workout, not a strand loose from the hair-band and a flip at the bottom. "It looks great. You should wear it down all the time, at least when you're not at work."

I brushed the layered strands back from my face. It had been blown out straight, but then the stylist had added some waves where they seemed to belong, and it looked like something from the fashion magazines I'd been leafing through while she worked. I had to admit, it seemed worth the effort.

"Not sure I'd go that far. I'm dying to scoop it up into a pony."

"Don't. Leave it alone. Everything you've got going here is perfect. Just . . . don't touch anything."

"I won't. Thanks, Ile." I started to push a strand out of my face, and Isla swatted my hand away, wagging a finger at me.

"Do you need anything else from me? Other than a confidence boost and a ride?"

"Mostly the ride, but also I don't know what to do with myself for the next hour. If you want to mess around with my coffee setup, you can make a latte or whatever." Isla owned a bakery café that had a high-end espresso maker, which she never used herself. She preferred an old drip carafe to make coffee for her bakers.

Five minutes later, Isla was sipping the thick foam from the top of a latte she'd made with the frothing attachment on my espresso machine. "This is so good." She took another sip.

"Right? I know it's more convenient to use the pods or whatever, but I like the classic old machine. And frothing is my new favorite thing. You can even use it to make scrambled eggs."

"Stop it."

"I speak the truth."

"Now I want to froth an egg."

I waved a hand at the refrigerator and sat at my kitchen table while Isla played around with the frother and a couple of eggs.

"I'm just warning you it's really loud, and you'll think the eggs are going to explode, but they don't," I told her, happy for the distraction from my nerves.

We played a few games of gin, and she made me a latte—decaf because I was already a bundle of nerves—and eventually, we made our way through the traffic into the city. When we paid the toll, and I stared up at the spires of the bridge, I felt content.

Isla stopped half a block away from the restaurant, where the valet parking was backed up, and a boisterous crowd was gathered on the sidewalk in front. "Is this okay?" she asked. "Or should I try to get closer?"

"Are you sure you don't want to come with me? We could swing by your place really quick, and you could shower and change." Maybe she was right. Maybe I did need a babysitter.

She shook her head. "You've got this. Go get that crazy prom date of yours. He's a keeper."

I traded the warmth of her car for the frosty San Francisco fog and closed the car door.

Seriously, I'd need to tie my hands together to keep from messing with my hair or makeup. I was nervous, and it didn't help that I had no idea what Blake was planning with his whole prom idea.

But since he'd redecorated my backyard, I'd had some time to think. *How many men go to the trouble of trying to recreate a missed moment, right down to hauling rocks to someone's house for a prom-posal?* I could only think of one.

Isla was right. I'd gotten a lot of mileage out of hating him and using him as an excuse for all the limitations in my life. It was time to take responsibility for myself. And the one thing I knew was that I wanted my life to include Blake.

Those were the thoughts swirling in my head as I wove through the throng of exuberant guests on the sidewalk in front of the restaurant and found a space in the crowd to reach the front door.

It took me a moment to figure out what was different. Obviously, the last time I'd seen the restaurant, it had still been under construction, and Blake and I had been there alone. But that wasn't what struck me as I craned my neck to see over the heads of the other guests and peek in between them.

The restaurant had been completely redesigned. Instead of the heavy brown-leather Chesterfield sofa booths, French curtains bifurcating the windows, and globe lights hanging over mirrors, the room was open and warm with industrial touches.

He'd kept all the brick and left the reclaimed wood unsanded and unpainted. The iron staircase in the center of the room wound around a Jerusalem marble planter with a large olive tree.

The tables had black iron legs and unfinished wood tops, with black-painted bistro chairs. Open cabinets displayed handmade plates. A wall of wine bottles stood behind the bar, and tiny twinkling spotlights highlighted all the tiny details perfectly—the ceramic jars of succulents; small, colorful abstract paintings on the walls; blooming lavender in planters beneath the front glass windows.

Blake had taken my Pinterest board and my napkin sketches and turned them into a gorgeous space.

I tried to find a space devoid of people so I could take everything in again.

"If I didn't like cooking so much, this is the kind of place I could get used to." I knew the voice before I turned to see Carla, decked out in a gorgeous silk caftan over flowing pants and kitten heels.

"I love that you're here." I kissed her on the cheek. And I loved Blake for knowing how important she was to me and inviting her.

Carla looked me over from head to toe and nodded approvingly. "I'm not staying long. I've tried the appetizers, and I can tell you that man can cook . . . but you already knew that. And he's a delight . . . but you knew that too."

"I do know." I cast a look around to find Blake, but I didn't see him. I turned back to Carla, who was still looking me over.

"Well, I never thought I'd see you in a sexy black dress, but you do it better than anyone. It makes me happy."

"This is what it takes to make you happy? All these years making coffee and keeping the yard neat, when all you wanted was me in a cocktail dress? You're a little nutty, lady."

Carla wrapped her arms around me and whispered in my ear. "Enough talking to me. Go find your date." Then she pushed me into the crowd.

It was hard to make it out, but if I had to guess, I would say the music coming through the hidden speakers was vintage 2007, the year we graduated high school.

It was probably lucky the room was so loud because it wasn't the kind of music that generally played at a swanky restaurant opening, and if people had really focused, they might have found it strange.

But I didn't. It was the kind of music that would have played at our prom.

CHAPTER THIRTY-FIVE

Blake

ALL I KNEW for sure was that Becca would be there at some point. Isla had assured me of that, but she hadn't said much more. Fine. I'd take it over worrying she was never going to see me or talk to me again.

Then again, I'd made it clear how much blood, sweat, and tears I'd put into opening the San Francisco restaurant, and she knew how important it was to me. Maybe she was just coming as a friend, being supportive. I would just have to wait and see.

The place looked great, and by seven, the crowd spilled out onto the sidewalk.

Meantime, I had plenty to distract me, namely my investors, who made a beeline for me as soon as they walked in the door. With the open plan of the dining room and kitchen, I was easy to spot.

Manny Elevado pulled me into a bear hug, which was his preferred greeting. "Congrats on another great partnership. Glad to be in this with you."

"Hoping three's the lucky number for us," I said.

He'd invested twice before, but the stake he'd put in this restaurant was the biggest. I wanted to make sure he got his money on schedule.

"Oh, I'm not worried. If anyone's a good bet in this crazy business, it's you." Then he introduced me to his wife, which he did every time we were in a room together.

"We've met," she and I said at the same time. Then we laughed at the same time.

"Always good to err on the side of caution. Besides, I know I'm lucky to be with her." He leaned toward me like he didn't want her to hear but talked loud enough to make sure she did.

"You're a good man, my friend. Thanks for coming out. Nice to see you again, Rachel." I kissed his wife on the cheek.

I pointed them toward where the bartender was holding a tequila tasting, and they moved along. I strained for a view through the packed house to see if Becca had arrived. I didn't see evidence of her sun-streaked hair, and I was pretty sure my nerves would be fucking with me until she showed.

This was what my evening would consist of—shaking hands, accepting congratulatory wishes, and craning my neck over the crowd until Becca walked in the door.

Jim Lambert grabbed my hand and simultaneously slapped me on the back with the other. "Hey, man, looking good." He glanced around the place. "And I'm referring to the restaurant, not you. You look haggard and exhausted. As your backer, I'm thrilled, but as your friend, should I be concerned? You've usually got every-thing in hand by this point."

Jim and I had worked together since my early days, and he'd been a partner in six different restaurants. He'd made serious venture capital money in the early days of Silicon Valley, and now he only invested in restaurants and hotels. He was tall like me and had been a swimmer in college. Now he spent his free time scuba diving in the world's most exclusive dive spots and looking for the bluest water. He kept his silver-brown hair slicked back, and his two-day scruff always made him look like he'd just come back from vacation.

He was pathologically single, and I knew he intentionally hadn't brought a date to the opening because he preferred to keep his options open. *Hey, if it wasn't broke . . .*

I scrubbed a hand over my face, hoping to remove whatever haggard traces he was referring to. "Yeah, this one's been a bear. I wanted to get everything right in my hometown, I guess, so I made myself crazier than usual." I chose not to tell him that I'd also been agonizing over Becca and how to salvage the relation-ship I wanted with her. He didn't need to know I was stressed *and* whipped.

"Well, the place looks great, and I heard it's getting a write-up in the Style section and the Food section of the *Times*, so good on you."

"Thanks, man. There'll be passed apps all night, so you can taste a good part of the menu," I said.

Normally, he would come in several times for tastings before we opened a new place, but he'd been traveling lately, and at the end of the day, he trusted me.

"Good deal. I'll come grab you later." Then he raised his hand in the air and squeezed past a group of people to greet another chef, who was a mutual friend.

Then my heart lodged in my throat, where I worried it might choke the life out of me. Becca stood in a corner of the room, chatting effortlessly like she was born to mingle at cocktail parties and restaurant openings. She looked confident, content, and fucking gorgeous. To say nothing of her dress.

If I'd thought her denim miniskirt was a turn-on, this little black slip of fabric with the spaghetti straps was a stunning, electrifying hard-on masquerading as evening wear. And I was pretty sure she wasn't wearing a bra. I must have saved a fleet of drowning puppies in a prior life to deserve this.

Once she entered my line of sight, I didn't see anyone else in the room. I might have shoved people out of the way. Who even knew? I couldn't remember. I did what I had to in order to be near her in the most expeditious way possible. It may have included jumping over tables.

"Hi." I put a hand on her bare arm and inserted myself between her and the guy who was trying to have a conversation with her. He could have been the biggest restaurant critic alive, and I'd have trampled him to get closer to Becca.

She turned, and the warmth in her eyes washed over me. "You found me."

"Wasn't hard. You stand out in a crowd."

"I was trying to blend in." She started to brush a tendril of hair from her face but stopped midway.

I reached out and tucked it behind her ear, marveling at her beauty. "Impossible."

She gulped, and her pupils dilated. Good. I still needed the proof that I affected her as much as she leveled me—every damn time. Then she shook herself. "You changed the whole design . . ." she said, incredulous. "What happened to the globe lights and the curtains?"

"I trashed ' em."

"Seriously?" She looked horrified at the waste.

I guided her out of the crush of people to a quieter spot near the kitchen. "I was able to return most of it. Design companies are used to changes, and I'm sure they charged a restocking fee."

"But why? I didn't mean to make you think the design wasn't good. I was just spitballing. For fun," she said.

I could tell she felt guilty. I had to make her understand. "Becca, you're really good at this. Look around you. It's gorgeous."

She scanned the room, taking in all the design touches that gave warmth and character to the place, all touches she'd inspired. "I do love it."

"I do too." I wasn't looking around. I was looking at her.

"Are you sure?" she asked.

She still didn't get it. I wanted everything she wanted to give me. I grazed her jaw with two fingers. Her eyes immediately pulled to mine, their deep oceans daring me to float away in them.

"Never been more sure of anything. When it's right, you know." I hoped she knew I wasn't just talking about the design.

She trembled under my touch. I wanted her lips, but I didn't want to mess up her perfect red lipstick.

Scratch that. I wanted to ruin it.

"Okay," she said. "I'm glad you think it's right."

"I think it's perfect." And also fucking awful timing because I was supposed to be hobnobbing with everyone in the place and not plotting how to sneak off and make out with my high school crush, who I wanted to spend my life with. It was a problem. It had always been the problem where she was concerned—I was in a roomful of people, and I only saw her.

I pulled her in close and held her face in my hands. When I leaned in to kiss her, my lips were enveloped in the heat of her mouth, the gentle brush of her tongue. I needed to feel her skin against mine, and her bare arms weren't enough. But she pulled away.

"We can't do this here."

She was right. I could be a grownup for a couple more hours. "I agree with the thought behind that, but for the record, kissing you is all I want to do."

That made her smile, and I didn't need her to tell me she felt the same way. I trusted that it was true.

The rest of my night was amazing because I didn't let go of Becca's hand, and I introduced her to my investors, my publicist, and the chefs I'd known for years and worked with during our early kitchen days.

"Well, this makes me happy." The voice came from behind me, but I didn't need to turn around to recognize my sister. She smiled at Becca and leaned in to hug her. "Do you remember me from the hospital?"

"Of course I remember you. How are you doing? How's little Katie?" Becca asked.

"Katie's great, the best, but this is the first I've been out since she was born, if that tells you anything." I took in my normally boisterous, high-energy sister, and she looked drained. I immediately felt guilty that I hadn't been to her house in a few days. I'd have to do better.

"I can't believe you came," I said. "If you only get one night out, is this how you want to spend it?"

"Um, is there a bar? Does it have alcohol?"

I nodded.

"Then yes. I need a break from being a walking dairy farm. Although I'll be engorged within the hour and need to pump and dump."

"Does every conversation need to be about your breasts?" I feared for the guests she might decide to talk to about engorgement.

"Yeah. 'Fraid so. And since I know how uncomfortable it makes you, I'll be sure to include all the details." She smirked, knowing I wouldn't yell at her in a room full of people.

"Come, let's get you a drink." Becca led her away, smiling at me. She walked my sister over to the tequila tasting while I gladhanded a few more investors. I still had to work about half the room before I could wrap up the evening and take her home, and I intended to take her home.

I made sure she was by my side as often as possible. I knew how awkward it felt to kill time at someone else's party, and I didn't want her to get tired of making small talk with strangers and leave. But more than once, she told me she was fine and urged me to chat with all the people who'd come to celebrate the opening.

"I get it. This is your night. Don't worry about me. I'm not going anywhere." She left me to talk with a potential investor and went to greet Burt when he walked in.

I worried a little bit when I saw the two of them later with their heads bent together like they were conspiring about something. Then Becca tipped her head back, laughing so hard that I could see tears glistening in her eyes.

Burt looked over at me, gave me a thumbs-up, and mouthed, "Don't fuck it up."

He didn't need to tell me twice.

She seemed content, tasting the food, trying the tequila, chatting with anyone in her immediate radius like the outgoing, charming woman she was. I vowed that night to never do anything to curtail that in her. No more vampire hours on the night shift. She was born to shine in daylight.

CHAPTER THIRTY-SIX

ecca

I STAYED until the last investor bear-hugged Blake and left the restaurant. The wood door closed behind him, and we were alone. "Hey There Delilah" by the Plain White T's was playing on the sound system, which was a throwback to high school, and it made me smile.

"Nice music," I said.

"Glad you like it." He smiled and pulled out his phone. With a couple of swipes, he turned it lower and dimmed the overhead lights. He left the spotlights, which made the room feel like it had been kissed by fairies.

"Did you get to try any of the food?" he asked.

I hadn't realized until then that I'd been busy all night, chatting with new people, hanging with Sydney, and holding his hand while he introduced me to everyone who came to talk to him.

"Actually, no. But not for lack of interest. I hope you know that."

He nodded, pulling me toward him, wrapping one arm around my waist, and snaking his other hand through my hair. "Thank you for being here tonight. It meant a lot to me."

"Seemed like it went well. Were your investors happy?"

He nodded again, eyes moving over my face, lingering on my lips. "Very happy."

"You feel ready for the crush of customers?"

Another nod, tracing his finger over my cheek, sending a chill down my spine.

"Are we done talking?" I asked.

He put a finger over my lips and traced their shape, pausing when I opened my mouth and licked his finger. He dipped his head and kissed me hard, with all the urgency that had built over the two hours with him in the same room.

So this is what it feels like, I thought. This is what it feels like to kiss someone without reservation, without thoughts of whether it's the right thing to do or what the next conversation should be. I was fully lost in the moment and couldn't fathom being anywhere else. It felt good.

We could have used any one of the tables in the room and pulled each other's clothes off right there, but Blake drew back slowly. Then he changed his mind and kissed me again.

And again.

He tried once more to back away, then groaned his agony and returned once more to ravage my lips. "I can't resist you," he said, his voice a growl that turned my insides to molten lava.

"Then don't." I had no issue with using an unfinished wood table for what I felt certain was its intended purpose.

He kissed me again, taking his time, brushing his lips against mine and holding my face in his hands, turning it to find the angle he wanted. His lips were soft and tasted like honey. I sucked his bottom lip into my mouth, and he groaned.

"Ahh, I want to keep doing this, but . . ." It was the second time he'd hesitated.

"What?" I asked.

"Just . . . come." He kept his arm wrapped around my waist while he moved us toward the staircase.

"Careful. I'm wearing some big heels here." I looked down so I wouldn't miss a step.

"Don't think I missed a single chance to gawk at your legs in those shoes and that dress. Not to worry, darling. I won't let you fall."

We got to the top of the staircase, and he turned me toward him so I couldn't immediately see the second floor. It hadn't been finished when we were there before, and Blake had dismissed it as his office and a small party room that I didn't need to see. But after he'd leveled me with one more soul-melting kiss, he gently directed me to look at where we were.

"No way," I said, unable to put anything else into words.

He'd turned the empty room into a model of the Blue and Gold Fleet party boat, with life preservers hanging on the walls, a cheesy prom banner and streamers, and a keg sitting in the corner. A table for two sat in the center of the room with a Class of 2007 centerpiece made of Styrofoam and old photos of senior class antics from our high school yearbook. Each place setting had a silver lid on the plate and a champagne flute next to it.

I spent several minutes with my mouth agape, taking in everything he'd done to recreate the prom neither one of us had attended, before noticing that he was holding a plastic box in front of me. "This is for you. I understand the wrist corsage is the preferred option." He opened the box.

Inside was a spray of tiny red roses interspersed with baby's breath and some sprigs of green. I laughed. At one time, having the right corsage and the perfect prom dress would have been so important to me. Then I'd rejected it all and almost all of life's worthwhile moments along with it. But there I was with a guy who wanted to give me all of it—my past, my present, and maybe even a future. I didn't need a prom redo to know I wanted him to be my date forever.

"It's beautiful." I slipped it onto my wrist.

Blake lifted my hand to his lips and kissed it. "Now, I'll have you know that it took some doing, but I was able to find out what they served on the Blue and Gold Fleet back in the day, and I wanted this to be authentic. So get ready for some rubber chicken in a mushroom gravy and some gray beans and mashed potatoes in the shape of a flower."

"Wow, as a master chef, will you really be able to stomach that? Because it sounds awful."

"It sounds like you don't want to eat it, so you're trying to make it sound like I'm the food snob."

"Maybe so. Maybe I am doing that." I couldn't help laughing at him. "But I'll eat anything you cook, even if the green beans are gray."

With a flourish, Blake took the lids off the two plates. The food was a perfectly plated selection of all the appetizers that had passed around the room all night. "Okay, I admit it. I am a food snob. And I happen to think the food from my menu is better than what they served at prom. Can you stand to be with me?"

"I only want to be with you."

"Then lucky me, because I only want to be with you. And when I say 'only,' it's because I mean forever. You're it for me, Becca. You're the one." His eyes locked on mine and I let the words sink in. Before I realized it, I was nodding.

"Shall we?" He walked behind one of the chairs and pulled it out for me.

"Do you think the Blue and Gold party boat has nice chairs and tables like this? Not that I doubt your reenactment at all. I love it."

"They have chairs and tables, but they're below deck and kind of ordinary. I have a feeling that if we'd gone to our prom, we'd have been outside on the deck. It would've been cold and wet, and we wouldn't have noticed because we'd have been drunk on cheap, illegally-pilfered champagne and teen hormones."

"Kind of sad I missed that, but this is so much better," I said.

"Chasing Cars" by Snow Patrol started playing.

"Aw, I loved this song back then. Although it made me cry."

"No crying at prom," Blake said. He took a champagne bottle from a chilling bucket and poured some into each champagne flute.

I raised my glass for a toast, and he did the same.

"To a successful new restaurant," I said, holding my glass a little higher.

He shook his head. "No. We can toast to that later. Right now . . . to us."

311

EPILOGUE

ecca

Three Months Later

I never knew if guys kept track of significant dates the way I did. In the years I'd spent dating, I'd rarely been with anyone long enough to celebrate a one-month anniversary or a two-months-since-our-first-kiss anniversary. And when I had, the guys in my life at the time had never given the date any significance.

So I had no way of knowing whether February twentieth would ring any bells for Blake. I had zero expectations, but I did ask if we could go out to dinner, my treat, and I would pick the place. He didn't object and didn't ask where I planned to go, which was a little unlike him, being the foodie he was. But I chalked it up to him being busy with the restaurant, which had been booked out two months in advance since its opening night. It had been written up in several magazines and prominent food blogs, and it looked like it was on its way to being a James Beard award contender.

We'd spent almost every night together since our prom redo, splitting the time pretty evenly between our two houses. Blake's was more convenient to the restaurant, but I knew he loved my back patio. My house was closer to the hospital, but I loved the views from his house and the guy who lived in it. It took a lot of commuting, but that never bothered me.

This would be one of our East Bay nights at my house, so Blake drove over in the afternoon, once he'd wrapped up the tasting menu for the lunch seating. He'd been working about three daytime shifts a week, which coordinated with the new day shifts I'd picked up at the hospital. On those days, I still marveled at my regular-person life of working in the daylight and having nights off. We stayed up late and rediscovered the joys of the drive-in movie theater.

But it turned out I didn't need to give up my vampire ways entirely. Blake loved working the dinner shifts because that tasting menu was a little more complicated, and on the nights he worked dinners, I took the overnight shifts, which left us both exhausted but free during the day for some hiking and sailing on the bay.

"Are you going to give me any hints about where you're taking me?" He slipped into the passenger seat of my car.

"Nope." I started driving, but as soon as I turned from Shattuck to University and headed west, I glanced at Blake and saw the smile creep over his face. He knew where we were going.

"Does it have a view of the water? I hope so," he said, playing along.

I kept my gaze straight ahead. "It might. We're heading west, so there's a decent possibility."

He tilted his seat back a few inches and leaned his head back on the headrest. I snuck another glance his way. His eyes crinkled, and his smile was wide. He looked so open, so content. Gone were the hints of self-consciousness that I only picked up on because I'd known him when he was all self-consciousness. Watching him now, I could tell he'd finally forgiven himself for the past and was firmly looking forward.

I pulled into the parking lot of Skates on the Bay, and I was surprised at how little it had changed since our dinner there all those years ago. "Do you still eat fish and chips? Or does your 'chef's palate' forbid stuff like that?" I air quoted it because I would never be done ribbing him about his fancy food taste and the fact that he'd loved the dinner I'd recently cooked that consisted of spaghetti with sauce from a jar and salad with blue cheese dressing.

"I'm not even gonna answer that."

I hadn't thought to call ahead to reserve the table in the back by the windows where we'd sat before. It seemed a little too cute, and that wasn't me. But the table was vacant, so I agreed to give a tiny nod to fate and its apparent role in my life.

We briefly looked at the menus and ordered a few things, but neither of us seemed to care what we ate. The magic was in the place—and the sun setting on the bay, and us, there, together.

"So you may be wondering why I invited you here." I felt suddenly nervous. For a guy I loved, he really had a way of making me nervous. I wondered if that would ever change.

"I figured the reason was dinner."

"That's part of it. But I wanted to revisit the pact we made . . . I mean, it was kind of a brilliant idea, and I think I'll always regret that we didn't keep it."

He looked confused. "Me too . . . but aren't we both a long way past that? Or if you're suggesting we reenact our first night together, I'm game to do that. Pretty much every day until the end of time."

That made me smile. "I can get on board with that, but I have something to add." I grabbed the sheet of paper I'd stuffed into my purse earlier and unfolded it. The page was covered in scrawl, some of it crossed out, other parts circled. I should have recopied everything I wanted to keep onto a fresh sheet, but I'd run out of time.

I could tell Blake couldn't read anything from where he sat, which was just as well. "What is it?" he asked.

"It's a new pact. Some ideas I had for things I'd like to promise only to you. And it will replace our old pact since we kind of blew upholding that one. This one is for keeps."

His expression softened. "I like that idea. What's on the list?"

I looked down and read, "I, Rebecca Finley, promise that you can always call me Rebecca. In fact, I insist on it. I love hearing the way you say my name. I also promise to invest in one cute nurse's outfit, which I will wear only for you, as long as you never breathe a word of it to anyone else. I also will never take you to another family dinner. You are banned. I love you too much, and I won't risk the curse."

"I like that pact," he said quietly, considering my words. "But to make it an official pact, don't I have to agree to some things?"

"I mean, in an official pact, yes, but I didn't want to put words in your mouth. This is my side. You're welcome to add whatever you'd like, but no pressure. I'm not trying to put you on the spot. Take time to think about it."

"Okay, thanks. I will." He nodded and drummed his fingers on the table. I got the feeling I'd made him nervous with my declarations. "You know, your pact sounds a lot like vows." He looked a little wary.

That made me blush. "Yeah, I was kind of afraid of that. Please don't take it that way. I was going more for cute."

He nodded. "Okay then, because I wouldn't want you to steal my thunder."

What kind of thunder?

I was still trying to figure out how to backtrack so it wouldn't sound like I was pushing marriage vows on him, which was why I didn't immediately register when he got out of his chair. But then he knelt down in front of me and lifted my hand from my lap.

"When you suggested dinner tonight and wouldn't tell me where you wanted to go, it gave me an idea."

"Oh. Um . . ." My heart started thundering because he was kneeling, and I couldn't think of too many reasons why a guy would do that. *But this guy? The one who'd punished himself for so long because he didn't think he was deserving of love?* He had to be kneeling because he'd lost a contact lens or something, even though I was pretty sure he'd had Lasik surgery. *He'd said that, right?*

"The kind that starts with me countering your pact with my own. I, Blake Fulton, will call you Rebecca because that's the name of the girl I fell in love with when I was sixteen, and I punished myself for fifteen years and told myself it was my fate to be miserable without her because I'd hurt her unfairly. But now, I'm choosing a different fate. And it includes every day and every night with the beautiful, fabulous, hilarious, bright light that is Rebecca Finley, if you'll have me as your husband. I will never abandon you. I will never run from you. I will love you forever. And I hope that when you look at this ring, you'll know that you own my heart."

He'd taken a small box from his pocket and held it out to me. A solitaire diamond in an antique setting gleamed in the waning sunlight. My eyes pricked with tears, and I tried to speak, but my words caught in my throat. I nodded and threw my arms around Blake's neck.

If he wanted forever, I would give it to him. "I won't ever break that pact."

"I think it's a good one." Blake pulled me into his arms and bent to kiss me as the sun cast its golden stripes over the bay.

If a waiter came with our entrees or refreshed our water glasses —or played the national anthem on a tuba—I didn't notice.

I only wanted the guy who had me wrapped in his arms. I had forever for everything else.

THANK you so much for reading Second Chance at Us!

Ready to find out what happens with Isla's relationship on the rocks? CLICK HERE for her story, FALLING FOR YOU! Read on for a sneak peek!

ACKNOWLEDGMENTS

Readers, thank you. I'm grateful for every word you read, every kind review, every thoughtful click and like and comment. Love you all.

Jay, Jesse and Oliver: I've multitasked during movie night, I've crawled into bed when the sun was coming up and I've forced a few too many Trader Joe's lasagnas on you. Thank you for forgiving it all and loving me anyway. My deepest love goes to you three giant men with the best heads of hair I've ever seen.

To my beta readers, editors, proofers, givers of feedback, and supporters—Amy V., Kelé P., Amy D., Amanda and Laura at Red Adept Editing.

And enormous thanks to the SOS crew — a group that expands with every book — no matter when I send a desperate text or email, you respond and talk me off the ledge: Adriana L., Kimberly K., Christine D.R., Dylan A., and Melanie H. I'd be a pile of unpublished mush without you.

Jenn and Shanoff Designs, you outdid yourselves with this cover - thank you, thank you.

Thank you Jenn and the Social Butterfly team for expert advice, brilliant execution, and other superpowers. Hilary and Shan, I'm happy to have you in my corner - you make the PR part a breeze.

Bloggers and bookstagrammers—thank you for embracing my books and exposing my writing to readers. I couldn't Glad to have you in my village.

And to my fellow authors: as always, I am honored to type among you.

SECOND CHANCE AT US PLAYLIST

BECCA AND BLAKE - SONGS FROM HIGH SCHOOL

Sophomore Year

Beautiful Day - U2

Since U Been Gone - Kelly Clarkson

Karma - Alicia Keys

All That You Can't Leave Behind - U2

Boulevard of Broken Dreams - Green Day

Stuck in a Moment - U2

Best of You - Foo Fighters

Prom Night

Who Knew - Pink

Hey There Delilah - Plain White Ts

Waiting on the World to Change- John Mayer

Chasing Cars - Snow Patrol

ABOUT THE AUTHOR

Stacy Travis writes sexy, charming romance about bookish, sassy women and the hot alphas who fall for them. Writing contemporary romance makes her infinitely happy, but that might be the coffee talking.

When she's not on a deadline, she's in running shoes complaining that all roads seem to go uphill. Or on the couch with a margarita. Or fangirling at a soccer game. She's never met a dog she didn't want to hug. And if you have no plans for Thanksgiving, she'll probably invite you to dinner. Stacy lives in Los Angeles with her husband, two sons, and a poorly-trained rescue dog who hoards socks.

Facebook reader group: Stacy's Saucy Sisters

Super fun newsletter: https://geni.us/travisNL

Tiktok: https://www.tiktok.com/@stacytravisauthor

Website: https://www.www.stacytravis.com

Email: stacytraviswrites@gmail.com - tell me what you're reading!

facebook.com/stacytravisromance
instagram.com/stacytravisauthor
bookbub.com/authors/stacy-travis
goodreads.com/stacytravis

The Summer Heat Duet

1. The Summer of Him: A Mistaken Identity Celebrity Romance

2. Forever with Him: An Opposites Attract Contemporary Romance

The Berkeley Hills Series - all standalone novels

1. In Trouble with Him: A Forbidden Love Contemporary Romance (Finn and Annie's story)

2. Second Chance at Us: A Second Chance Romance (Becca and Blake)

3. Falling for You: A Friends to Lovers Romance (Isla and Owen)

4. The Spark Between Us: A Grumpy-Sunshine, Brother's Best Friend Romance (Sarah and Braden)

5. Playing for You: A Sports Romance (Tatum and Donovan)

6. No Match for Her - an Opposites-Attract Friends-to-Lovers Romance (Cherry and Charlie)

San Francisco Strikers Series - standalone novels

1. He's a Keeper: A Grumpy-Sunshine Sports Romance (Molly and Holden)

2. He's a Player: A Second Chance Sports Romance (Jordan and Tim)

Standalone Novels - Adult Contemporary Romance

French Kiss: A Friends to Lovers Romance

Bad News: An Enemies to Lovers Romance

FALLING FOR YOU

Chapter 1.

Isla

Wednesday felt like a great day for a breakup.

To the kind of person who thinks things through—like knowing in the morning which dessert I planned to eat after dinner that night—Wednesday made the most sense.

For the record, it was apple pie, preferably à la mode.

Wednesday was far enough away from the previous weekend to blur the memory of the beautiful brunch Tom and I had eaten at Sam's in Tiburon and far enough from the upcoming weekend that I wasn't worried about sitting on my couch alone with no plans.

If I waited until Friday, there was a chance I'd get lazy, decide that kissing the wrong guy was better than kissing no guy, and decide to wait another week.

Like I'd done for the past two months.

So Wednesday it was—the day I'd tell my unfairly handsome, highly accomplished, noncommittal boyfriend to pack his things and find someone else to shower with lukewarm affection and expensive jewelry bought by his assistant.

But first, I needed to bake two hundred and fifty loaves of bread.

My day started at three in the morning, as it always does, when my babies needed my full attention, and I arose before the sleeping roosters to feed them. I threw on a pair of comfortable cotton pants and a long-sleeved shirt and tied my long, blondish brown hair up in a knot to keep it out of my face.

My morning wasn't flexible, and I had the routine down pat, including a little wiggle room for the unexpectedly long red light, the coffee spill in my car, or whatever other trouble could befall me at three in the morning.

The first snafu came in the form of bad parking karma.

My usual parking spot was occupied, odd considering it was a non-space wedged between a blue dumpster and a telephone pole in an alley. I managed to find a semi-legal space that only covered a quarter of someone's driveway.

In San Francisco, which had zero parking ever, that was practically valet.

The sourdough starters were sleeping when I opened the back door to Victorine, my bakery and café, and felt the cool outdoor air mingle with the warmer humidity of the industrial kitchen.

And there they were, lined up in jars under a length of burlap cloth. So pretty. So much potential.

"Hello, loves," I said, uncovering them and smiling at the way they'd bubbled overnight.

Yes, I knew it was a little crazy and they weren't actually human children, but honestly, they were as well-tended as some of the kids whose parents I knew. And they behaved a lot better.

If I took care of them and kept their lives consistent, they did exactly what I wanted. I paid close attention to their development, I fed them, I made sure they had what they needed to grow and thrive . . . and the result was an award-winning sourdough that sold out every day since I opened my first bread bakery seven years earlier.

In the time since then, I'd ended up authoring a couple cookbooks and selling my bread to restaurants—some of which had the most sought-after reservations in San Francisco. That led to write-ups in epicurean magazines, invitations to bake for events at the mayor's residence, and a devoted following of sourdough die-hards who treated me like a celebrity—a bread celebrity.

Normally, when I turned the key in the back door, I felt excited—new day, new loaves. Each time I baked, it was a chance to discover something, even though I was starting with the same ingredients every time.

Flour. Salt. Water.

It might seem like there were only so many ways baking a sourdough round could go. But depending on how a farmer changed the soil or how the grains were ground, or which strains of wheat were blended with other ones, the bread would taste different. If there was a heavy fog in the city that day or a light rain, the bread would be different. Normally, I loved it all.

Not today.

Today, I was so fixated on the impending breakup that it was ruining everything else.

"Bonjour, copine." Camille, my pastry chef, was the only other one who got to work as early as me. She had her own morning ritual that consisted of laminating dough for croissants, which meant layering cold butter between sheets of dough and folding, chilling, and folding umpteen times before they were ready to bake. Then she'd start on the other baked goods that we sold in the pastry case in front.

Classically trained in Paris, Camille wanted to open her own shop, but she needed her green card and some financial backing before she could do it.

We'd struck a deal early on—she only baked for me, which allowed my café to offer some of the best pastries I'd ever eaten, and I showed her the ropes of running a business.

Today, a blue beanie covered her blond hair because it was forty degrees outside and she was crazy enough to ride to work on a moped. Even with the beanie under a helmet, thick gloves, and a leather jacket, the fierce chill had her shivering.

"Hey, Cam. You get wet out there? The fog was practically rain."

"Yeah, it was a treat. No big, though." She unwound a scarf from her neck and started hanging her layers up on a hook in the back. I'd already put my jacket and scarf there.

Camille had moved to the Bay Area from Paris four years earlier and I'd hired her immediately. Her English was flawless, thanks to a few years she'd spent at a high school in England, and she still didn't know many people in San Francisco, so she spent a lot of time at work. Like me.

"You're a beast. Someday, I aspire to be you," I told her.

"You want to ride around in the cold because you can't afford a car or a parking space?"

"No, I just want to be cool and ride a Vespa and pretend I'm French. But first I'll have to learn how to ride one," I said.

"It's easy. I'll teach you. The key is balance." As if proving her exceptional skill in that area, she climbed on a stool and stood on one foot as she leaned to grab a fresh box of parchment paper off a high shelf.

"Hey, can you grab me a stack of baskets while you're up there?" I asked. I had a special order for a dozen extra loaves.

She handed down the baskets and I added them to the stacks that were waiting on the lower shelves for the day's bread. Then, I fed the starters and waited while they consumed the new flour and water and started to bubble.

"*Alors, quoi de neuf?*" she asked. I'd gotten used to her habit of interspersing conversations with French. I understood she was asking me what's new, but despite a few years of high school French, I always answered in English.

"Same old. I think I dreamed of bread starters."

"Waste of a good dream. You should listen to poems read by French men before bed, dream about that."

I went to the front where we had an industrial coffee brewing setup and turned on the machines. The crew of bakers who'd be coming in over the next hour would want coffee and I always made sure there was an urn filled in the back for us.

When I came back with the urn, Camille was in the walk-in fridge foraging around for her butter. She was almost as crazy about the origin and provenance of her butter as I was about my flour. She imported five-pound slabs of it through a cheesemaker with a connection to a dairy farm in Normandy. "It's practically black market. Probably illegal," she told me. "But it's worth it for the perfect butter."

"I won't tell a soul. Can't afford to have you hauled to jail for trafficking in illegal dairy."

Camille slammed the door to the walk-in. "So . . . how'd it go with Tom?"

"I didn't do it," I said, quickly moving to the other stacks of baskets and counting them. It was pure avoidance because I knew exactly how many baskets were in each stack.

I hated telling her I'd chickened out of the breakup. Again. But Tom had brought me flowers from a place I liked, and I'd wilted like last week's blooms.

"Tonight. I'll do it tonight."

"You're a broken record, you know."

She cast a judgmental stare my way. I didn't even mind. I deserved judgment. "I know. I was just exhausted by the time I got home and didn't feel like dealing with a confrontation."

She shrugged. "So what, you left him sleeping in your eight-hundred thread count sheets under your warm down comforter so you could come to work and he could live to dream of having lukewarm sex with you another day?"

Admittedly, it wasn't a pretty picture.

Part of the problem was that from the outside Tom and I looked perfect.

I was tall, he was taller. Both of us were driven and independent. Most people figured that no one in her right mind would dump a billionaire venture capitalist with a hard jawline and searing green eyes.

Hugely successful and gorgeous, Tom knew how to live well.

He was exactly the kind of guy I'd dated over and over again, the captain of industry types. They liked that I baked—they thought it was cute and homey—and they thought I'd accomplished enough, but not too much. I could be arm candy at whatever business thing they dragged me to, but not too pretty, smart, or accomplished to overshadow their physical splendor, brilliance, and success.

And once again, the relationship left me wanting.

Wanting what, I wasn't exactly sure, but I had a feeling it had something to do with the wild melding of minds and the hot, sexy melding of everything else.

Tom and I didn't have that.

For a year, it didn't matter.

Then I'd rounded the backstretch of thirty-four and was heading into my last months before thirty-five. As the oldest of five sisters, I felt responsible for setting some kind of example for women as we aimed for work-life balance. Our brother, the oldest, was already engaged, and by the logic of our birth order, I was supposed to be next. Or at least taking meaningful steps in that direction.

Somehow a bell started ringing in an empty belfry in my brain I hadn't visited before. *Clang, clang, clang. Commitment, adulting, babies.* It was loud and annoying, and it got my attention.

I knew I should stop wasting my time if Tom wasn't the guy. He wasn't. I just hadn't done anything about it.

My phone buzzed with a text.

Tom: Call me.

I felt a pang of nerves rush through my body. Breakup time.

I had to do it. I would.

But my fingers wouldn't dial.

A few minutes later, another text.

Tom: Please.

I felt my resolve weakening just at that one word. *Please* tugged at my heartstrings. Maybe I could wait another week. Maybe something would change, and Tom would want something more than arm candy.

Maybe I was deluding myself. Again.

Falling for You is available to read NOW